The Art

of the

Decoy

The Art

of the

Decoy

A SCANDAL MOUNTAIN
ANTIQUES MYSTERY

Trish Esden

**CROOKED
LANE**

NEW YORK

Copyright © 2022 by Patricia A. R. Esden

All rights reserved.

Published in the United States by Crooked Lane Books, an imprint of The Quick Brown Fox & Company LLC.

Crooked Lane Books and its logo are trademarks of The Quick Brown Fox & Company LLC.

Library of Congress Catalog-in-Publication data available upon request.

ISBN (hardcover): 978-1-64385-964-4
ISBN (ebook): 978-1-64385-965-1

Cover design by Alan Ayers

Printed in the United States.

www.crookedlanebooks.com

Crooked Lane Books
34 West 27th St., 10th Floor
New York, NY 10001

First Edition: April 2022

10 9 8 7 6 5 4 3 2 1

For my grandparents, Dr. John and Helen Rice, whose genes I suspect may be responsible for both my love of writing as well as my passion for antiques.

In the world of art and antiques, it's all about the story.

For example, when an antique or piece of art is stolen from a museum or home, and then vanishes underground, the rumors and stories deepen into legends and mysteries. The crazier the story is, the higher the piece's value climbs.

Think about it, I'm not lying. The Mona Lisa *only became famous after she was the victim of a high-profile theft. What would happen if she were stolen again and went underground for, say, twenty years? What would she be worth then? Billions, maybe?*

Do you think the thirteen pieces stolen in the infamous Isabella Gardner Museum heist are worth more today than they were the day they were taken? Of course.

Same goes for last month's robbery at the Canadian Museum of History. A police officer dead. A security guard left in critical condition. No clues to the identity of the robbers, who made off with over five million dollars' worth of Canadian and Aboriginal art: sculptures by Inuit carver Johnny Inukpuk, a hooked rug created by fabric artist Ozama Martin, a series of paintings, Dogs and Decoys, *by the renowned folk artist Jean-Paul Bouchard . . . The $250,000 reward for information is nothing compared to what the theft has done to the value of the stolen pieces. Previously worth just over five million. Now? Easily twice that.*

Stories add value.

Value means dollars.

And to us dealers in the art and antiques trade, it really all comes down to the cash. Well, that, plus the love of history. And the hunt. And the desire for beautiful things.

Not that I'd ever steal or trade in stolen goods. Not intentionally, at least.

—Edie Brown

Chapter One

The *brrring* of the phone bounced off the van's metal walls. Jolting from an adrenaline-fueled dream involving dumpster diving and a Fabergé egg, I fumbled under the pillow for the offending device. "Hello?"

"It's Tuck. You awake?"

Aaarggh. Of course I was awake. *Now.* If it had been anyone other than my uncle, I'd have bitten their head off for calling at two in the morning.

"Hang on a minute." Wriggling out of the sleeping bag, I squeezed toward the van's sliding door, past suitcases and an early nineteenth-century blanket box from a rummage sale. Though nowhere near as life-altering as discovering a Fabergé egg in a dumpster, the blanket box was a quality piece and an easy sell. I had a knack for finding such things, even when they were hidden amid piles of fakes and other junk. Perhaps it came from growing up in the antiques and art trades, now a fine-tuned instinct after years of tagging along with my grandparents. Maybe it was heightened by my education and internships. Whatever, the neurons at the back of my brain jumped to life every time I crossed paths with a genuine, quality piece.

As I slid the van door open, the overhead light flashed on. The smell of smoldering campfires hung in the damp air. Frogs chimed in the distance.

"You still there?" Tuck asked.

"Yeah. What's going on?" I settled down in the van's open doorway. As a rule, Tuck didn't keep normal hours. Still, this was late, even for him.

"I meant to call earlier. Kala and I were away at an auction."

"Who's Kala?"

"She's not why I called." His voice tensed. "It's about your mom."

I closed my eyes and prayed that the months of waiting and not knowing had come to an end.

"She took the plea agreement. Nine months. Federal prison. Art forgery."

The air bottled up in my lungs released. Finally. "So she decided not to risk going to trial."

"Didn't have much choice. It could have been a lot worse."

"You're right about that." Even the thought of jail terrified me. "I still don't understand how Mom got herself into this situation. She knows what's legal and what isn't."

Tuck was silent for a moment. "Edie, I need you to come home."

"I'd love to see you, but I'm camped out in the Berkshires, doing a flea market this weekend."

"Your internship at the auction house is over, right?"

"Yeah. Last week." A sick feeling knotted in my chest. He was up to something.

"I didn't mind helping your mom, but that doesn't mean I can do everything on my own. Plus, I have the gardens and my African violets . . ."

As he rambled on about retirement and his latest horticultural ventures, thoughts of the longtime family business seeped into my mind: Scandal Mountain Fine Arts and Antiques. For decades, collectors and dealers had flown in and driven up to northern Vermont to buy from us. Famous artists had held court in the shop and camped out in the spare bedrooms. I vividly remembered racing home from grade school to watch my grandparents unbox their latest finds: primitive paintings, folk art carvings, etched powder horns . . . so many stunning pieces created by master artisans, history and beauty melding together. I thought of the warmth and strength of Grandma's hands, and the scent of Grandpa's corduroy jacket, beeswax, lemon oil, and damp humus.

But along with success came rivals and trouble, and the plane crash that killed my grandparents. After that, Mom took over the business. She was hopelessly inept. It had been nearly three years since I'd lived at home and attempted to work for her. One of her lapses had culminated in my arrest for selling stolen property. Thank you very much, Mom.

Tuck cleared his throat, pulling me from my thoughts. "There's this appraisal event coming up. An *Antiques Roadshow* sort of deal. The shop's under contract to be there, but it's going to be hard to pull off without your mom's expertise. I really could use your help."

"I can't believe they'd want any of us there. Mom's arrest has been in the news for months."

"It's here in Scandal Mountain. Will you do it? Please."

I rubbed a hand over my face. I was good at saying no, but this was Tuck and he rarely asked for anything. "All right. When is it?"

"Tomorrow. Actually, today—it is after midnight."

"You've got to be kidding! I'm five hours away."

"That's why I called now. It's on the village green. Ten o'clock sharp." He hung up.

I stared at the phone, then laughed. Tuck, the slick bastard. He'd purposely called at the last minute so I wouldn't have time to wiggle out of the deal, and I'd fallen for it hook, line, and sinker.

And that definitely wasn't normal for me.

Chapter Two

The village of Scandal Mountain was nestled in the foothills of Mount Mansfield, about an hour north of Burlington, east of St. Albans, and just south of the Canadian border. In the Victorian era, it was a thriving community thanks to the logging industry. Then, as its wealth diminished, so did the village. But it was on the rise again, with organic farms, quaint homes, and artsy storefronts drawing new families and, more recently, tourists searching for an old-fashioned sense of home. It was the ideal spot for an antique business to thrive. Or at least it should have been.

I yawned for the sixty-fifth time in the last two miles, then tapped the van's brakes, slowing as I neared the village. In retrospect, Tuck waiting until the middle of the night to call about the plea agreement should have told me he was up to something. However, I did agree with him. If the squirrelly event organizers assigned Tuck to a category that wasn't in his wheelhouse, the shop might come off as limited in scope, or even incompetent. He needed my help. Besides, it wasn't like I had any pressing plans. Everything I owned was already packed in my stripped-down minivan, the perfect rig for hauling inventory and camping on the road.

I passed Quickie's Quick Stop, then the side street down to the abandoned railroad yard, currently home to Fisher's Auction House. Next weekend they'd hold their traditional Memorial Day extravaganza auction. I hadn't been in years, but I'd never forget the time I went and outbid slippery Martina Fortuni. I'd been sixteen. She was in her mid-forties. I hadn't really wanted the box of vintage jewelry we were bidding on, but she'd been a pain in my family's side forever, elbowing her way into church sales before they opened and undercutting us when it came to house calls. Turned out there was a pair of Tiffany cufflinks in the box worth three times what I'd paid for the entire lot. It was a sweet victory for me, and really ticked off Martina.

Traffic slowed to a crawl. Parked cars lined both sides of the road. The sidewalks brimmed with people walking toward the village green. A boy pushed a 1970s Schwinn bicycle. A man toted a Victorian rocking chair—commercially made, maybe worth forty bucks on a good day. Other people carried tons of different things, but I didn't spot anything unique. I felt sorry for all of them. I could almost see the sugarplum daydreams of high appraisals dancing in their minds and feel the letdown to come.

The green came into view. A white canopied tent spanned its center, surrounded by crabapple trees bursting with pale pink blooms.

I flicked on the turn signal and swung toward the backside of the green, following a sign that pointed to a reserved parking area next to the town library. A deputy sheriff in an orange safety vest stood guard at its entry.

Smiling at him, I lowered my window. "I'm an appraiser. Edie Brown."

He flagged me on. "There's a spot back by the portable toilets."

Not ideal, but I was running late. I pulled into the parking place, then checked my makeup. Nothing overdone. Nothing smeared. I swept my frizz of brown hair into a ponytail and confined it with a length of black ribbon. White blouse. Dressy slacks. Casual but smart. My standard work outfit.

Satisfied, I wrestled my tailored jacket out of the dry-cleaning wrapper, slipped it on, and grabbed my iPad and bag. In truth, whether I looked professional or not, I still couldn't believe the people in charge of the event wanted anyone from Scandal Mountain Antiques to join them. Tuck might have the police record of a saint and mine might have been expunged almost three years ago, but it didn't mean rumors about our family weren't still running rampant.

I strutted toward the green, outpacing people and dodging cars. As I stepped out of the sunshine and into the cool shade of the tent's awning, a blonde woman in a powder blue cardigan raced across inches in front of me.

I skittered to a stop, not wanting to run into her. She clutched a dishtowel-wrapped bundle against her chest. Someone else might've been upset that the woman was so fixated on where she was going that she nearly ran into them. To me, our encounter—or more correctly, my encounter with the plump, grinder roll–size bundle she was carrying—was nothing short of pure joy.

As I zeroed in on the bundle, the neurons at the back of my brain went crazy, snapping and prickling, one excited synapse electrifying the next. It didn't matter that I couldn't see beneath the cloth; the way she was holding the bundle told me it was lightweight and not easily broken. Wood, most likely—and treasured.

The woman veered in the direction of the registration line. I lengthened my steps, trailing behind her, but I thought better of it and turned toward the appraiser check-in instead. As much as I longed to peek under the dishcloth, and perhaps offer to buy what it concealed, doing so when the woman was about to register for an appraisal fell into the not cool category. Technically, the unethical category. If only I'd spotted her before she reached the tent, the piece would have been fair game. Not that I intended to cheat her by offering to buy it on the sly, but it was important to make good deals when possible. Buy low. Sell high. Be as knowledgeable as possible and sharper than the next person. Have lots of connections. Rules to live by if you want to survive in the antiques and art trades.

I shoved my hands in my pockets and kept going. What was beneath the cloth? Instinct whispered: Perhaps not incredibly old, but genuine for sure. Probably—

My elbow bumped a man's arm, startling me from my thoughts.

"Sorry," I said.

He swiveled to face me. Middle-aged. Expensive suit. Silk tie accented with an onyx and diamond stickpin. I went cold as I raised my gaze to his face and saw familiar salt and pepper hair and a plastic smile. Felix Graham.

"If it isn't Edie Brown." His voice slithered over me as refined and glossy as a Rolls-Royce salesman's. He stepped closer, invasively so. "Last I knew you were in New York studying something."

I held my ground. "I was working at Christie's." No need to clarify that I was only an intern at the renowned auction house's New York City branch. That was none of his business. I drummed up my own counterfeit smile. "I didn't realize you were appraising today."

"I do this event every year." He ran a hand over the stick-pin. "A shame your mother isn't going to be here."

Anger simmered inside me. I kept my smile in place and shrugged. Tuck had heard that Graham was the one who'd talked Mom into forging the artist's name on the painting the FBI's Art Crime Team seized during their sting operation (*Afterglow* by Maxfield Parrish). Mom admitted to replicating the painting but denied signing it. I would have believed her, except that not long before the arrest I'd come home for a visit and walked in on her practicing Parrish's signature. I could still remember her putting me down for questioning what she was doing and flippantly claiming that writing his name was noth-ing more than a way to get into character before she began to paint in his style. Maybe true, but it sounded ridiculous at the time and wasn't something I'd ever seen her do before.

Mom was extraordinarily skilled when it came to replicating art. Graham had even hired her to create pieces for his clients in the past. She'd been worried about money and the possibility of being forced to sell the family's personal collections, not to mention the house and business. Still, I never dreamed she'd do something as crazy as attempt to sell a copy as original.

I met Graham's eyes. "I'd love to stay and chat, but I'm running late."

"I need to get going myself." He fluttered his fingers, indi-cating a gazebo that rose up in the middle of the tent, beyond the scattered appraisal tables and the lines of people waiting with their treasures. "I'm being interviewed shortly. *New England Antiques Magazine*—or some TV station. There've been so many events and interviews lately I can't keep them straight."

"Such a pity." I bit my tongue, then half turned in the direction of the check-in table. "See you later."

"I look forward to it."

"Sure you do," I mumbled.

I should've expected Graham to be here. I'd run into him over the years at antique shows and auctions throughout New England. But his shop—Golden Stag Antiques & Gallery—was in Burlington, Vermont. He was the definition of a self-satisfied jerk. He was also very well connected and extremely successful.

As I approached the appraiser check-in table, the gray-haired gentleman working it glanced up. He wore a yellow pullover sweater and plaid golf trousers, rather dapper in appearance, until his eyes met mine and his expression pinched disdainfully. "You must be Edie Brown from Scandal Mountain Fine Arts and Antiques. I was just telling Mr. Graham that I suspected you were going to be a no-show."

I clenched my teeth. Between his sour pickle face and the mention of Graham, it wasn't hard to imagine they'd been discussing more about me than whether I would be there or not.

I scanned the man's nametag. *Jules Ramone.* "Well, Jules, sorry about that. I drove up from Massachusetts this morning. It's a rather long trip."

His lips pressed together as he took an envelope out of a folding file. My name was written on it, but he pulled it to his chest instead of handing it over. "You've been assigned

your mother's usual 'New England Decorative Arts' category."
His eyes narrowed. "The other Scandal Mountain Antiques
appraiser is already set up. Perhaps you'd feel more comfortable assisting them with their category?"

I leaned forward, looming over him before snatching the
envelope. "Decorative Arts is perfect, thank you very much."

"Alrighty then," he said with a huff. "Your nametag and
a voucher for lunch are in the envelope, along with the event
itinerary. Your table is at the rear of the tent, past the gazebo."

"Thank you." Smiling, I wheeled away and headed across
the tent. While working on my master's degree and during various internships, I'd specialized in New England folk art and
furnishings. My intention was to become a leading authority in
those areas. If I couldn't make it on my own as a dealer, at least
I'd have the credentials to get a job at a top-notch museum or
auction house. There was no other category I'd have been more
pleased to get.

My steps lightened, eagerness jittering inside. I glanced
around, hoping to see the woman in the cardigan. It would be
cool if she came to the shop's table. I'd love the chance to see
what was under that cloth.

I wove through a crowd gathered in front of the gazebo. A
TV crew was setting up microphones and camaras, probably
for the interview Graham had bragged about. A couple of buff
guys in suit jackets were hanging out there as well. They had
short hair and wore dark glasses. One look said security, even
if they were attempting to blend in.

Beyond the gazebo, the crowd thinned. It took me a second
to spot the Scandal Mountain Fine Arts and Antiques banner.
It hung behind a long rectangular table. Five, maybe six people

in total gathered in front of it, including a teenage boy. An unfamiliar, short black woman stood behind the table. She was young, twenty-one at most, a good six years younger than me. She had on overalls and a sleeveless purple T-shirt. Gigantic gold hoops hung from her ears. A bandana-print headband held back an enormous puff of hair. She looked cheerful, but not professional in the least, and she appeared to be appraising the contents of the teenage boy's raffia beach tote—at Scandal Mountain Antiques' table. What the hell?

The woman's eyes grew wide with excitement as she took something from the boy's tote. A small doll. Long pink hair spiked out from the top of its flat head. A troll?

I blinked and blinked again. I couldn't be seeing right. Who was this woman? For sure not an employee. It had been years since Scandal Mountain could afford to hire anyone beyond family. For that matter, if she was an employee, then what was she doing appraising trolls? They were low-end at best. And where was Tuck?

I took a fresh grip on my bag, marched to the table and around behind it. Grandpa would roll over in his grave if he knew someone was valuing mass-produced junk at Scandal Mountain's table. Sure, trolls were cute and collectible, and supposedly good luck—but they weren't antiques or fine art. What was next? Plastic Funko bobbleheads?

As the woman swiveled toward me, I caught a glimpse of her nametag: *Kala Acosta*. Kala, the woman Tuck had mentioned going to the auction with last night. Clearly, she wasn't one of Tuck's normal lady friends. She was a good three decades too young.

A wide smile brightened Kala's face; even her eyes sparkled with excitement. She moved over, making room for me to join her. "I'm so glad you're here. Tuck said to expect you. You're Edie, right?"

"Yeah. Nice to meet you." I kept my voice light. Whatever was going on, it wasn't Kala's fault. "Is Tuck here?"

She grimaced. "He helped me set up, and then took off—something about a Burlington Garden Club meeting. He said he'd try to come back at noontime."

I laughed. If Tuck had gone all the way into the city to a gardening event, there was almost zero chance of seeing him at lunch or anytime soon.

Kala's attention went back to the teenager and his tote. She took out a white-haired troll as carefully as if it were a fine Daum Nancy vase. "As I was saying, this one is special. It's a Dam Thing troll. Made by Thomas Dam. Very desirable. However"—she pointed to the troll's fluff-tipped tail—"this makes it extra valuable, easily five hundred dollars."

Five hundred dollars? I stared at the plastic creature. I'd never have guessed it was worth more than twenty bucks. Maybe if it was a Star Wars collectible, mint-in-box, but a troll? Perhaps I needed to pay more attention to them in the future.

Kala waved her hand over the beach tote. "All together, the newer trolls are worth less than a hundred dollars. But including the unusual pieces, I'd insure the entire collection for two thousand."

The onlookers gasped. The teenager let out a whoop. "My mom was about to throw them in the trash. She's going to be so mad she gave them to me."

I nodded. I could hardly believe it either.

Glancing up, I scanned the onlookers, hoping to spot something that fell into my New England Decorative Arts category. A woman clutched a vintage postcard album decorated with red poppies. The album could contain a small piece of artwork, I supposed.

Out of the corner of my eye, I caught a flash of powder blue. The woman in the cardigan was meandering toward me. *Yes! There was a god.*

"Excuse me. Are you Edie Brown?" she asked when she reached the table. Her eyes were slightly downcast, her voice tentative. "I was assigned to a different appraiser, but they said you specialize in folk art."

"Yes, I do. I'm glad they sent you over." I motioned for her to set the bundle on the table.

She glanced at the onlookers, now all focused on her. "Um—I didn't mean to cut ahead of anyone. Is there a line?"

"It's fine," I said emphatically. "They're waiting for Kala."

Kala beamed. "I don't know a thing about folk art. Midcentury is my jam."

"As long as I'm not stepping on anyone's toes." The woman put the bundle down, then touched her nametag. "I'm Nina Graves-Bouchard." Her voice lowered to a whisper. "I'm not sure if what I brought is worth anything. It's not in very good condition—kind of ugly."

Sweat slicked my palms. "Why don't you unwrap it and let me take a look?"

She began to untie the string that held the towel in place. "I was going to talk to the Shelburne Museum, but then I heard about this event . . ."

My awareness narrowed to a pinpoint, centered on the woman's fingers and the string being slowly unknotted. Nina's voice and the murmur of the onlookers faded under the hammer of my pulse.

As she pulled the string off the bundle, she said, "It's actually not mine."

I snapped from my focus, sick worry rising inside me. It was hard enough to discreetly initiate a purchase in a situation like this without added complications, and even without having seen the object, I knew there was a possibility I'd want to do exactly that.

I swallowed dryly. "Who does it belong to?"

"It's complicated. It was—*is* from my father-in-law's collection. He has dozens of them. My ex-husband, Frank, and I are trustees. Well, he's not exactly my ex." Anger clenched her voice. "He hasn't lived with us since last fall, but we aren't divorced—" She took a sharp breath, then her tone returned to its previous meekness. "It's a long story."

"Why don't you let me see what you've brought?" No need for details at this point. Trustee sounded good. Not divorced meant still part of the family, and that's what mattered at the moment.

She unfolded the cloth, revealing the body of a carved shorebird. A plover decoy. No legs. No stand. Just the body. About ten inches long. Paint worn from use. Worse for wear, but as honest as they came.

"Beautiful." The word tumbled out, before I could snap my mouth shut and will my expression back into a mask of reserved professionalism. Fortunately, my ongoing focus on folk art had given me a fair amount of exposure to decoys from across North

America. Not that all decoys were folk art; certainly, modern mass-produced plastic ones weren't. But pieces like this were prime examples, reflecting the region and culture of the carvers who had created them. Beautiful and sometimes primitive pieces not made purely as aesthetic works of art, instead sold and used by hunters, at least in the case of early decoys.

I glanced at my bag, considering whether I should take out a pair of gloves before handling the piece. But the prospect of touching the decoy with naked fingertips made me quiver, and in truth clean bare hands were better for dexterity.

I wiped my hands on my pants, then picked up the bird and ran a finger down its side. Solid wood with a hairline split from age. The paint stippling was distinctive, as was the angle of the brush marks under the tail. There were two holes in the belly where wire legs had previously been attached. No maker's brand. No signature or marks of any sort . . . At some point, a spot on the top of the bird's head had been scraped clean and then repainted. A mortal sin. I cringed.

"So?" Nina broke the silence. A hint of desperation filtered into her voice. "Is it valuable?"

"Ah—" I mulled over the best way to phrase it. It was lovely, but . . .

"It's a shorebird decoy, right?" Kala interrupted.

"Yes—a plover," I said. "But there are concerns."

Behind Nina, a mobile TV crew wandered in our direction. A swarm of people broke away from the group gathered around the gazebo and followed the crew to Scandal Mountain's table.

Nina glanced at our new audience, then back at me. She bit down on a smile as if pleased by the attention. "My father-in-law insists it's special."

I squared my shoulders and raised my voice slightly, addressing Nina as well as the audience and camaras. "You have a right to be concerned about the bird's authenticity and value. There are a lot of inexpensive reproduction decoys out there, some purposely aged to look antique. This one has honest evidence of age and use. Did it come with a provenance?"

Nina gaped. "Um—I'm not sure what you mean."

"Do you have any documentation about who made the decoy or owned it in the past? Did it come from a reputable dealer or auction house?"

"I'm not sure."

"The reason I'm asking is that proof of those things would increase the value. The decoy is unsigned and damaged." I pointed to the tail. "There's a chip that was broken out and glued back in place. The glass eyes are an addition, and the legs are missing." I paused, dramatically. The bird was far from perfect, but Nina had said it was from her father-in-law's collection. If I could weasel an invitation to look at the rest of the decoys in private, I might be able to buy something more significant, and at a good price. In order to do that I had to come across as an expert—which I was, to a degree. I wasn't, however, experienced enough to study and value a shorebird in thirty seconds, especially one that fell outside the parameters of those I was closely acquainted with.

Disappointment filled Nina's voice. "Are you saying it's junk?"

I smiled. "Oh, no. Definitely not junk. It dates to the late nineteenth century." I reached into my memory, sorting through what I remembered from lectures and auction catalogues. Thank goodness, when it came to folk art and antiques in general, my retention level often surprised even me. "The holes in the belly indicate it would have originally had a style of wire legs most often attributed to Toronto Harbor shorebirds. Other aspects hint at a Massachusetts origin."

The audience pushed closer.

"Fascinating," someone murmured.

I continued, giving a flamboyantly lengthy but general overview on how the 1918 Migratory Bird Treaty Act ended commercial hunting of most shorebirds in North America, followed by more encompassing laws a decade later, that in turn essentially ended the production of American and Canadian shorebird decoys. When I ran out of trivia, I looked Nina in the eyes and brought my dissertation to a close. "A good shorebird decoy can sell in the three- to five-thousand-dollar range. But an exceptional New England plover with an impeccable provenance sold a few years ago for over eight hundred thousand dollars."

Nina gasped. "Oh, my goodness."

I let out a sigh, then gentled my tone. "Unfortunately, your decoy isn't a particularly good example. It's unmarked. Has no provenance. I'd value it at around five to eight hundred dollars at auction, tops."

Nina pressed her hand against her chest and looked down at the bird. The corners of her mouth curved into a slight smile. "Eight hundred thousand would be life changing, but eight hundred isn't bad. Honestly, it doesn't do much for me. Some of the other ones are more attractive."

As she folded the cloth back over the plover, I raked my hands down my pant legs. I had to wrangle an invitation to see the rest of the collection before she left. However, doing it discreetly was impossible with the audience and cameras fixed on us.

"Thank you for sharing the decoy with us today," I said, dropping my voice at the end to indicate I was bringing the session to a close. "It was a pleasure to see it."

Nina picked up the bird, wrapping the cloth tighter. "Thank you as well. This was very helpful."

The audience pushed forward, people lining up in front of the table, bags, boxes, and treasures clutched close to their chests, eyes bright with fantasies of similarly good appraisals. The TV crew remained focused on me. I glared at them. Couldn't they see the appraisal was over? Time to move on.

My jaw tensed, my resolve building.

I whipped out a business card from my pocket and thrust it at Nina. Whether soliciting was taboo at the event or not, I couldn't afford to blow this chance.

I lowered my voice, keeping it under the drone of the crowd. Hopefully, too quiet for the microphones to pick up. "Feel free to call if you have more questions or other pieces you'd like to ask about. The decoy might not appeal to you, but I'm very fond of such things."

"Ah—I'm not sure I can sell anything right now. If that's what you're getting at."

"I don't mean it like that." I waved my hands to stress the point. "It's important for you to know what you have for insurance purposes, if nothing else."

Nina set the business card on the table. "That makes sense. But I don't know."

"You should have the collection looked at. Seriously." My voice strained. *Damn it, this was going nowhere.*

"Thank you. I truly appreciate your honesty," she said. Then, just as the TV crew finally moved on toward a different appraisal table, she abruptly turned and sped in the direction of the gazebo.

My excitement drained, shoulders slumping. When Nina and I had been talking, I'd figured the odds of finagling an invitation to see the collection were high, but now it felt like the chance was slim to none. Why had she taken off so suddenly? I'd tried to not come on too strong.

I looked to where Nina was vanishing around the back of the gazebo. *Nina Graves-Bouchard.* Maybe I could track her down online. Or I might be able to locate her soon to be ex-husband or the father-in-law . . . *Graves-Bouchard.* The name did seem vaguely familiar.

My train of thought shifted as I noticed a well-built guy leaning against the railing of the gazebo, looking directly at me. Sandy brown hair, curly and rebellious, just long enough to run fingers through when wet—at least that's how I remembered it. As always, his oxford shirt was trim-fit and the sleeves were rolled up, leaving muscular forearms bare. Even at a distance, I knew the cartoon-style tattoo on his right forearm was an angel, and the one on his left a devil.

A liquid wave of heat swept through my body, tumbling and pooling just below my belly. Shane Payton. My ex-probation officer.

He touched two fingers to his brow, a salute acknowledging the connection. A smile flickered across his lips as if memories of our brief romance were playing in his mind as well. Memories that even now stirred more heat inside me.

It had started right from my first probation check-in. We'd been in his office, him seated behind his desk, black shoes polished to a business-like gleam, firm jaw, calm voice, kind eyes, a vintage Omega wristwatch—1950s, military, nice condition, unexpectedly distinctive for a man I'd assumed would be blandly conventional—and that damn oxford shirt. From the very first moment, I'd fantasized about ripping that shirt off and running my hands over what lay beneath.

Not long after, meetings in his office changed to less formal check-ins at Irwin's Deli in St. Albans. He was handsome, stable, and seemingly sane. He got that I'd never have intentionally bought or sold stolen goods, that the charge against me was justified but senseless, and that the judge was right to give me probation and no jail time. We had similar interests and tastes: primitive antiques and art, exploring museums and remote mountain lakes, rich foods and fresh ground coffee. With each passing month the connection between us intensified, a raw ache urging me to pull him over the line into forbidden territory, him stalwartly attempting to keep everything professional.

Then Labor Day weekend happened . . .

I'd gone to an antiques show in the Adirondacks, the van packed with folk art and a variety of sporting antiques that I hoped to sell to vendors. He was there as a collector, scouting for things to buy. We ran into each other early Saturday morning, and that was that.

I risked violating probation and he risked his job for three days in a rented cabin. Three days of being ourselves and doing what we'd longed to do—followed by unbearable awkwardness the next week at my probation check-in.

A week after that appointment, I was released from probation and the expungement of my record was set in motion by the court. I suppose I could've stayed in Scandal Mountain. Shane and I could've kept our distance for a few months, then started seeing each other once it didn't look so questionable. But he had his career and I had a master's degree to finish. We were both down in the dumps about it. Still, my leaving was for the best, for him and me.

There was also the issue of my relationship with Mom. My patience with her business mistakes and self-centered bullshit had reached the boiling point. It was time to go before I said something that caused an irreparable rift in the family. For my sake, Mom's, and for Tuck.

"Excuse me." A man's voice pulled me back to attention. He set another decoy on the table in front of me—a duck this time, hand carved, probably last week in China. "You still doing appraisals?"

"Of course, sorry." I gave Shane one last look. If I stuck around for the balance of the weekend there might be a fringe benefit, other than getting a chance to visit with Tuck. That was, if Shane was still single.

Chapter Three

I'd expected to catch myself obsessing over Shane once the appraisal event wound down. Haunting him online had been my pastime for a good six months after I'd left Scandal Mountain, a hobby I intended to take up again beginning tonight. But as I started for home, it was Nina Graves-Bouchard who consumed my thoughts.

My skin tingled and my heartbeat quickened at the idea of the plover decoy coming from a collection of unknown size and quality. Beautiful birds—ducks, shorebirds, maybe even something as amazing as a swan or a great blue heron—created and painted by master carvers, treasured and hunted over for decades. I had to locate Nina. That's all there was to it.

I slowed and turned onto the road where my family's shop and home sat up on a hill. Taking a long breath, I slowed even further and glanced at the grass airstrip that stretched along the right-hand side of the road. Memories flooded my mind. Ten years ago. The hum of my grandparents' distant plane as it emerged from behind a veil of white clouds, and descended toward the airstrip—

I clenched my teeth, blocking out the moments that followed. The explosion. The flames.

That summer, I'd kept vigil over the airstrip, watching as the scorched earth left behind from the plane crash gave way to an upsurge of new grass. I'd chosen then to see the field as a living memorial, each unrelenting green blade dedicated to my grandparents—to their strength, their unwavering determination, their love of beauty and history, and their devotion to family. Death is like loneliness. It's up to each of us how we choose to deal with it.

"Love you, Grandma. Love you, Grandpa," I murmured.

I tapped the accelerator. Ahead, the shop sign came into view on the edge of the road. "Scandal Mountain Fine Arts and Antiques." At the base, a lush planting of pink impatiens and blue lobelia spilled from a cast iron urn. The whole display was classy and beautiful, except that the "Open by chance or appointment" placard beneath the sign dangled awkwardly by one hook.

I pulled into the driveway, parked, and rehung the placard. Before I returned to the van, I glanced back down the road at the airstrip. Odd how much I could miss a place that carried such painful memories.

As I stood there staring toward the field, a metallic blue Audi swung out from the driveway across from ours. I looked down, pretending to study the urn of flowers until the car drove off. Rene St. Marie, no doubt, fifty-something, real estate developer and general town muckety-muck. His sister, Celine, was Mom's best friend. But there had never been any love lost between Rene and our family. The mutual dislike had only grown after Mom publicly and very disdainfully rejected his offer to buy the airstrip. Instead, she leased it long-term to the family that owned the Drunken Turkey Inn. They'd be responsible for the airstrip's taxes and other expenses; in exchange, the property couldn't be developed like Rene envisioned. Generally, I disagreed with Mom's business decisions. This one both shocked and thrilled me. Thank you, Mom, for sticking it to Rene St. Marie—and saving the field.

I got into the van and continued up the steep driveway. My family's large brick house sat at the top of the rise. It was built in the 1830s and had changed very little since then. As always, the gardens and lawn took my breath away. Irises and peonies overflowed beds and escaped cages. Ferns, hostas, and wild rose bushes crowded the edges of the lawn. No matter what time of year, the gardens never failed to remind me of Claude Monet's home in France, a location Grandma and Tuck had intentionally emulated when they'd planned the landscape. But what brought a prickle of tears to my eyes was the familiar sloped panorama of Scandal Mountain Valley, framed by the gardens and hills of lush-green trees.

A heavy sense of being right where I belonged closed in, as welcoming and weighty as the crazy quilt I'd napped under as a child, satin and velvet, embroidered with dates and symbols of past events, torn where time-frayed threads had laid open its cotton heart.

I took a steadying breath, then parked in front of the carriage barn that housed the shop. I retrieved a suitcase from the back. Its wheels clattered as I pulled it up the walkway toward the kitchen door. I'd barely been able to stand coming home for short visits, a day or two at the most, since I'd moved out. But this time Mom wasn't around—and that would make all the difference.

As I went inside, the rich aroma of simmering spaghetti sauce made my mouth water. I left my bag beside the kitchen table. As usual, it was piled with stuff: old oil lamps, leather-bound books, horseshoes, a pitcher decorated with hounds and hares, clay pots, seed packets—and a worrisome number of unopened bills and receipts.

A clank of dishes came from the pantry. Tuck mustn't have heard me pull in.

"Hello," I called, not wanting to startle him, especially if he was armed with a frying pan.

He lumbered out of the pantry, a bear of a man with tousled gray hair and a neatly trimmed beard. The apron he was wearing declared: *Powered by Plants.*

"Edie! I was starting to think I'd have to eat alone." He plunked down the colander he was carrying beside the sauce-filled crockpot and hurried toward me, arms open for a hug.

I met him halfway across the kitchen, resting my head against his broad shoulder as he squeezed me close. Despite the fabric softener scent of his cardigan, I caught a whiff of damp humus, like the smell of a plant-filled solarium.

"I've missed you," he said.

"Same here." I wriggled from the hug and mocked a glare. "You realize you owe me several explanations."

He grimaced. "I hated calling you at the last minute."

"Not just that. I expected you to be at the event—and where did Kala come from? She told me she's living here."

Tuck glanced at the door. "She's not back yet?"

"She said something about picking up a raspberry pie on her way home, my favorite—and don't even try to tell me you didn't put her up to that." I was glad when I discovered Kala

28

had her own car and planned on running some errands. I liked her and had enjoyed working with her, but I needed some private time with Tuck.

Tuck laughed. "Can't pull anything over on you, can I?" He went to where a loaf of French bread waited on a cutting board. "Kala showed up on our doorstep a few weeks ago, begging for a job. Your mom hired her."

"Figures. No matter how nice Kala is, it makes absolutely zero sense to hire an employee when you can't pay your bills."

Tuck drew a knife through the bread, most likely readying to transform it into crispy garlic toast, another of my favorites. "That's where you're mistaken. Kala's more than nice," he said. "She's listing low-end items for sale online. She's a whiz when it comes to research, computers, social media, and all those thingamabobs." He stopped slicing, looked at me, and raised his eyebrows as if holding back the best for last.

"And?" I prodded him to go on.

"In exchange, Kala gets five percent of those sales, room and board, and a chance to learn other aspects of the business from us."

"So, she's more like an intern than a full-fledged employee?" He went back to slicing. "She's a good kid. Eager."

"Agreed. Except"—I searched for a way to word my concerns without making us sound like a pack of criminals. Making money in the antique trade called for finesse, for certain moves and finagling that might be misinterpreted as illegal by someone not familiar with the business, especially with Mom's situation thrown into the mix.

Tuck chuckled. "Don't worry. Kala knows not to share private dealings with anyone. She's as sharp as they come."

"She was great at the appraisal event," I relented.

"I knew she would be."

I got a baking pan from the cupboard and set it next to the cutting board, then folded my arms across my chest. "Speaking of the event, Kala said you weren't there because you went to a garden club meeting. What if I hadn't showed up?"

"I know you better than that." His eyes twinkled. "I talked the club into hosting an African violet symposium later this year. The first step in my plan to take the gesneriad world by storm."

I laughed. It seemed his love for African violets was even overshadowing his interest in outdoor gardening. I wasn't sure how that fit into his plan for supplementing his retirement, but I had the feeling I'd soon find out.

He waggled a finger at the spaghetti sauce. "I was going to pop in to help you and Kala before I came home, but I decided you'd rather have a hot dinner waiting."

"It smells wonderful," I said.

His voice lowered. "I talked to Shane Payton for a minute while Kala and I were setting up. Did you see him?"

Heat crept up my neck. I'd never been sure how much Tuck had figured out about my relationship with Shane. However, he had always been perceptive when it came to my high school crushes, not to mention the guys I'd hooked up with when I was home on college breaks.

I shrugged as if it were no big deal. "I saw him, but we didn't talk."

"I've always liked that guy. He's got something going on in his upper story."

Tuck was right. Shane had a natural intelligence that went way beyond the degrees that hung on his office walls, not to mention a bunch of other appealing qualities. Still, right now, there were more pressing and less personal things Tuck and I needed to discuss—things that might lead to an infusion of cash for the business. "Do you know someone called Nina Graves-Bouchard?"

He thought for a second. "Can't say that I do."

"I met her today . . ." While Tuck coated the bread slices with garlic butter, I told him about Nina and the plover decoy. "She left my business card behind. But if we could locate her and talk her into hiring us to appraise the collection, at a minimum we'd get paid for that and she might recommend us to other people. If the collection has some exceptional pieces, maybe we can convince her into letting us cherry-pick something good in lieu of payment. I got the feeling she's strapped for cash."

Tuck paused, knife going still for a moment. "Does this mean you're going to stay and help out?"

I swallowed hard. I'd walked right into that one. "Well, I—"

"Your mom will be gone for nine months. If you stayed until then and took over running the business, we could get it back on track." He hesitated. "Even with Kala's help, I don't have the skills or time to keep everything afloat for long. Property taxes are coming up real soon. The septic tank needs pumping . . . Your mom thinks we should start selling off family pieces."

A chill went through me. *Grandpa's books. Grandma's stoneware collection. No way.*

I squeezed my fingers into fists, anger simmering. If I had half a brain, I'd take over like Tuck was suggesting, use the time Mom was away to show her how a business should be run.

My thoughts shifted to when I'd come home last Christmas and mentioned the very same possibility to Mom. "Don't be ridiculous," she had said. "Running a business isn't as easy as getting an 'A' in a marketing class. It's hard work. I should know. I live it every day while you gallivant around taking classes and interning at those posh auction houses."

A sick feeling rolled in the pit of my stomach. I looked at Tuck. "I'm not sure."

"It would be fantastic. We'd have fun, you and me." He raised his eyebrows, waiting for my answer.

I nibbled my bottom lip. I didn't really have any commitments or plans for the foreseeable future, other than freewheeling around New England, picking and selling. But what if Mom was right and my taking over dealt Scandal Mountain Antiques its final deathblow?

Another possibility occurred to me, a compromise. If I stayed and helped track down Nina, then I might get to see the decoy collection—and the thought of that was more than a little enticing. If we scored the appraisal, I could stay for that too. Income from something like that could pay a lot of back bills.

I flipped my palms up in mock surrender. "Alright, if we can locate Nina and talk her into letting us do an appraisal, I'll stay. But no other promises."

Tuck smiled as broadly as if one of his violets had won best of show at the upcoming symposium. For a moment his forehead wrinkled in thought, then he switched back to talking about Nina as if there'd never been any question about my sticking around. "You said this woman was assigned to a different appraiser at first, but they referred her to you. She didn't happen to mention who that appraiser was?"

"No. Why?"

"Probably nothing. It just strikes me as a little strange. After everything that's happened with your mom, we need to be extra cautious. What about the estranged husband and a father-in-law involved?"

I waved his question off. "There's no reason to worry. The other appraiser probably didn't know a lot about decoys. Nina was very open about everything. If anything, she acted a bit desperate. I think we should find her and jump on it. Folk art is hot right now."

"*Hot* is one of the things I'm concerned about."

I laughed. "The plover definitely wasn't stolen or part of an FBI sting, if that's what you're getting at. It was in rough shape, and Nina's an open book." *Man, it felt good to talk with Tuck like this.*

I saw a flare of brightness out of the side of my eye, light glinting through the kitchen window. I glanced toward it in time to see an older Prius pull in and park near where the carport jutted out from the carriage barn. "I'm guessing that's Kala."

"Sure is." Tuck shoved the pan of garlic bread into the oven. "It's a good thing dinner's almost ready. She gets snappy as a razorback when she's over hungry."

"A razorback?"

He chuckled. "She made me watch this horrible old movie the other night. *Razorback*, the feral hog, ripping apart cars and devouring people. Made me think of that serial killer up in Canada a while back, murdering people and disposing of their bodies by feeding them to his pigs."

Tuck must have downed more than a few bourbons before agreeing to watch something as disgusting as that. I laughed. "In that case, we shouldn't keep her waiting."

"Do you mind getting the spaghetti bowls while I—"

The upsweep of an instrumental ringtone interrupted him: "Serenade to Spring" from *A Secret Garden*, from somewhere on the kitchen table.

"Why don't you get that?" Tuck said. "It's probably your mom. She's scheduled to call around now."

Every muscle in my body went rigid. "I'll talk to her next time."

"Go on. She could use your encouragement. For heaven's sake, prison isn't day camp."

I looked down. "I know. I'm just not up to it right now."

Another sensuous sweep of music sounded. Tuck wiped his hands on a dish towel, then dashed for the phone. I felt like an ass for refusing. When I'd been arrested, I'd lived in terror of ending up exactly where she was right now, lived with it day and night until the judge agreed to probation. And I couldn't forget how cavalier Mom had been during my trouble, like what I was going through was no big deal, and she wasn't responsible for it to start with.

The melody stilled as Tuck answered. "Hello, Viki—" He stopped. "Oh, I'm sorry. I was expecting someone else to call. You want to speak with Edie? Sure, she's right here."

I frowned and mouthed, "Who is it?"

He shielded the phone with his hand. "Nina Graves-Bouchard."

I bit back the urge to squeal with joy and snagged the phone. "Hello, this is Edie."

"This is Nina from the appraisal event. I had the decoy."

"Yes, I remember you." I had to force myself to speak slowly.

"I got your number from your website. I hope it's all right to call so late in the day."

I pulled a chair back from the table and dropped onto it. Nina had to mean the Scandal Mountain Antiques website, since I didn't have one myself. "I'm glad you did. I enjoyed speaking with you earlier. I'm assuming this is about a possible appraisal of your other pieces?"

Nina's voice softened to a regret-filled tone. "I'm sorry I rushed off. I was getting a migraine from all the people and the cameras. I don't like crowds . . ."

As I listened to her drawn-out apology, Tuck noiselessly opened the kitchen door and signaled for Kala to stay quiet as she came up the walk and into the room.

I smiled a greeting to Kala, then said into the phone, "Don't worry, Nina, I totally understand, and I get your concerns. There are dealers in the antique business who would take advantage of people in your situation. If it makes you more comfortable, I'd be happy to look at the collection, tell you if it's worth having a written appraisal done and how much it would cost. There's no charge for doing that."

"Really?" I could hear the relief in her voice. "That would be wonderful. Ah, there is a slight problem: I have a very hectic week coming up—doctor appointments, my daughter's dance class. You don't happen to be free tomorrow?"

"Oh." I hadn't seen that coming. I'd figured—if we'd managed to locate Nina—I'd have time to scan some books and auction catalogues, refresh my knowledge of values and decoy makers, not to mention giving Nina and her family a quick background check online. I might have disagreed with Tuck a few moments ago about there being anything to worry about, but in principle I agreed it was better to be cautious ahead of time than run into trouble later.

Nina hushed her voice to a confidential whisper, "After I left the event, I kept thinking about the collection and insurance. What if it is worth a lot?" She hesitated, then finally continued, voice strained. "But I should warn you. My father-in-law is a hoarder. We—my daughter and I—live at his farm. He's letting us clean things up. But the house is—it's a disaster."

"Tomorrow's fine," I said gently. A hoarder's house, a place packed with stuff. A collection of decoys of unknown quality and origin. I licked my lips. "How about ten o'clock?"

Chapter Four

"Remember, when we get there, play it cool," I said to Tuck the next morning, as we headed forty-five minutes north to the boonies where Nina and her daughter lived, not far from the Canadian border.

Tuck glanced at me and smiled. "Are you talking to me or yourself?"

"Both, I guess." He was right. Anticipation knotted my stomach. Sweat slicked my palms. I stepped on the accelerator, leaving the cluster of houses that formed the village of Franklin behind. We cruised past barns and fields, brightened by lines of sprouting corn. The distance between the farms lengthened and a road sign announced the impending Quebec *frontière*.

"You didn't tell me to bring my passport," Tuck teased.

"Don't get your heart set on a Montreal vacation quite yet. The turn's right here." I swung down a dirt road.

He grabbed hold of the dash as we thumped over a hump where a large culvert ran under the road. "You might want to slow it down before you kill us both."

"Sorry." I reduced speed as we approached the hunter-orange mailbox Nina had said to keep an eye out for. The name

"Bouchard" was painted across its side. Next to it was a narrow gravel driveway hemmed in by dense underbrush.

A wave of fresh excitement tumbled through me. "Cross your fingers that this is our lucky break."

"Double crossed already," Tuck said.

Waist-high ferns whisked against the van as I started up the drive. A beaver pond materialized, skirting dangerously close along one side of us. The van lurched as we drove over a short makeshift bridge built out of barnboards and old pallets.

The pond retreated, surrendering to a swampy jungle of black alder shrubs, too thick for anyone to even bushwhack through and probably swarming with mosquitos. Warning signs covered a wooden gate and peppered dilapidated fence posts:

Private Property. No Trespassing.
No Hunting. No Soliciting.
Violators will be shot on sight.

Tuck leaned forward and peered out the windshield. "I hope Nina told her father-in-law we were coming."

I nodded. "It sure doesn't look like the kind of place she'd live. She seemed more like the suburban mom type, three-car garage, playdates, game night with the neighbors."

"Didn't you say her husband abandoned them here?"

"I'm not sure exactly what happened. She said he moved out last fall."

The black alder swamp yielded to fields and glimpses of an old farmhouse, darkened by the shade of aging maples. The front porch sagged under the weight of firewood and dilapidated recliners. A rusty chest freezer sat by the cellar bulkhead. Satellite dishes clung to the eaves. Nearby, a rundown cow barn and chicken coop were rotting back into the earth.

"Paradise," I murmured. "Absolute paradise." It was exactly the kind of place that might hold real treasure.

I pressed on the accelerator. In a minute, we'd be inside, checking it all out. This was going to be amazing if we could—

A huge animal lumbered into the road, directly in front of the van.

"Shit!" I jammed on the brakes.

The van skidded forward, gravel sliding under its tires. I put all my weight on the brake pedal. I couldn't steer around the animal without going into a ditch. A bear? A black lab? A family pet?

The tires finally caught, stopping our forward momentum a second before the van collided with the creature. What the hell was it?

Swallowing dryly, I craned forward. It was so close to the front bumper I could only see the ridge of its back, coated with a bristle of dark hair.

"Holy freakshow," I muttered as it moved into view. A monstrous pig, easily five or six hundred pounds. Leathery, mud-flap-sized ears partly covered squinty eyes. Its snout was slick and covered with dirt.

"Razorback," Tuck announced proudly.

I shot a glare at him, though his comment was kind of funny. "Kala's going to be jealous for sure when she hears about this."

One inch at a time, I let the van creep forward. But there was no way around the creature, and it showed no interest in going anywhere.

Tuck reached for the door latch. "I'll shoo it out of the way."

"After you telling me about that movie and the serial killer's pigs? No way." I pressed the car horn, a short beep. I hated to do anything that might seem rude this close to the house.

The pig glared at the van.

Stupid animal. I punched the horn, letting it blare.

The pig staggered forward into the roadside ditch and out of the way.

I stepped on the accelerator, then gave the pig one last glare in the rearview mirror. Only its outline was visible, a huge shadow trundling into the thicket of black alders. *Definitely pork chop material.*

"Edie." Tuck's tense voice brought me back to attention.

"What's wrong?" I said, but in the same instant I spotted what had disturbed him. Near the Bouchards' front porch steps, in the deep shade of the maples, a bulky twenty-something guy in a baseball cap and camo sweatshirt was tossing cardboard boxes into a dumpster. My teeth clenched. "Just what we need."

It never failed to astonish me how many people threw things out without thinking about potential value, artistic merit, or even historical significance. People heaved books, art, and furniture into dumpsters or trash fires, one at a time or by the cartload. They flung good stuff over banks and hauled precious items to recycling centers—whatever was easiest, especially when they were in a hurry to clean a place out. Sure, Nina had brought the damaged plover to the appraisal, but that didn't mean she wasn't allowing other things to get trashed. After all, she hadn't really liked the decoy until she found out its value.

"Maybe they're getting rid of legitimate trash," Tuck offered.

I narrowed my gaze on the dumpster. "I'm going to get a look in that thing on the way into the house. If they're getting rid of good stuff, I'll—"

Tuck cut me off. "You sure about that? Wasn't it you who said something about playing it cool and acting professional?"

I huffed out a frustrated breath. He was right. Dumpster diving definitely wasn't a part of the plan. We needed to focus on the decoys and getting the appraisal job. That's where the sure money was. Once we had a contract in hand for that, then we could think about taking a look-see around for other things. Still . . . "A quick peek couldn't hurt. I'm not talking about jumping in headfirst. It might keep them from tossing out something important."

Tuck chuckled. He waggled a finger at my outfit. "Glad to know under that fancy jacket, you're still my little picker girl. Remember when you used to dig bottles out of the old dump on the St. Marie property?"

I laughed. "I got good money for those bottles."

"Rene would have skinned you alive if he'd caught you trespassing—dumb bastard."

"That's for sure."

I parked the van beside a pair of cars and an older pickup with a jerry-rigged wooden tailgate. The driveway continued around toward the back of the house, but a trampled path across the lawn to the front porch made it clear that was the entrance of choice.

As we walked toward the porch, the bulky guy shambled away from the dumpster and vanished down the cellar bulkhead, like a woodchuck escaping into a burrow.

I bent close to Tuck. "Guess he didn't want to talk to us."

"Seems not," he said.

We stood in silence for a moment. The nonstop buzz of a chainsaw echoed from in back of the house, but no voices or sounds came from inside.

My mouth dried. "Do you think anyone's going to come out and invite us in?"

"She did say today?" Tuck asked.

"Yeah, definitely."

I took a few more steps toward the porch. A metal sign nailed to the front door reiterated the message of the ones we'd seen on our way in: *Solicitors shot on sight.* A chain and industrial size padlock hung nearby. The lock wasn't secured on the door, but it certainly didn't look welcoming.

Just when I began to worry this visit might amount to nothing, the pale face of a woman appeared behind a nearby curtained window.

A second later, the door inched open and Nina crept out. The shade of the porch faded her outline to nothing more than a faint silhouette, but the shadows failed to diminish the sharp blue eyes and brassy curls of the little girl tagging along beside her. If there was a spark of life and normality in the place, it belonged to the child.

"This is a lovely spot," I said to Nina as we reached the bottom stair. I motioned to Tuck. "This is my uncle, Angus Tuckerman. He's an expert in books and a wide variety of other things."

She nodded. "Nice to meet you. Angus, is it?"

"Tuck is fine." He smiled at the girl. "Who is this little sweetheart?"

The girl scowled. "I'm Gracie. I'm five years old—and you can't have Mr. Blue."

"Don't worry," Tuck said, totally deadpan. "I wouldn't dream of taking your things."

As we climbed the porch steps, Tuck reassured the girl we were only there to help her mommy. I nodded along. Most likely Mr. Blue was an aged-out toy Nina had threatened to sell or throw in the trash.

That thought reminded me of the dumpster. I glanced back. Thanks to the added elevation of the steps, I could see the contents. Empty cardboard boxes. A plastic tricycle. Plywood paneling. A broken laptop. Not a single interesting item.

Satisfied, I turned back and followed everyone inside, into a maze of garbage bags and stacks of yellowed newspapers. Rolled carpets filled one corner of the entry. Cardboard boxes climbed halfway to the ceiling. I reflexively covered my mouth and nose with my hand to keep out the stench of mildew and cat urine.

Thinking better of it, I forced my hand back down. As repulsive as the smell was, I didn't want to look impolite.

Nina grimaced. "I opened the windows earlier to air the place out. It's better than usual."

Tuck waved off her apology. "It smells like a rose garden compared to a house I was in last week."

"It's fine, really," I said. On the scale of disgusting odors, this was an eleven out of ten.

I felt a tug on my sleeve. Gracie was looking up at me. She whispered, "Pepe wets his pants."

"Gracie," Nina snapped. "That's not true. I told you not to listen to Mudder. The smell is from the cats, not your grandfather." She rolled her eyes. "Feral cats. I've chased them out a thousand times, but they keep sneaking back in."

"At least it's not the pig," Tuck said lightly. "We saw it on the way in. That's one heck of a porker."

"It certainly is, and not a particularly friendly one either." Nina took Gracie by the hand, towing her toward a narrow staircase that led to the second floor. "If you'll follow me. The collection is in the attic."

I hung back, letting everyone go ahead. Penetrating odors—especially tomcat—along with dampness and a multitude of other sins were enemies when it came to keeping antiques and art in good condition. This could be a real problem, even for decoys—even up in an attic, which generally was my favorite place to get into in any house, not counting the cellar and the outbuildings.

"Mommy, can we show them my room?" Gracie's voice echoed down from near the top of the stairs.

"Maybe later, dear."

As I gave the entry one last scan to make sure I hadn't missed anything important, I was surprised to see that the curtained window Nina had glanced through was closed tight. All the doors that led out of the entry room were also shut. If this was Nina's idea of airing out a house, she was doomed to fail.

I headed up the stairs and rejoined everyone as they started down the hallway. Like the entry, the hall was narrowed by mounds of trash. Plastic crates. Magazines. Old crockpots. A worn-out mattress. A crib. Nothing good.

"You'll have to forgive Gracie for the pee comment," Nina said, as the girl flew ahead of us, around a corner and out of earshot. "Mudder is forever telling her stories about her grandfather." She hesitated, then glanced at Tuck and me. "You must have seen Mudder when you drove in. Big guy with a baseball cap? He's my husband's cousin. Step-cousin, actually. He's been coming down from Canada to help me clean things out."

"Your father-in-law doesn't object to you doing that?" I asked. Given that she'd previously called him a hoarder, this seemed like a strong possibility. His objection might also make it hard for us to cherry-pick anything in lieu of them paying us cash for the appraisal.

"Getting rid of things is an ongoing battle with Jean-Claude. But he's fond of Gracie and has agreed to some changes for her sake."

"We have an older home too," Tuck said with a sympathetic bob of his head. "They're expensive to keep up. Always something to fix or clean."

Nina stopped walking and looked directly at us. "A couple of months ago, I was surprised when Claude let another dealer buy a few things."

I did a double take, not sure I'd heard right. That wasn't good. The best things might already be gone. "Did they buy any of the decoys?"

"My husband brought the dealer up here to look at some jewelry. I don't believe they went to the attic." She pressed a finger to her lips, thinking for a moment. "It was a woman from St. Albans. She owns a pawnshop. Fortuni's . . . something or other."

Slippery Martina Fortuni. My body went cold, and a bitter taste crawled up my throat. I hadn't run into her in years, but I'd thought of her just yesterday when I'd driven past the road to Fisher's Auction House. Now here she was again today turning up like a bad penny.

Tuck cleared his throat. "Are you talking about Fortuni Pawn and Treasures?"

"That's it. Martina Fortuni," Nina said. "My husband told Jean-Claude that he only sold her a handful of costume jewelry. Claude didn't believe him. It was just junk, I think."

"Jewelry—and coins—are her mainstay." I toughened my voice. "You want to be careful with her. She's honest enough, I guess. Just make sure she's not offering you scrap value instead of antique or numismatic value, in the case of coins."

"Numismatic value?" Nina shook her head. "I'm not sure what you mean."

"A coin's numismatic value is determined by rarity, condition, and demand rather than purely by its weight and the type of metal. Like with antique jewelry, a rare coin is worth more than just the value of the material it's made from. In other words, more than scrap value."

"Thank you for telling me that," she said.

"No problem. I can't stand dealers who aren't up-front with people." Any day I could warn someone off Martina was a good day, for the client and for us.

Nina turned the corner and stopped where Gracie waited in front of a narrow door. An oversized padlock, like the one by the front door, secured in place an equally large deadbolt.

Gracie bounced up and down. "Can I unlock it, please, please?"

Nina took a key from her pocket and gave it to Gracie. "Be careful, sweetie. Put it in, then turn gently." She smiled at Tuck and me. "My husband was a teenager when his mother married

46

Claude and they moved down here from Quebec. I'm sure Frank saw the decoys at some point, but I hadn't noticed them until a few weeks ago when I was in the attic looking for old photos. There really are quite a few of them. The birds, I mean."

My pulse picked up at the mention of a larger quantity. Still, there was another question begging to be asked. "What made you decide to bring the plover yesterday?" Why choose a worse for wear, legless shorebird? Was it because the rest of the collection was in even worse condition?

"It was the only thing Claude would allow me to take out of the house. He's very fond of his things." She nudged Gracie's hand out of the way, finished unfastening the padlock and deadbolt, then opened the door. "Watch your step. There's only one light in the stairwell and the steps are a deathtrap, especially coming down."

I hesitated, catching Nina's eye instead of moving toward the stairs. It was time to start edging toward the ultimate goal with a bit more vigor. "Before we go up, I want to stress that there's no such thing as a silly question. We're happy to answer anything as best we can—at any time."

Nina smiled, clearly pleased. "Thank you. I appreciate that."

"Tuck and I aren't here to buy today. All we intend to do is look at the collection and tell you if it's worth the cost of appraisal."

Tuck expanded on my comment, taking over with well-rehearsed ease. "I'm not sure if you're aware, but there are several types of appraisals. Appraisals based on replacement value are used for insurance. That's different than the value the pieces might get at auction or in a retail setting."

She nodded. "I'd like one for insurance purposes—and maybe the auction value too." She pressed her hands over her face and shook her head. "Honestly, even if the collection is worth insuring, I'm not sure I can afford to hire you."

I rested a comforting hand on her back. "Don't worry. Once we've looked at everything, if you like what we have to say, we'll work something out."

"We could always take something in trade," Tuck suggested, as casually as if it had never occurred to him before. "A decoy in lieu of a cash payment, perhaps."

Nina lowered her hands. "Really? That might help a great deal."

I bit back a smile. Cherry-picking items in exchange for work wasn't technically illegal, as long as the values were equal. And it was abundantly clear Nina—living in this squalor with a small child—could benefit financially from a trade as much as we would. The only thing we needed to make sure of was that we ended up with a premium piece or pieces, a fair trade with wiggle room to spare.

I quieted my voice. "Nina, do you mind if I ask you something else?"

I wasn't fool enough to assume she was unaware of my family's encounters with the law. If she had any concerns, it was wiser and easier to address them now.

"Of course not. Anything." She crossed her arms and tucked one leg behind the other, drawing it up until she stood on one foot like a stork. Until that moment, I'd taken her for an open book. Now she seemed defensive, worried I was about to ask a question she didn't want to answer. Sometimes the most innocent looking people are the best at hiding secrets.

I looked her in the eyes. "Why us? Why didn't you invite a larger shop or more well-known appraisers to look at the collection? I know, you met me at the event. But clearly you and Claude have connections with other dealers."

Nina unfolded her arms and untucked her leg, standing on both feet and looking at me squarely. Her voice became steady, full of truth. "Your knowledge at the appraisal was a large part of it. I also believe you can relate to my desire to keep my current living situation under wraps, more perhaps than other dealers."

"Appraisals are kept private. Always," Tuck said. He gave me a sidelong look as if to ask whether I was wondering how much more there was to this story.

"You see," Nina continued, "my husband—Frank—is a charming man. He could charm the pants off the Queen of England. My parents warned me about him, but I didn't listen. Frank drained my trust funds. He sold the home we received as a wedding gift. He pocketed that money and moved us here. Then he took off with the Corvette." She waved her hand, indicating her situation in general. "This is something I don't want to have leak out. I don't need anyone knowing, especially my parents and old friends. Even if the collection is valuable and we decide to sell it in the end, I want complete discretion."

Though I could only assume she came from serious wealth, I related wholly with her desire to keep personal embarrassment private. "You have our guarantee. No matter where this leads, not a word will get out about your situation."

"You don't know what a relief that is," she said. "I knew you'd understand."

Her shoulders rose and fell as if taking a deep breath. Then she turned on a light switch at the bottom of the stairwell and gestured for Tuck and me to go first.

To say the attic stairs were steep was an understatement. They would have challenged a mountain goat. As we climbed, the air became fresher, perfumed with the scent of wood and oiled leather rather than urine and mildew. Halfway up, my instinct was nagging me to move faster. I could smell old books and cardboard now, sense the warmth of a dusty and crowded place. There were good things in the attic, lots of them, I could all but taste it in the air.

At the top of the stairs, Tuck and I entered a long narrow space. The ceiling was low, with exposed beams and light bulbs stationed down the middle. Cobwebs coated mountains of forsaken furniture and trunks. It must have been a horrific chore to get the larger pieces up the stairs or through a window, or however they'd done it. Still, I'd seen similar piles in confined spaces before.

I glanced around. I couldn't spot anything incredibly valuable right off, but one thing was for sure—this was the definition of an untouched stash. Not a hoarder's mess.

"Go to your left," Nina called from where she and Gracie were still making their way up the steps. "The collection is on the table under the window."

I ducked past a curtain of tangled marionettes that hung from a beam and stepped around a pile of muskrat traps. A stack of hatboxes and suitcases. A broken eighteenth-century chair.

My hands trembled from excitement. My whole body felt on fire as I moved farther away from the stairwell. I leaned close to Tuck and whispered, "The decoys are good. I just know it."

I didn't hear his reply. I couldn't wait any longer. I rushed through the warren of spiderwebs, bedframes, and dressers, past a barrel filled with old wool jackets and around a broken bassinet brimming with plastic dolls, their chopped-off hair held flat by dozens of bobby pins. Floorboards creaked under my weight as I skirted mop buckets and agate basins, most likely intended to catch any rain that leaked through the roof.

Out of the corner of my eye, I noticed an armoire set deep under the eaves. One time my grandma had discovered an outstanding eighteenth-century sampler tucked away in a cabinet just like it. I needed to look in there. But not first.

First came the decoys.

Finally, I saw the table, a six-foot-long aluminum folding gizmo, too clean to have been in the attic for more than a few days. A light bulb illuminated it from above. Sunlight streaked across it from the nearby window, spotlighting the collection.

I froze, nearly too overwhelmed to move before I stumbled toward them, like a sleepwalker drawn into a dream.

A drake mallard, a goldeneye hen, a pair of teal, a lone black duck, shorebirds, including the plover from the appraisal event, and others. Not all in outstanding condition, but stunning nonetheless. A dozen of them, maybe a few more, lined up across the table. Honest, old pieces. Amazing. Simply gorgeous.

My gaze went to a wicker laundry basket nearby, full of newspaper-wrapped items. Next to it, unopened boxes and a large trunk waited. Were there more decoys in there? *Yes*, my instinct whispered.

"Ballerina bird!" Gracie screeched. She rushed past me toward the table, her small arms straining as they reached for one of the shorebirds, a yellowlegs with exceptionally long wire-and-cloth legs and outstanding paint.

Nina took her by the shoulders, pulling her back. "Remember what we talked about. If you can't behave, you'll have to go to your room."

Gracie shoved her hands into her pockets and grumbled, "I love the ballerina bird. It's my favorite."

My heart went out to her. The bird's head tipped at a jaunty angle. Its dark eyes gleamed slyly. I would have killed to have it at her age, or now for that matter. It was exquisite. And worth serious, serious money.

Tuck crouched by the wicker basket. He glanced at Nina. "Are there more in here?"

Nina nodded. "Gracie and I didn't have a chance to unpack everything. You're welcome to take the rest out, if you'd like."

"We can't give a realistic estimate without taking a look." I smiled. "However, I can already tell you this much: It is worth having an appraisal done. You have some very fine pieces here."

"Oh—that's wonderful."

I tilted my head to indicate Gracie, and said to her, "This isn't going to be a fast process."

Nina snagged Gracie's hand. "I'm guessing it would be easier without distractions."

"As long as you're comfortable leaving us alone," I said.

She waved off the comment. "I just appreciate you being willing to do this, especially on a Sunday. We'll be in the kitchen if you need us. We have some cooking to do, right Gracie?"

"*Sucre a la crème!*" Gracie cheered. "Pepe's favorite."

"Yes, it is. Except this batch isn't for him. This is for dance class."

Tuck stood up straighter. "That's one of my favorite treats too."

Nina grimaced, a tinge of pink flushing up her neck and across her cheeks. "I'm using a recipe from Frank's mother. She was an amazing cook. Mine, however, will probably come out more like rocks than sugary fudge."

I clenched my teeth, resisting the urge to glare at her and Tuck. I was as fond of *sucre a la crème* as they were. Mom's best friend, Celine St. Marie, always gave us a box of it for Christmas. But we were here to score a job, not talk about sweets. And I was all but shaking from a desire to handle the decoys.

"We better get going," Nina said.

As she propelled Gracie back across the attic, I exhaled in relief. I waited another second until their footsteps faded down the stairwell, then swiveled back to the table and scooped up the drake mallard. Pure joy rippled through me as I ran my hand over its painted surface. It was solid-bodied, smooth beneath my fingertips, and heavy from lead ballasts, the weights used by hunters to keep the birds upright in the water.

"Better than *sucre a la crème*?" Tuck asked, chuckling as if he knew how frustrated I'd been by the previous discussion.

"You do realize *how* nice these are, don't you?" My voice was breathy.

"I'm guessing not factory made?"

"Definitely not."

I studied the mallard more closely. Its paint was in pristine condition with a dry, mellow patina—simply exceptional. Hollow-carved and glass-eyed. Delineated bill. My entire being tingled from the honor of handling such an amazing piece of workmanship.

But, like the plover Nina had brought to the event, this decoy's style didn't perfectly mirror any that I'd studied in detail before. It had earmarks of some New England carvers, yet other details pointed to a Canadian origin. Still, it seemed like I'd seen similar pieces, perhaps in a museum, a book, or an auction catalogue.

I turned the mallard over. Maybe this time I'd find a maker's signature. Then the mystery would be solved, or at least easier to research.

"See anything?" Tuck asked.

A black brand marked the duck's belly. I wiped my thumb across it, cleaning off the surface to make it easier to read. "There's a circle with an initial inside it. It looks like—"

A brusque masculine voice with a rolling French Canadian accent interrupted me. "It's a '*B*' for Bouchard."

I wheeled around to find a small, older man three-quarters of the way across the attic from the stairwell, ambling toward us. He was somewhere in his mid-seventies, with a narrow, wrinkled face and a pointy nose. Faded green work pants were belted high on his waist and coated with fresh sawdust. The scent of chainsaw exhaust, beer, and marijuana hung in the air around him. Judging by his brashness, I assumed he was Nina's father-in-law. Mostly, I was surprised we hadn't heard him come up the steps.

His rheumy gaze went to the mallard. "*Pépère* Jean-Paul carved that one. *Mon oncle* painted it."

My throat contracted, shock stealing my ability to speak. I'd been so blind. *"B" for Bouchard.* This man's grandfather was Jean-Paul Bouchard—as in the famous Québécoise carver. And his uncle—undoubtedly another Bouchard family member—had painted it.

I gaped at the mallard in my hands as the connection between it and the folk art world sent electricity snapping through every cell in my body. Nina's use of Graves-Bouchard had thrown me off. Still, I should have realized. Of course I knew who'd made the decoys, or at least the two I'd studied so far. This family was related to *the* Bouchards, a renowned family of artists and carvers whose work dated from the late nineteenth through the mid-twentieth century, maybe a bit later. Being Canadian, they were a little out of my New England wheelhouse. But I'd heard of them and admired their works once or twice in person, most recently in Christie's end of the year listing of auction highlights.

I went numb as I remembered something else about the family, a story murmured in avid folk art circles, a rumor about pieces made at the peak of the Bouchard family's careers. The very best of their decoys, displayed at folk art events and hunting shows, and then secreted away. A legendary collection unseen for decades. A group of exceptional decoys that dealers, collectors, and museums would give anything to own.

Was I looking at that collection? Had I stumbled onto those legendary pieces in a dilapidated farmhouse in Vermont?

It certainly looked like I had.

Chapter Five

My hands trembled as I set the mallard carefully back on the table. Dear God, the long-missing Bouchard collection had to be worth hundreds of thousands of dollars. Perhaps millions.

Sweat rolled down my spine. As exciting as this possibility was, it made the need for caution even more vital. This could be the saving grace for my family, or the final bullet in our reputation if I misstepped.

I glanced at Tuck, widened my eyes, and pressed my lips together, hoping he'd take it as a sign that this was good, but that we needed to be wary. He nodded, almost imperceptibly. Then I looked back at Jean-Claude, softened my tone and asked a question similar to the one Nina had answered earlier. "Why didn't you let Nina bring one of the better pieces to the appraisal event? Most of these are much nicer than the plover. It's a privilege to have the chance to examine them."

He narrowed his eyes, his whole face crinkling as he pointed a weathered finger at me. "I wanted to see what kind of antique dealer an unmarked bird would lure in—a tricky magpie or a wolverine."

"Oh." My face heated. I wasn't totally sure what he meant, but he clearly was far more suspicious than Nina. "You are okay with us being here though, right? Nina just wants us to give our opinion."

Tuck sidestepped closer to me and rested a protective hand on my shoulder. "We were led to believe your daughter-in-law and son are overseeing your interests."

Claude snorted. "*Bon Dieu!* Frank's not my son. He's a step-son. The worst mistake I ever made was marrying his mother."

I folded my arms. As excited as I was by the possibility of what we'd discovered, Claude wasn't easy to take. However, I'd dealt with abrasive people like him before, and something told me the only way to earn his respect would be to ignore his blustering and meet him head-on.

Unfolding my arms, I pulled my shoulders back. "You know as well as we do that the decoys are valuable."

Tuck glanced my way. "I'd say *crème de la crème*, wouldn't you?"

"Very much so, judging by the mallard and the plover." I willed my voice to stay firm and pinned Claude with a hard look. "Are all the decoys from your family's personal collection?"

He stalked closer. "That's why I kept them up here. Away from prying eyes." His tone quieted, almost to a whisper. "For Gracie."

My heart seized in my chest, then it pounded so hard it felt like I might pass out. He'd verified my suspicion. This was the long-missing Bouchard collection.

I took a steadying breath. "I don't know what you have for insurance on this place or what else you have of value besides the decoys, but you're doing yourself a disservice if you don't have adequate coverage." His last and quietest comment pushed into my mind, a whisper that held more power than any shout. "A disservice to yourself—and to Gracie."

The sour expression dropped from his face. He took a step back and smiled as if I'd passed his rather odd litmus test. "You are a crafty one for sure. *Mon rusé carcajou.*"

I pretended I didn't understand; being called a sly wolverine seemed better than him thinking of me as a trickster magpie. I went on: "You need a professional appraisal. A rock solid one." I jerked my chin at a nearby mop bucket, half full of rainwater. "Frankly, even with full documentation, I'm not sure any insurance company is going to touch this. But you should try, and I'm willing to do the appraisal without it costing you anything out-of-pocket." Bouchard collection or not, Tuck and I weren't here for an ego boost. We were here to make money.

"You mean a trade?" A shrewd look brightened his eyes.

It was rapidly becoming clear Claude was not a man to be judged on crotchety behavior or appearance alone, or by the various odors that clung around him. He was very much like an old antique dealer who'd been friends with my grandparents: Bucky Sanders. Bucky always stank of liquor and streaks of tobacco juice stained his beard. In the winter, he wore tattered snowmobile suits to local auctions. In the summer, he switched to overalls and T-shirts with stretched-out collars. But he was brilliant, one of the smartest and sharpest dealers I ever knew. The biggest names in the industry traveled to Vermont to visit him.

I met Claude's eyes. "Once Tuck and I have seen everything and have a better idea how much time the appraisal will require, we can discuss the possibility of a trade further. The appraisal's not going to be a fast process. We'll need to photograph and document each piece, then research current values. My guess is that it'll take us a week to ten days at minimum."

Tuck touched my hand. "Do you want me to go downstairs and get Nina? I think it might be a good idea for her to hear this part."

I glanced at the table of decoys, avoiding Claude's glare. It didn't matter if he acted as if this was his decision alone to make. At the appraisal event, Nina had mentioned that she and Frank were co-trustees. I needed to know more about that situation. On top of that, even if everyone's signature wasn't legally necessary, I was going to require it. I wanted to make absolutely sure every angle was covered. Besides, family members were more likely to cooperate with each other when their names were on the same binding document, and I didn't need to be a therapist to see this family had more than its share of issues.

I looked back at Tuck and nodded. "Yeah. I think getting Nina is a great idea."

* * *

"I'll send the e-contract to you later today." It was a few hours later, and we'd finished a preliminary look at the collection. Nina was walking Tuck and me out the front door to the steps.

"I appreciate you doing this so quickly," she said.

"You'll need to sign and have Jean-Claude sign as well," I continued to explain. "Then it'll just be a matter of waiting for your husband to respond. You're sure the email you gave me for him is current?"

"I'm positive. Frank might take his time, but I can't imagine him not signing. He used to rant all the time at Claude about the property being underinsured. The collection being valuable enough to warrant an appraisal proves his point, and there's nothing Frank loves better than being right." She rubbed her bottom lip, quiet for a moment as if uncertain she wanted to say more. Finally, she said, "I suppose I could try calling him, just to let him know the contract is coming."

"That's a great idea," Tuck said.

She let out a loud sigh. "I never dreamed anything of Claude's would turn out to be valuable. My goodness, can you imagine if we'd had a fire?"

My thoughts went to the leaking roof and the decoys on the table, along with those we'd uncovered in the trunk and boxes. More ducks, two spectacular Canada geese, a preening hen merganser nothing short of breathtaking, and a group of shorebird flatties. Plus, if I was reading Jean-Claude's hints correctly, there were a few other pieces elsewhere in the house—one of several reasons I'd refused to give them even a general value for the collection. Instead, I'd only referred to the value as significant.

"Once we have all the signatures," I said, "we'll come back and start the appraisal process right away."

The guy who'd been tossing stuff into the dumpster when we arrived galumphed out the open front door with a roll of reeking carpet slung over one broad shoulder. *Mudder*, I reminded myself of his name. Frank's step-cousin. Claude's great-nephew. Hired to do the dirty work.

I stepped aside, making room for him to pass.

"Need a hand with that?" Tuck asked.

"Ya, no. I got it," he grumbled, his French Canadian accent even stronger than Claude's.

Nina tagged behind him as he lumbered down the porch steps. "Don't forget to pull all the tacks out of the floor once you're done getting the carpet up. The boxes in the entry need to go before you leave for the day."

Mudder heaved the rug into the dumpster. "Ya, no problem."

I bit my lip to cover a smile. Poor Mudder. Not only did he have to put up with his great-uncle Claude's brusqueness, but he had to deal with Nina's supervision. Fortunately, Tuck and I would be working in the attic, hopefully without an audience.

I turned to Tuck. "Unless you can come up with something I've forgotten, I think we've done all we can for today."

"As far as I can see, we're all set," he said.

Nina beamed. "Thank you again. Thank you so much."

As Tuck and I walked to the car, it took every ounce of willpower to keep my pace relaxed and my mouth shut. I wanted to hoot for joy and pirouette across the lawn. The Bouchard collection. The appraisal job of a lifetime—and it was all ours. Well, ours as soon as I got the contract together and they all signed it.

Still biting my tongue, I turned the van around and headed out the driveway. I kept one eye on the rearview mirror, waiting until the house receded into the distance before I thumped the steering wheel and let out an enormous cheer.

"Can you believe it, Tuck?" Warmth radiated through me. "If we play this right, we might walk away owning a piece or two. You do realize how important this collection is?"

He swiveled toward me, face eager and ruddy from excitement. "I gathered it was good news from the way you were glowing up there in the attic."

I jumped in, unable to contain myself. "Those decoys are probably one of the most important collections to ever surface. The Bouchards are legendary. These pieces haven't been seen in decades."

He shook his head, as if trying to take it all in. "I could see they were quality pieces, but that's—incredible."

I reached the mouth of the driveway, waited a second as I turned onto the road, then told him everything else I could remember about the long-missing decoys. "The collection represents the family's work at the peak of their skills. Dealers, collectors, even museums haven't known where the pieces went off to. They just vanished . . ."

When I was finished, Tuck gave a low whistle. "I was going to suggest that we offer to look through the rest of the house once we're done with the appraisal, to see if we find any general merchandise worth buying. Now I'm thinking it's silly to hunt for scraps. Instead, we should talk them into putting the collection in a top-notch auction with us acting as their intermediary agent. For a healthy commission, of course."

"That's probably the best route. Right now, I'm mostly worried about Frank not opening the email. We need everyone to sign. We can't afford to make any mistakes."

"Nina said she'd phone him. Maybe Frank won't respond instantly to the call, but he'll want to make sure she wasn't phoning about Gracie. No man in his right mind wouldn't worry about a little princess like her. Gracie even makes old Claude weak."

For a moment I couldn't say anything. I just stared at the road ahead as an ache of unspoken pain twisted in my chest. Not all men were as good as Tuck, or so weakened by the innocent eyes of a child. Some men didn't think twice about the children they created. Some men didn't even wait around to see them born. Some men, like my father.

Tuck sanded his hands together eagerly. "How about we celebrate by getting some lunch? I'm starving."

I laughed. "I was going to ask if you were okay with driving home by way of St. Albans. I need to pick up a couple of things in the city. If you can wait that long, I'll treat you to bagels and soup. While we eat, I want to scout around online. I vaguely remember something in the news recently about a Bouchard piece." St. Albans wasn't that far out of our way. It had a movie theater and bigger grocery stores, a better selection when it came to necessities than Scandal Mountain's smaller shops. It was also where I used to meet up with Shane, both at his office and for coffee, back when I was on probation.

Tuck patted his stomach. "Fine by me, as long as lunch comes before shopping."

"Don't tell me you're going to turn hangry like Kala," I teased.

He chuckled. "Like a razorback."

* * *

By the time we reached St. Albans and Irwin's Bagel Deli, Tuck had devoured the entire stash of granola bars I kept in the glove box. I felt a bit guilty for not stopping someplace closer, but Irwin's was my favorite lunch spot and I hadn't been here since I'd gotten off probation.

I ordered a toasted sunflower bagel with artichoke cream cheese and a raspberry iced tea. Heaven on earth in my book. Tuck muttered about turkey pastrami being a crime against nature but ordered the twist on the classic Reuben anyway. Food in hand, we claimed a table at the rear of the deli's seating area.

"I'm all for Kala coming with us when we go back to do the appraisal," Tuck said between bites. "That would leave me free to focus on documentation while she helps you set up and take photos."

As he continued to eat and give suggestions, I nibbled my bagel and searched on my phone for recent information about Bouchard pieces. Later, I'd have to go through auction catalogues carefully to get an accurate idea of values, especially since this collection fell into the long-missing and legendary category.

I added the words "Quebec folk art" to the search, and a slew of newspaper headlines popped up. I blinked for a second, suddenly aware of another reason the Bouchard name had seemed familiar:

> *"Theft of Quebec Treasures Joins Ranks of Brazen Museum Heists"*
> *"Canadian Museum of History: Over 5 Million Dollars in Art Stolen"*
> *"Cultural Treasures Vanish. No Leads in Shocking Robbery"*

The robbery had happened at the beginning of April, when I'd still been an intern at Christie's. Everyone had talked about it for weeks. One of the stolen pieces was a Bouchard painting.

"Hey, Tuck, do you remember the robbery at the museum in Quebec last month?" I asked.

He stopped chewing and frowned. "Vaguely. Wasn't someone killed? Why?"

"Yeah. A police officer. It looks like another wounded person died just yesterday. Let me read this to you." I clicked on the most recent article:

"Gatineau, Quebec—The security guard wounded during the heist last month at the Canadian Museum of History has died as a result of his injuries. There are still no suspects in the dramatic robbery that left Canada in shock. No information about how the thieves got into the museum has been released and the suspects remain at large. A two hundred and fifty thousand dollar reward is being offered for information that leads to the safe return of the stolen cultural treasures and/or the arrest and arraignment of the thieves. Among the missing pieces are sculptures by Inuit carver Johnny Inukpuk, a hooked rug created by fabric artist Ozama Martin, and a series of paintings known as Dogs and Decoys *by the renowned folk artist Jean-Paul Bouchard."*

"I assume that's the same Jean-Paul who made decoys?" Tuck asked.

"Definitely. There are several Bouchards from the same family who were both painters and carvers. He's the most famous."

Tuck set his bagel down, then wiped a stray piece of turkey pastrami off his sleeve. A wistful look came over his face. "You said a two hundred and fifty thousand dollar reward?"

I laughed. "Wouldn't that be nice."

"I could add a solarium onto the carriage barn for that kind of cash—complete with grow lights and a watering system."

"Or pay a mountain of bills?" I suggested.

Tuck's wistful look faded. He sat up straight and glanced toward the checkout area. "Interesting . . ."

"What is it?" I wasn't sure I wanted to look. Knowing Tuck, it was a fifty-something woman in bicycle shorts or a low-cut shirt. It didn't take much to get him going.

He waggled his eyebrows suggestively. "Don't look now, but someone you should be dating just bought cookies and a coffee."

Heat rushed across my cheeks. "Are you talking about Shane?" I hardened my voice. "If he sees us and comes over here, don't you dare say anything that will embarrass me."

I ran my tongue over my teeth, searching for stray bits of bagel or sunflower seeds. I dabbed the corners of my mouth with a napkin, then began to suspect Tuck was pulling my leg. "He's not really here, is he?"

"Would I lie to you?" Tuck sat back, a glisten twinkling in his eyes. "You used to tell me this was his favorite spot. Isn't that why we came here? We drove past several other places where we could have eaten."

"That doesn't mean I was expecting to see him."

He smirked. "More like hoping."

I glanced at the checkout area. Shane had finished there and was sliding into a nearby booth with his back to us. His dress slacks, the iPad he was setting on the table, even the slightly isolated booth he was sitting in suggested he was meeting a probationer—at least, every detail mirrored how it had been when we met here. Once they arrived, he'd buy coffee for them and share his cookies.

My throat tightened. I took a sip of my drink and then another. What type of probationer was he meeting outside of the office, and on a Sunday? Someone who worked during the week. Someone who'd earned special treatment. It might even be an attractive young woman who didn't belong in the system.

My stomach tensed.

I shoved that thought from my mind. Even if Shane was meeting a woman, it wouldn't be the same as it had been with me. What happened between us was an anomaly, something he'd never done before and was probably even less likely to do again. He was beyond a good person. In fact, I'd always felt guilty about encouraging him that weekend in the Adirondacks. Not that he couldn't have said no, and not that the relationship wasn't mutual. There was no question he had been as into me as I was into him.

Tuck nudged my hand. "Go talk to him."

"I planned on calling him later this week," I said. I took another look.

Shane scrubbed a hand over the back of his head, rumpling his hair, curly and as sandy brown as spiced honey. My mind went to that weekend, his damp hair clinging to his neck as he came out of the moonlit lake, his body as naked and excited as mine. His hair was shorter now, but no less enticing.

He shifted in his seat, checked his iPad, then glanced toward the bakery's front door. Perhaps he feared his appointment would be a no-show. Maybe he was getting ready to leave.

Damn it. Why shouldn't I talk to him? I thought as I got up and marched across the room. Tuck was right. I'd been hoping we'd run into him.

"Hey, Shane," I said when I reached his booth.

He turned toward me, eyes brightening. "Edie! What a nice surprise. I felt bad I didn't get a chance to talk to you yesterday."

The warmth of his voice set off flutters in my belly. "Me too. But it was kind of busy."

"That decoy you appraised was right up your alley, wasn't it?" he asked.

"The plover? Definitely, I was really excited to see it." I wasn't surprised the plover was the first thing he asked about. Decoys were one of the things he collected.

"It made quite a splash on TV this morning," he said.

I frowned, confused. "What do you mean?"

"The appraisal event. The segment with you and the plover aired on the *Morning Show*. You looked great."

Fear knotted in my chest. The plover had appeared on TV before we had the contract with the Bouchards signed. That wasn't good. Not at all. A dealer more experienced than I was with Canadian decoys might recognize the plover as a Bouchard piece on sight. Sure, I'd watched countless TV appraisal shows and they never announced the names of the pieces' owners on the air. Still, that sort of dealer might have connections and be able to find out who Nina was. They could try to slide in under us and buy the entire collection. My voice choked. "I didn't realize the episode was going to air so soon."

Shane smiled at me, totally enticing. "What was that woman's name? The one with the plover?"

"Ah—I think it was Tina Gray or Gravel . . . something like that." I liked Shane, a lot. Not long after the first probation meeting, I vowed never to lie to him. Trouble was, he had lots of friends who collected antiques and acquaintances who'd kill for a chance to own a Bouchard. Not that Shane would intentionally sabotage us, but anyone can let information slip out and rumors fly.

Shane's eyes met mine. There was no missing the familiar smolder in their depths. "I was going to call, ask if you wanted to do something while you're home. Do you still have the same number?"

My heart stumbled. That voice could make me do anything. "Yeah. How about yours?"

"My personal one's the same." His smile grew into a proud grin. He reached for his iPad. "You want to see something I've been working on?"

He brought up a photo, then turned the iPad so I could see. The image was of a small, two-story log cabin. Twin Adirondack chairs sat on the front porch. Vines climbed up the wide stone chimney. That weekend in the Adirondacks, Shane had said someday he was going to build a log cabin. It had sounded like a pipe dream, but I wasn't shocked he'd followed through.

"It's really beautiful," I said.

"It's not finished yet. I'm living in the downstairs for now."

I studied the photo again. Last I knew, Shane lived with his parents. He moved back in with them after his mother suffered a traumatic brain injury. As a kid, he'd dreamed of becoming an FBI agent or a K-9 officer. He aimed in that direction after high school, then pivoted to becoming a probation officer because it guaranteed he could work close to home and help out his parents. "So, your mom's doing better?"

"She's almost fully recovered. She and my dad moved into a smaller place a couple of years ago. That's when I decided to build the cabin. It's here in St. Albans, just outside of town."

"Looks amazing. I'm assuming there's a big fireplace?"

"It takes up one whole wall." He touched my hand, strong fingers tightening around mine, forging a link between us. "I'd love to show it to you."

"I'd like that." My voice was breathy. And, for the briefest of seconds, I caught my bottom lip between my teeth. Then I let my shoulders slump. "I'm not going to be in town for very long."

He sat back. "I assumed you were here for . . . the summer."

I suspected his momentary hesitation had been him avoiding saying "nine months." No doubt he'd heard my mom's sentence on the news and assumed that was at least part of the reason for my return. "I'm thinking a week and a half. Maybe a little longer."

"We still should get together." His hand withdrew and the smolder left his eyes. He nodded at the empty seat across from him. "I'd ask you to sit down, but I'm expecting someone any minute."

I shrugged and smiled. "I figured as much. Besides, I'm here with Tuck. If I don't get back soon, he'll finish his lunch and start on mine."

Shane laughed, a deep, wonderful sound. "I've missed you, Edie."

"Same here. I really hope we can get together."

I looked down to avoid his eyes, but found myself staring at his oxford shirt, sleeves rolled up to reveal corded forearms. Angel tattoo on the right. Devil on the left.

Man, I'd missed those arms.

Chapter Six

I sank down on the edge of the bed to check my emails for the fortieth time. I'd sent the appraisal agreement to everyone three hours earlier, but so far no one had signed. I'd expected Nina to do it as soon as the contract hit her inbox. If Claude wasn't conversant with the process, she could walk him through it. Even if he resisted signing, she'd keep after him and eventually wear him down. Then there was Frank. It sounded like he'd wanted the insurance situation taken care of. Still, he might refuse to sign or delay just to irritate Nina.

I brought up my inbox. Three messages! Please, please, please be the contracts.

One was from Nina. She and Claude had signed. Fantastic.

The other emails were online auction listings. Nothing from Frank.

Grumbling under my breath, I deleted the auction listings, then got up and paced to the closest window.

A breeze drifted in, bringing with it the scent of lilacs. In the distance, the late afternoon sunshine caught on the treetops and brightened the edges of the valley below. I'd missed this view. The only thing that equaled it was how good it felt to be back in my old bedroom. For one thing, it was as large as my entire Brooklyn apartment. Thank goodness I'd been able to cut ties with that gerbil cage as soon as my last internship was over.

Sure, I'd liked a lot of things about living in the city: museums, auction houses, lectures and classes, and the exhilaration of working with first-rate experts. I'd never lacked for things to do or new friends to do them with. Still, it had often amazed me how deeply alone I could feel in a crowded room where I knew everyone.

Here there was no hustle or bustle. There wasn't even a distant hum of cars or voices, especially since Tuck and Kala had just left for St. Albans to stock up on groceries. Right now, there were no sounds except the flutter of the curtains and the trill of evening birdsong. Yet I felt content and connected to everything in a way I hadn't in New York. I felt at peace.

I smiled. At peace, especially since Mom wasn't here to drive me nuts.

Thoughts of another late May evening slipped into my mind. I'd just gotten home for my summer break between junior and senior years in college. Mom was waiting in the living room for a U-Haul full of antique furniture to arrive. She'd bought the contents of two storage lockers while on vacation in New Orleans and hired movers to drive the load back to Vermont.

"You did look over the stuff thoroughly before you bought it?" I'd asked. I knew the question came across as a little snotty, but the shop was rapidly filling up with her mistakes.

She scoffed. "I was under a time crunch. The man who owned the units reassured me they were full of quality rosewood pieces—John Henry Belter, high-end Victorian and Rococo Revival. The man's a very respectable local businessperson."

"But he couldn't get a local antique dealer to buy the stuff?" I didn't mention that Victorian furniture was currently not as popular as it once had been—or question where she met this bigwig man.

"Are you implying I don't know anything? I've been in this business longer than you've been alive."

I gritted my teeth. "No, Mom. I just wish you'd be more careful."

"I don't know why you always have to put me down," she said.

"It's not that." I rubbed a hand over my face. "I really do hope it's wonderful."

An hour later when the U-Haul arrived, it was clear the man hadn't totally lied. The furniture was antique and high end. It did include Belter pieces. But at some point, the pieces had shared a home with a malamute—or a pack of extra-furry, wood-chewing, and upholstery-shredding dogs, and fleas. Worst of all, the pieces were infested with wood-boring beetles. If I hadn't noticed the telltale sawdust leaking out from where the insects had tunneled into the furniture's wood, the shipment could've infested everything in the shop.

My thoughts were interrupted by the purr of a high-performance engine.

As I listened, the sound grew louder, coming up the driveway. Not Tuck's Suburban, that was for sure. A customer? It was late for that.

I leaned forward to catch a glimpse of the approaching car. It seemed unlikely, but could it be Shane? He hadn't said anything about stopping by. For that matter, he'd never been to the house before, any more than I'd ever visited his parents' home. Still, he knew my address.

Anticipation quivered in my stomach. I turned from the window, sprinted out of the room and down the front staircase. Guests didn't come to the front door anymore, not since Grandpa had laid the walkway up to the rear of the house. I bolted to the kitchen and opened that door, breathless.

A vintage red Corvette had parked next to my van and a man was getting out.

My excitement drained. He was shorter than Shane and much older, about Mom's age, with slick black hair and a strong clean-shaven jawline. He wore stylish tinted sunglasses and a polo shirt under an open lightweight jacket.

I glanced at the car's bumper, expecting to see a Quebec or out-of-state plate, an antique or art dealer arrogant enough to drive a flashy car and not call ahead or care that it was past normal shopping hours.

The plate was from Vermont.

Vermont. A Corvette. I felt my eyes widen. *Oh, my God.* Nina had said Frank took their Corvette when he moved out. Frank Bouchard, here? This might not be good.

He strolled toward me with the swagger of a person who knew exactly where he was going and what he was doing, as if stopping by the house was something he did regularly. Nina had said he could charm the pants off the Queen of England. Undoubtedly, his casual ease was a part of that game.

I pulled my shoulders back and stepped out of the doorway and onto the landing. Maybe he could win over other people with a flash of a smile, but I was onto him.

As he neared, I rethought that stance and let the fight go out of my spine. As much as I wanted to confront him, I couldn't come off as antagonistic. I needed to play this cool. I wanted his signature on the contract more than he probably felt compelled to give it to me. This would have been so much easier if Tuck and Kala were here for backup.

Frank smiled—perfect teeth, as white and sparkly as a piranha's. "Are you Edie Brown? I'm Frank Bouchard."

A bead of sweat tracked down my spine. "I assume you got my email or spoke with Nina?"

His tone deepened. "There's something you need to know. You have no idea what you're getting yourself into."

My mouth dried. That wasn't at all how I'd expected the conversation to open. "I take it you're talking about the appraisal. Nina says you've been concerned that your father's property isn't adequately insured. Rest assured, the goal of the appraisal is to move toward that end. Nothing else."

"So *you* think." Sincerity played in his eyes, but it was as believable as "*trust me*" coming from the mouth of an attorney arguing on behalf of a crime boss. "Your goal may be purely business; Nina's is never that simple. Don't let her fool you into thinking she's a defenseless victim. She's a bitter, vengeful woman."

My BS meter went off, shrieking at a hundred decibels. I couldn't let him sidetrack me from getting his signature. "I'm aware that you and Nina are co-trustees of Jean-Claude's estate, right?"

"Yes." His voice quieted. He nodded at the doorway behind me. "We should go inside? Clear off a place at the table. Sit down and talk?"

A chill swept my skin and the hairs stood up along my arms. How did he know the table would need clearing in order to sit?

The answer came to me and I bit back a smile. Of course. The door behind me was open. He could see the cluttered table inside, and he wanted to control the situation by putting me on edge.

I rested my hands on my hips. "Talking out here will do just fine. Is there something about the contract that bothers you? It's standard, but conditions can be added or removed."

"The contract's not the issue." He took his phone out, swept his finger across the screen, then held it up for me to see. "All signed."

I stared at the screen. He wasn't lying. "Thank you. Ah—" I considered saying his cooperation would help Nina and Claude as well as him, then thought better of it. "This will help ensure Gracie's future. The decoy collection is quite valuable." No sense hiding it. He'd know as soon as I sent him his copy of the completed appraisal.

"I don't doubt that. Claude, the old skinflint, has kept it close to his vest for a long time. Just don't forget to dot all your i's and cross your t's. Watch your step, Edie Brown."

His gaze lingered on mine. Normally, I was a good judge of people. But in that moment, I wasn't certain if my BS meter had judged Frank fairly or if Nina's opinion of him had poisoned my first impression.

"What do you mean?" I asked. Was he warning me to watch out for Nina and Claude? Or warning me to not try and pull anything shady. I really couldn't tell. I leveled my tone. "Everything will be well documented and aboveboard."

"Fine. Just don't forget what I said." With that he turned on his heel and strode back to his car.

As I watched him drive away, I wished he'd given me time to ask a few more questions.

Chapter Seven

I grabbed a bottle of beer from the fridge, returned to the back stoop, and sat down to mull over Frank's visit. Given our family's reputation, I understood why he might have concerns. I could also grant that Nina might not be totally without faults or above milking her situation to gain sympathy. But what was Frank truly getting at? Did he believe Nina and/or Claude intended to rope me into some sort of scheme, like bribing me to overinflate the appraisal so they could play arsonist and collect a larger settlement? Arson fraud, among other insurance type schemes, wasn't exactly unheard of in the arts and antique world.

In one well-known case a Beverly Hills collector took a Monet he owned to another location, then he hired an arsonist to burn down his house. Before the FBI Art Crime Team caught up with him, he'd collected the insurance on the Monet and afterward secretly sold it on the black market, netting himself additional cash.

I rolled my beer between both hands, feeling the chill against my palms. I had a hard time believing Claude would do anything that might hurt the collection. As crotchety as he was, he treasured the decoys. On the other hand, Nina didn't care about the birds beyond their potential value. Still, she didn't come across as bright enough to be a criminal mastermind.

I paced to the end of the walk and looked down the driveway, wishing I'd hear the crunch of tires and see Tuck's Suburban coming up the hill. I was dying to talk to someone, but most likely he and Kala wouldn't be home for hours. Tuck had prescriptions to fill and Kala had a massive shopping list, mostly what she called brainfood, also known as snacks. I mean, plenty of people have dietary restrictions, or don't eat meat or anything not organic. Kala required the opposite: salty, sweet, processed, and preferably fried. Ice cream. Bacon. Canned onion rings. Tuck seemed totally amused by this and eager to egg her on.

I hiked back to the door. I could text Tuck, tell him about Frank, but that wasn't the same as face-to-face time with a cold drink.

An idea blossomed. Maybe it was good. Maybe it was bad.

Before I could talk myself out of it, I snagged my phone and texted Shane's personal number. *Hey, I'm headed down to the Jumping Café for a drink. Want to join me?*

I didn't have to tell him details about the appraisal or Frank's visit. I could talk in generalities about that and Frank's warning. Shane was a great sounding board, open-minded and logical. If he didn't text back right away, I'd stay home and forget the whole idea. If he really did want to meet up, there was no better time than the present to talk through my worries, and reconnect at the same time.

I went inside and immediately my phone pinged, Shane texting back. *Give me a half hour. I'll be there.*

Great! See you soon.

My heart pounded a thousand miles per hour as I ran upstairs, did my makeup, fixed my hair, threw on good jeans and a sexy top. I was downstairs and out to the van in less than fifteen minutes.

Pedal to the metal, I drove toward the Jumping Café. It was on the main road, about three miles past the turn to our house. Scenes from the weekend with Shane in the Adirondacks floated into my mind, not just the cabin or the hot times in bed (and on the beach, and in the woods), but the other things we'd done together too. One day, we'd gotten up before dawn and canoed into a wildlife area. We'd watched the sun rise and the waterlily blooms open, then we'd drifted past an awakening heron rookery. Truly unforgettable. Later, we had a picnic on a rock outcrop and napped in each other's arms. So many wonderful moments.

I pulled into the Jumping Café's parking lot and found a spot near the open-air deck. The term "café" was a slight misnomer. The building actually contained a restaurant, a pub, and a reception hall. Most important—at least in my mind—was the café's outdoor flea market. It was where I had my first solo ventures as a dealer, selling the bottles I dug up on Rene St. Marie's property to collectors and dealers, including Bucky Sanders with his tobacco-stained beard and sharp eye for quality.

As I got out and headed for the front door, I noticed a poster thumbtacked to the café's event board.

Memorial Day Celebration! Starting at 11am.
Parade. Chicken barbecue. Kids games.
Live music. Cow plop bingo. Fireworks!

I could almost smell the barbecuing chicken and hear the fireworks exploding overhead. Flares of color would brighten the valley. Smoke from the black powder would haze the crowd. I'd always loved the Memorial Day celebration as a kid. With luck—and if we worked hard for the next few days—we'd finish the appraisal before the weekend. Instead of taking off right after that, I could stick around for old times' sake. Kala would love the celebration for sure. But first things had to come first, and a sentimental journey didn't outweigh everything else I had going on.

Inside, the café's air was warm. It might not have smelled like barbecuing chicken tonight, but it was filled with other tantalizing aromas, most notably their infamous brick oven pizza. My mouth watered as I made my way across the restaurant and into the adjacent pub. The place was as cozy and dark as I remembered. A clink of glasses and murmur of voices rose from the booths in the back, but I didn't see Shane anywhere.

The guy behind the bar stopped slicing a lime and smiled a greeting at me. He was pudgy and balding. His rainbow-hued T-shirt proclaimed he was a proud Hufflepuff.

"Nice night out there, huh?" he asked.

"Sure is." I scooched my butt half up on a barstool and glanced at the liquor on the shelves behind him. "I'll take a citrus vodka on the rocks with a twist."

"Would you like something to go with it? Tonight's special pizza is Vermont Hawaiian—red sauce, smoked ham, and pineapple with a drizzle of maple syrup. By the slice or pie."

"Sounds fabulous, but I'll just take the drink for now. I'm waiting for someone," I said.

The pungent smell of aftershave filled my nose, signaling a man had walked up behind me. Definitely not Shane. He was more of a subtle fragrance guy.

I winged around and found Felix Graham standing an inch away. He might not have been wearing an expensive suit and stickpin like at the appraisal event, but his jacket and white shirt unbuttoned at the collar appeared no less posh.

His gaze skimmed over me. "Fancy meeting you here," he said. He leaned past me, his arm brushing mine as he spoke to the bartender. "I'll take the usual, and put it on my tab."

His closeness sent a shudder of revulsion through me, and I wanted to ask when he'd become a regular at the pub. For sure, Tuck would have mentioned if Graham had moved out of Burlington and into Scandal Mountain. I resisted asking that and instead searched for something innocuous to say. "Good turnout for the appraisal event, don't you think?"

"Very much so. I saw one of your appraisals made it onto TV."

"Yeah. It should be great for promotion." I looked away from his probing eyes, glancing past his shoulder as if watching for someone and only half interested in him. I shouldn't have said anything about the event. The last thing I needed was to draw his attention to the plover and the Bouchards. That said, I did have a nagging question, and he might have heard behind-the-scenes chatter that I wasn't privy to. I glanced back at him. "The woman who brought that plover had originally been assigned to a different appraiser. You don't happen to know who that was?"

He preened, smoothing back the distinguished gray at his temples. "As a matter of fact, I do. It was me."

"You?" No way could I keep the surprise out of my voice. "Well, thank you. I thought you knew a fair amount about decoys yourself."

"Enough to get by," he said with false modesty. He sighed heavily. "To tell you the truth, I heard a number of people had refused to go to your table for appraisals—on account of your mother's situation. I hated to see you sit there all day for nothing, so I sent the woman over."

The bartender chose that moment to set my drink in front of me—and I was beyond grateful. I wasn't sure if Graham expected me to grovel in appreciation or spit fire at him for his condescension. I knew which one I felt like doing, and it wasn't the former.

I pushed back my anger and coolly slipped off the edge of the stool, claimed my glass and handed the bartender my debit card. While he processed it, I swiveled toward Graham and took the middle ground. "I appreciate your help. Actually, I was busy all day after that."

Graham nodded. "That's nice." His voice toughened. "To be clear, since then I've questioned whether encouraging you was the kind thing to do. You're a smart girl, Edie. You'd be wise to go back to New York before your reputation gets tied to your mother's mistakes."

My fingers tightened around my drink, clenching it hard. Too bad the glass wasn't Graham's neck. Strangling him until he started to gurgle would have felt pretty good.

I glared at him and didn't try to hide my sarcasm. "Thank you for the advice, but I plan on staying." For how long was none of his business.

Graham bent nearer to me, speaking slow and concise as if to make sure I understood each word. "Over the years, I've referred clients to your mother for replica paintings. I tried to help her out. But this forgery charge is something Scandal Mountain Antiques isn't going to recover from. I'm only being honest, Edie."

"From what I've heard, you encouraged her to sign the Parrish painting," I snapped.

"What your mother did was her own bad judgment. It had nothing to do with me."

I gritted my teeth. That was a point I couldn't argue. I wasn't convinced of his innocence, but he was right about it being her choice. I dismissed his comment with a wave. "Whatever."

His voice lowered even further. "Your grandparents were excellent dealers, good businesspeople. But times have changed. The antique business isn't the same as it once was. Mark my word, you'd be doing yourself and your family a favor if you unloaded the shop's inventory and moved on." His voice lightened. "Speaking of which, when you do liquidate, I have a client who might be willing to purchase your grandfather's library as a single lot. Your mother didn't sell it off yet, did she?"

I let that go over my head. *Jerk.* I glanced past him toward the restaurant, like I'd done earlier. "I'd love to talk some more, but I need to save a place to sit. I'm expecting someone."

"That makes two of us. See you around, Edie Brown." He turned and strolled away before I could do the same to him.

Out of the corner of my eye, I spotted the bartender returning from the register with my debit card. He grimaced sympathetically. "I'm assuming you two aren't here together?"

"You've got that right." As I took the card, I watched Graham sidle into a booth at the back of the pub. The last thing in the world I'd ever do was sell Grandpa's books to any friend or client of Graham's. No way in hell.

Two seconds later, I was more than grateful when Shane walked in. I was even happier once we were stowed in a nearby booth with our drinks.

"The timing of your text was perfect," Shane said. "I was in town at Fisher's. I was hoping to get an early preview of some rifles they're running through next weekend's auction." He sighed as if disappointed.

"They wouldn't let you look at them, would they?" I guessed. Fisher's previews were usually only online and in person on the morning of the auction, or sometimes the day before.

"It's not that," he said. "More like I fell in love with a couple of guns I'm sure I won't be able to afford. They've got a pristine Winchester Centennial, hand engraved . . ."

His voice faded into the background as a man strode past and went off toward the back of the pub. He was older, physically fit, dressed in trim gray slacks and a stylish leather jacket. Even without the addition of his Audi, I knew it was our neighbor, Rene St. Marie.

He headed straight for Graham's booth and slid in across from him. My jaw tightened. First Frank Bouchard at my house. Now two asses meeting up in my favorite pub. What was this town turning into, a hot spot for toxic middle-aged men?

I felt the warmth of Shane's hand on top of mine. "What's wrong?"

"Nothing," I said.

He scoffed. "You never were very good at lying. You looked particularly happy this afternoon at the deli. Now you're distracted, edgy." He tilted his head, studying me. "Meeting up wasn't purely about us, was it?"

"It is. I really did—I mean, I do want to see you." I took a long breath. I was boxing myself in this time. I supposed I could use the confrontation with Graham as an excuse for being off. It wouldn't be a lie. But I'd come here in hopes of getting Shane's advice on something else.

"And?" His voice filled with concern. "Does it have something to do with the appraisal event?"

"Ah—" Shane was too perceptive for his—my—own good.

"The TV show?" he asked.

I looked down at my drink, withholding my thoughts for another heartbeat, then I glanced around to make sure no one was within earshot before I whispered, "The woman from the appraisal, Nina Graves-Bouchard?"

"Yes?" he said, equally quiet.

I let out a silent breath, grateful he hadn't reacted to the significant change I'd made to Nina's name since I'd previously mentioned it. I leaned forward, resting my arms on the table as I gave him the Cliff's Notes version of the trip to the farm, about Nina, Jean-Claude, and even Mudder and the dumpster, lots more than I'd originally planned to divulge. When I finished, I met his eyes and added. "Seriously, you can't mention this to anyone."

"Are you positive it's the missing Bouchard collection? Are you sure they aren't decoys Claude assembled recently from private sales or auctions?" His voice stammered and he gawked at me as if he were Lancelot and I'd just told him the Holy Grail was in the fridge next to the leftover spaghetti.

"Ninety-nine percent sure. They were packed away in the attic. The newspapers they were wrapped in were from the early 1990s and before. But I didn't straight-out ask Claude if that's what they were." I took a sip of my drink, savoring the tang and bite of the liquid as it flavored my mouth, then cooled my throat. "I planned on spending tonight hunting the internet for articles about the collection. There must be photographs and documentation, at least of the best pieces. I want to verify as much as possible before I broach the subject with Nina or Claude."

Shane lowered his voice, deep and serious. "Who else knows about them?"

"No one, besides you, and Tuck and Kala—and of course Claude and Nina. I'm not sure either of them fully comprehends how important the collection is."

"Are you certain there's no one else?"

"There's Frank. Nina's estranged husband and co-trustee of Claude's estate. He knows about the decoys and that they're valuable, but nothing more." I wet my lips, readying to tell him more. "Frank's kind of the reason I texted you. He showed up at the house earlier."

"He did? What did he want?" Shane asked.

"I'm not totally sure. That's what upset me. He was evasive, warning me to be leery of Nina and at the same time telling me not to try and pull anything. At least, that's how it came across to me." I thought for a second. "They didn't mention Nina's last name on the TV, right?"

"No. But her husband, this Frank, has a point—you need to be careful. Even the best intentions can go haywire. I don't want to see you end up in trouble."

"I really don't think Nina or Claude are out to screw us."
I picked up my drink and sat back, pulse thudding hard. "But
Frank did make me think about some things I hadn't consid-
ered, like insurance fraud."

"You said the collection's in the attic?"

I nodded. "The roof's a little leaky, but they're fine for now."

"How about burglary?"

"You haven't seen the place. Claude's not into high tech,
but I doubt even Jehovah's Witnesses dare go up his driveway.
There are no trespassing signs everywhere. They keep the windows shut. There are massive padlocks on the doors, including
the one to the attic. I also don't think Claude would hesitate to
shoot an intruder—or maybe even chainsaw them to death."
I rolled my eyes. "That's not even mentioning the nasty hog
roaming around."

Shane laughed, then his voice gentled and his gaze turned
warmer, more personal. "You might have had an ulterior motive
for luring me here, but I had my reasons too."

Every inch of my body flushed with anticipation. This
looked and sounded promising. My voice went husky. "What
would that be?"

"Did you leave anyone behind in New York, someone special?" he asked.

"No. How about you?" I laughed at myself, both nervous
and excited. "I don't mean that you left someone in New York,
I meant here. It's cool if you're dating."

"No one recently. I've been pretty much solely focused on
the cabin and work." His Adam's apple rose and fell as if he'd
swallowed hard. I replayed that bit of body language in my
head. *Guilt* was the word that came to mind. That didn't make

sense. I was certain he was telling the truth about not dating. Shane didn't lie. Maybe he had been seeing someone and they had broken his heart. Maybe he wasn't totally over them?

I looked deep into his eyes, then reached across the table and rested my hand on top of his. "You want to order a pizza—to go? Nobody's at my house right now. We'd have the whole place to ourselves to talk, at least for a while. Or we could go to your place."

He shifted back, moving out from under my touch and taking his hand from mine. His gaze, however, didn't retreat. It remained warm and welcoming, if darkened with a sort of wistful sadness.

"I'd really like to." His lips tilted into a sexy lopsided smile that I remembered from that weekend. "Seriously, I'd like to. But I can't. In fact, I can't stay for more than another few minutes. That's why I was glad you texted."

"Ah—I'm not sure what you mean," I said, confused.

"I wanted to see you in person to make sure you knew that I wasn't giving you the brushoff if I didn't reach out. I've got a lot on my plate this week. Mostly work related."

I would have complained it sucked that he was so responsible, but that was also one of the things I liked about him. I let my eyes linger on his. "But we can do something before I leave town, right?"

"I hope so." He rubbed his wristwatch, hesitating. His voice turned deep and as rich as velvet. "I really am glad you texted."

A coil of desire tightened just below my belly as that voice brought back memories of us, lying naked and doing a lot more than just talking.

"Same here," I rasped.

He slipped out of the booth, but instead of standing up as if readying to leave, he slid onto my seat. His fingers brushed my jawline, a light stroke that melted every inch of me.

I scrunched closer to him, resting my hand on his upper arm as he leaned in. His lips touched mine, pressing lightly. I parted my lips, inviting more.

Chapter Eight

About ten minutes later, I was in the café parking lot pressed up against Shane's Land Rover. I was caged in by his arms and we were getting into a second kiss, when the *toot-toot* of a car horn interrupted. I glanced toward the sound in time to see Tuck's Suburban speed past. Shane laughed and I did too, but I knew the fallout was going to be unmerciful once I got home. Which it was. In fact, Tuck and Kala were still picking on me about getting a quickie in the café parking lot when we arrived at the Bouchard farm the next morning. It didn't matter I'd told them the truth—about Frank's visit and my needing to talk with someone, and that it had only been a kiss, nothing else, and that I'd deserved a little something, especially after my encounter with Graham.

"You do realize I'm not going to forget this harassment," I said, opening the van's back door. I took out the camera bag and thrust it into Kala's arms. "New girl on the block or not, revenge will happen."

She dramatically tossed her hair back. "As if you'd dare."

Considering how briefly I'd known Kala, it was amazing how comfortable I felt around her. She fit in at the house and as part of the team as if she'd been born into it. I supposed Mom had been smart to hire her. Kala and Tuck were also right to keep the mood light, even if it was at my expense. With all the work we needed to accomplish, an upbeat attitude was better than focusing on the possible trouble we were walking into.

Still, I wasn't foolish enough to totally abandon my caution, and neither was Tuck. He moved with purposefully slow steps on the way up from the first floor to the attic door, scanning everything we passed with even more scrutiny than the day before. Like Frank had said, we needed to dot all our i's and cross our t's, then everything would be fine.

The only thing that made me even vaguely uneasy happened after Nina unlocked the attic door and stepped aside to let us go up the stairs. I waited to go last and, as Kala clambered up the steps, Nina squinted at her and shook her head. It came across as condescending, perhaps even wary, but it wasn't anything to worry about. When I'd been young and gone on house calls with my grandparents, people had sometimes eyed me the same way. I supposed Kala did come across as young. Her overalls and flashy T-shirt certainly didn't add maturity to her look.

Mostly I was grateful when Nina left us alone and we got down to organizing our workspace. First, I set up my laptop and the camera tripods on the table while Kala damp mopped the area and stretched extension cords for the lighting. The natural light wasn't that bad, but we couldn't rely on it alone for photographing the decoys.

"I'm going to run down to the van and get some foam board for a backdrop," Tuck said, starting for the attic stairwell.

"Can you grab a couple of white sheets while you're down there?" I called after him. "They're in one of the blue plastic totes."

"You got it."

As I watched him disappear into the stairwell, my gaze was drawn toward the depth of the eaves and the armoire I'd noticed yesterday. My instinct prickled, urging me to check it out. There was something good inside it, I was certain. More decoys? Maybe something totally different? An old hooked rug. A schoolgirl sampler like my grandma had found in that other armoire.

I scowled and clenched my hands—as if by squeezing them I could wring the urge from my mind—and went back to unpacking supplies. First things first. I needed to focus on the job at hand. There'd be time to look in the armoire later.

Kala glanced up at me from where she hunched on the floor, extension cord in hand. "I was just kidding, you know. I don't really think you had sex in the parking lot."

"What?" I said, unsure where her comment had come from.

"You look upset. I thought maybe we'd taken the razzing too far."

"It's not you. That armoire's driving me nuts. I can't shake the feeling there's something interesting inside it."

"There's an easy solution." She sprang to her feet, cobwebs dangling from where her knees had wiped the floorboards.

I held up a hand to stop her. "Forget it. We can look after we finish taking the photos."

"Like it's going to stop distracting you?" She danced between the piles of junk, heading for the eaves.

"It's probably locked." I followed her under a low beam and up to the armoire. It was burled mahogany veneer, double-doored, with a single small brass knob. It was beyond me how anyone had managed to squeeze it up the attic stairs and into place.

Kala tried the knob. It didn't turn. She huffed. "See, you jinxed us. It's locked tight."

"Next time we see Nina, I'll ask her for the key."

Kala's smile turned sly. "Why wait?"

"No," I said. "Whatever you're thinking, absolutely *no*."

"It's a simple lock."

I eyed her. "Should my mom have done a background check before she hired you?" I said it jokingly, though I could almost see the headline: *FBI's Art Crime Team locates notorious international gem thief working with local antique dealer.*

"Ha ha—very funny." A slight gleam of sweat shone on her temples. "When I was in high school, my folks had this old camp outside of town, on a lake. The perfect place to party, only it was locked. My folks also hid their liquor in a cupboard similar to this one, and I had this hot girlfriend who had a brother who . . . Let's just say we never had any trouble getting into the camp *or* the cupboard."

"Oh." I glanced at the armoire again. She was talking about picking the lock, a very bad idea. Only I really did want to see what was inside. "Alright. As long as you don't break the lock."

Kala took a Leatherman-style multi-tool from a pocket in her overalls and opened it to a narrow screwdriver. "The only other thing I need is a bobby pin or a paperclip."

"Just a second," I said as my mind raced back to where I'd seen one yesterday. I dashed to the bassinet filled with dolls and swiped a bobby pin from the hair of a big blonde one with glassy eyes. I'd probably just gone from jinxing Kala and me to being cursed for stealing from the Bride of Chucky.

I handed the hairpin to Kala, then watched in amazement as she straightened it and used it along with the tiny screwdriver to open the lock with only a few wiggles and jiggles.

She grinned. "See, easy-peasy. No harm done."

"Hurry up. Open it." My heart thudded like crazy. I couldn't wait to see what was inside.

She rested her hand on the knob, turned it, then began inching the door open with the dramatic flair of a game show hostess—

Voices floated up from the stairwell. Tuck and Mudder.

Kala gaped at me, then shoved the armoire door closed. We whipped around in unison, facing the stairwell with our backs to the armoire as Tuck appeared at the top of the steps, foamboard under one arm. Mudder was behind him, lugging a blue tote.

I plastered on a smile. "That didn't take you long."

Mudder eyeballed us suspiciously from under the brim of his cap. His gaze flicked to the armoire and he mumbled, "Claude's in the kitchen if ya need the key for that."

"We haven't even checked to see if we need one," Kala said. Without missing a beat, she wheeled around and tugged on the armoire door, opening it an inch. "Look at that. It's not locked."

As she swung the door all the way open, my breath stalled. I pressed a hand against my chest. The shelves were covered with a menagerie of carved songbirds: goldfinches, cardinals, chickadees . . . beautiful pieces of art bringing life to the dark interior of the armoire. A couple of shelves near the bottom held books, leather bound and mostly related to waterfowl and hunting, judging by a quick glance. My instinct had been right to keep pestering me. This was a discovery I needed to uncover and include in the appraisal.

Mudder dropped the plastic tote on the floor and lumbered over to us. "Those used to be at the old farm in Quebec. My *mémère* says they were always kept in the china hutch, don't ya know."

He pushed past Kala and snatched a chickadee, cradling it in his callused hands. It struck me then how those big hands had descended from the same gene pool as the artists who had most likely carved and painted the delicate songbirds, and the decoys for sure. Mudder was Claude's great-nephew. A direct descendant of the legendary Jean-Paul Bouchard himself.

A sense of history and wistful thoughts of times gone by swept over me. Here we all stood under the eaves of a Vermont farmhouse, probably not much different in appearance than the Quebec home where these birds once sat in their china hutch. They'd most likely been carved and painted in that same home, perhaps on a table under a sunny window or by the light of a kerosene lamp. Rural history. Quebec history. The history of families who lived along the *frontière* of two countries. The Bouchard family's history.

Thoughts of my grandmother, a Mayflower descendant, not French Canadian, slipped into my mind. I clearly remembered her turning over the "closed" sign on the shop door so we could go for walks in the forest behind the house. Chickadees, goldfinches, yellow-throated warblers, brown creepers . . . she taught me to recognize all the native birds by their flight patterns and calls. Her favorite was the pileated woodpecker, bold, big, and noisy. The hooded warbler was the last bird she'd added to her life list of sightings, only a month before the plane crash.

"This one was my *mémère*'s favorite." Mudder's voice broke through my thoughts.

I jolted back to the here and now. His hands were closing in around the chickadee, like a gigantic Venus flytrap ensnaring its prey.

"Should've been hers," Mudder went on. "Claude don't give a fig about them, no more than he did about the home farm."

I lunged, snagging the bird before he could drop it by mistake. "Actually, it's a good thing Claude's kept them tucked away—out of direct sunlight. That kept them in gorgeous condition."

"Ya, I suppose." Mudder's shoulders slumped, but his eyes remained as sharp as if he wasn't totally resigned to the fact that he couldn't lay claim to the chickadee. His voice brightened. "*Mémère* says Claude has other things. Paintings. A blue heron, big as a real one."

"A life-size heron?" I bit my tongue to keep from sounding too ecstatic. Paintings would be amazing, tremendously amazing actually. And a full-scale blue heron decoy? It might well be the crown jewel of the whole collection. "Do you know where the heron is?"

"Probably up here, if Claude didn't sell it." Mudder glanced over his shoulder at the stairwell as more voices trailed up from it. Nina and Claude this time.

Embarrassment and worry pushed heat across the back of my neck. It had been easy to convince Mudder that the armoire was unlocked, but it seemed impossible that Claude, the keeper of the keys, wouldn't realize what Kala and I had done.

Nina emerged from the stairwell first.

"Perfect timing," I said as cheerfully as I could. One of the best moves, when caught in the act of doing something wrong, is to find a way to shift the focus off your crime and onto something that will benefit the person you trespassed against. "I was about to ask Tuck to look at these books. I know we're just supposed to be appraising decoys, but you have some significant value here." I crossed my fingers and hoped I wasn't lying.

Tuck made his way to the armoire. He stooped and scanned the books. "*Johnson's Natural History*, *Manual of Ornithology* . . . There are some good ones." He straightened and rested a hand on my shoulder. "It wouldn't take me long to document them, if you'd like."

Claude stalked away from the stairwell, eyes narrowed. He scowled at me, then the armoire. "How did you get in there? It was locked."

"Don't be like that," Nina scolded him. "You told me yourself the keys are kept on top of it."

Unsure what my best move was now, I looked to see what everyone else was doing. Kala had retreated toward the worktable. Mudder was headed in the opposite direction, poking into cardboard boxes, more interested in snooping than calling Kala and me out.

I looked directly at Claude and chanced shifting the focus again. "I was told there were paintings around here somewhere. We should include them in the appraisal. Mudder also mentioned a blue heron. We haven't found it yet."

Claude bristled, like a rooster readying to fight. His voice turned caustic, even more so than normal. "There are two paintings. One's hanging in my bedroom. The other's in the parlor. You won't find no heron." His gaze fixed on me, challenging me to contradict him. There was no question he knew the armoire had been locked earlier, but his fierce defensiveness made me wonder if he was hiding something himself. Was the heron here somewhere? It was the only thing he'd denied having.

I looked him in the eyes and gave a slight nod, lips tight to let him know that I didn't wholly believe him. Still, I didn't question whether he'd told the truth or not, a peace offering of sorts. It was ridiculous not to include his best piece in an appraisal, but my gut said there was more simmering beneath the surface here. Claude claimed only to tolerate Nina for Gracie's sake. He disliked his stepson Frank. Yet he'd made them co-trustees of his estate. Why had he done that—and why was he being so difficult?

My mind went to my good friend Jimmy. I'd met him at an art auction in New York a couple of years back. He'd grown up in Greenwich Village, where he now owned his family's funeral home. Occasionally, I worked for him as a greeter—cash money, not a bad job. Jimmy was a super nice person, but the man he was married to at that time was as abrasive as Claude, and prone to flares of anger, totally erratic. I saw him give away a valuable piece of art, then stubbornly refuse to throw out a smelly pair of sneakers. When I first met Jimmy, I didn't understand why he put up with the guy, until I discovered his partner had been diagnosed with cancer. Before the drugs and chemo, before the death sentence, according to Jimmy, his partner had been the sweetest man on the planet.

I eyed Claude again. I hadn't stopped to consider there might be some other pressure, an underlying medical reason for his behavior. He always smelled of marijuana. It was a total guess, but could Claude be smoking for pain relief and not just to get high? I hoped not. I hoped he was healthy. Truthfully, I liked the old codger.

I gentled my voice. "The paintings should be included in the appraisal, along with the songbirds and your more valuable books, if you're open to having them looked at."

He harrumphed. "You're not going to weasel your way into including everything in the house. I'm wise to you, *mon petit carcajou*. Appraising more means I have to pay you more."

He nodded curtly at the armoire. "Include those and the paintings, but nothing else."

"If that's what you want," I said, but as my thoughts turned to the heron again, something else occurred to me. When we'd first met Gracie, she'd said something about us not taking Mr. Blue. I'd assumed it was a toy. What if I was wrong? Claude loved Gracie. He might have already gifted the blue heron to her.

Chapter Nine

As morning moved toward midday, Mudder left the attic. But Nina and Claude continued to hover over our shoulders, firing questions and coming up with suggestions while Tuck worked his way through the books and Kala and I attempted to document and photograph the decoys. At one point, Claude dug an old alarm clock out of a camelback trunk, wound it, and then set it on the nearby windowsill.

The clock's incessant *tick-tock-tick-tock* reverberated in the confines of the attic. It reminded me of the patience-shattering tap-tap of an SAT monitor's fingernails on the edge of a desk. I had really hated those tests.

I'd just become immune to the noise and was zooming the camara in on the drake mallard's head, when Nina cleared her throat. "I wonder if the decoys in the stolen Bouchard painting were mallards? You heard about the robbery at the Quebec museum, right?"

I nodded as if not surprised to hear she knew about the robbery. In truth, I was taken aback. Sure, the theft had been all over the news when it first happened, but it was strange that Nina had paid attention to it. As far as I could tell, folk art and the family's connection to it was a newfound interest for her.

"Mudder mentioned it yesterday," she went on. "His grandmother said the thieves took several paintings by Jean-Claude."

I smiled. So she hadn't known about the robbery before. I glanced over my shoulder at her. "It was actually a series of related paintings, *Dogs and Decoys*," I clarified. "It's horrible that they were stolen, but the fact that they were in the news lately helps when it comes to value and appraisal accuracy."

"That's wonderful," she said.

Claude grumbled, "Don't know what's wonderful about something getting stolen."

"That's not what I meant, Claude," she said, disgusted.

Kala caught my eye and cringed. I shook my head. I couldn't take any more of this. If Nina and Claude wouldn't leave us alone, we'd never make any progress on the appraisal. And it was only a matter of time before some other dealer or collector who'd seen me evaluate the plover on TV realized it was a Bouchard piece and showed up on Claude's doorstep, asking questions and offering cash. Besides, Nina talking about the stolen Jean-Claude pieces had turned my previous curiosity about the paintings they owned into a distracting need.

I thumped the camera down on the worktable and turned to Claude. "I'm going down to the second floor to use the restroom. While I'm there, maybe you could show me the painting in your bedroom?"

He glowered at me. "I got better things to do. I need to get my truck to St. Albans while Mudder's around to fetch me back home. *Maudit* muffler went to hell."

I bit my tongue, resisting the urge to ask why, if that was true, he had been standing around for hours watching us work. I flashed a smile. "It will only take a minute. I can bring the painting back here if you don't want to wait while I photograph it."

"You're not going to let me out of this, are you?" he asked.

I widened my stance. "I really have to see it."

He blew out an exasperated breath. "Women. Always wanting more when they've got all they need in front of their faces."

I pretended not to hear that and followed him downstairs. After I faked a trip to the bathroom, I made my way along the cluttered hallway to where his room sat on the east side of the house.

Even at a distance, I could see an enormous hinged hasp screwed to the frame of his open bedroom door. It was the sort of hasp designed to lock a barn door shut. Before now, it had been clear Claude was serious about keeping trespassers out. But this particular overkill made me wonder if he was a bit too paranoid.

When I reached the doorway and looked inside, this seemed even more likely. Compared to the rest of the house, his bedroom was empty. There weren't any bookshelves weighed down with decoys like I'd hoped. No piles of junk. No overfull totes or garbage bags. There wasn't even a cat hair or a dust bunny on the floor. No carpet. Only bare painted floorboards, a slipper chair upholstered in red velvet, and a three-piece Victorian bedroom set—bed, dresser, and washstand. Solid walnut, but not worth much nowadays.

I cautiously sniffed the air. Nothing other than a trace of stale perfume, and a stronger mix of chainsaw exhaust, beer, and marijuana emanating from Claude.

"Are you just going to stand there?" he asked.

I hurried into the room. Claude waited next to a medium-size oil painting that hung over the washstand. It was a dark oil on board, depicting loons swimming under an autumn moon. Intricate details. Subtle touches of color to reveal the time of year. Rich tones similar to the stolen Bouchard series. I could have gotten lost in its beauty for hours.

I looked away from it and skimmed the rest of the room to make sure I hadn't missed something important. Next to the bed, a velvet tapestry of a deer hung on the wall—midcentury, gaudy but not valueless. Kala might have liked it. My gaze paused on a vintage card tucked into the mirror of the nearby dresser. It was a holy card depicting the Sacred Heart of Jesus. I didn't need anything else to tell me that Jean-Claude was Catholic, not surprising given his roots were French Canadian. However, this detail made me do a double take when I noticed the framed wedding photograph on the dresser top.

The photo was of a short, wiry-looking groom in his late thirties with a young bride in a white gown. They were being married outdoors under an arbor by an older gentleman in a gray suit and tie, definitely not a priest. On the dresser, next to the wedding photo, a tray held a pair of corsage pins and the crumbled remains of a pink carnation.

"Is that you, Claude?" I nodded at the photo.

"Worst day of my life," Claude grumbled. He'd said something similar when he'd mentioned Frank was his stepson. However, this time, a quiver of a smile passed over his lips. He was lying again. He missed his wife. Plus, he'd cared about her deeply enough to marry outside of his family's church—a pretty woman in her late twenties with a teenage son, and him an older Catholic bachelor.

I pressed further, hoping to discover if my burgeoning theory about how the decoys ended up in Vermont held water. "Mudder says his grandmother remembers the songbirds being kept in a china hutch, back on your family's farm in Quebec."

"His *mémère* is my sister—Maria. She and I were two peas in a pod when we were young."

"You aren't any more?" I asked.

His tone hardened. "Maria didn't like me marrying Frank's mother. Didn't like me leaving Canada. Didn't want to sell the farm . . . She's only happy as long as she's getting her own way."

"Oh." I wasn't sure what to say, other than that I suspected Claude's sister's side of the story would involve something about him deserting his family to marry a non-Catholic with a brat child.

Claude's voice lowered to a growl. "Mudder's not bright enough to pound sand in a rat hole. I hired him to keep him from leaching off my sister. To her, Mudder's a saint. To me, he's just sucking down money I don't got enough of already."

My face heated with embarrassment for him, and out of surprise that he'd revealed so much personal information.

I turned away, studying the painting more closely. What he'd said made my theory about the collection's provenance seem likely. Granted, inheritance traditions had changed over the last few generations, but old-fashioned beliefs were still common enough that they'd been touched on in my classes about estate appraising. In such cases, the eldest son or the sons inherit pretty much everything from their father: the property, the family's most valuable heirlooms, like a collection of decoys. The daughters divvied up the remaining household trinkets and maybe some cash. If I combined Claude marrying a non-Catholic and moving away from Quebec with him inheriting everything and then selling the farm, an irreparable rift between him and his sister, Maria, seemed more likely than not. Mudder was perhaps the last thread of connection between what once had been two peas in a pod.

"When your father died, was that when you brought the decoys to Vermont?"

His gaze turned stony. "They were mine. Maria's greedy daughter had already sold the geese to a neighbor before I got there. I had to buy them back." He yanked open the washstand's drawer, snatched out a pair of lightweight work gloves and shoved them into his hip pocket. "Why don't you take the painting down. You can look at it all you want up in the attic. I've got to find Mudder. Get my truck to the garage, then get back. There's a mountain of logs waiting for me to cut them into firewood."

I stood up straighter and chanced making him angry. "Maybe it's not too late to heal old wounds. Life is too short to hold grudges." The words just tumbled from my mouth, tugging at my own heart for a second. I'm not sure why I said them. Most likely, it simply felt like the right response after him telling me so many private things.

He snorted. "That will be a cold day in hell."

"I guess I understand that," I said. And I did. I couldn't even pick up the phone when Mom called from prison.

I took the painting from the wall. It was heavy in my hands and left a trail of cobwebs behind. It's a horrible thing to say, but sometimes family really doesn't deserve forgiveness.

Chapter Ten

After that first day at the Bouchards, the novelty of watching us work wore off and we were able to make faster progress than we'd expected, with extra thanks going to Kala for her internet research talents. The woman had real skills when it came to locating and comparing information. She searched collector forums and blogs, as well as online auction catalogues and tons of other places. Me? I had knowledge, experience, and a natural eye for details, but I tended to get distracted. For me, researching folk art was like setting a beagle free in a park full of squirrels. Oh! Look at that—and over there, and that!

At any rate, on Thursday afternoon Kala stayed behind at home to work online when Tuck and I headed for the Bouchards' to finish up a few loose ends. For one thing, I was worried that the photos I'd taken of *The Hunting Blind*, the Jean-Paul oil on board that hung in the so-called parlor, hadn't adequately documented the damage it had suffered from exposure to nicotine and woodsmoke.

We'd gotten through Franklin and were passing the impending Quebec *frontière* sign when I decided to broach a subject I'd been mulling over for miles.

I glanced at Tuck. "We should sit down with Nina and Claude today and talk seriously about selling part or all of the collection at auction—with us acting as their intermediary agent. I don't expect getting Claude to cooperate will be easy, but he told me himself that he can barely pay Mudder for the work he's doing. If Claude intends to get the roof fixed, that alone will cost him a small fortune." I nodded in agreement with myself. "It's time to put the idea on the table."

"Today?" Tuck frowned. "Are you sure that's a good idea? Why not wait until tomorrow when we present the completed appraisal? As far as I knew, we hadn't decided against taking a couple of pieces in trade for our work and being satisfied with that."

"It's just . . ." I slid my hand along the steering wheel, deciding how to best phrase my concern. Ahead, a coyote trotted across the road with something clamped in its jaws. In a flash, it disappeared down a farm lane, the kind of overgrown place the county sheriff hid when he set up speed traps. I wet my lips. "It's probably just normal jitters, but I've got the feeling something bad is going to happen if we don't sew things up today."

"What are you afraid of?"

"It's a gut feeling. I'm worried we won't get a second chance if we don't get it done now."

"Are you thinking they'll contact an auctioneer themselves once they see what the collection is worth? Cut us out of the deal?"

"No. Nina hired us because she wanted to keep things under wraps. Claude's even more private. Frank? I'm not sure about him."

"Are you concerned he might call Martina Fortuni?"

"Not really. Well, I'm not ruling that out as a potential problem. But we also can't forget that Felix Graham sent Nina over to my table at the appraisal, so she kind of knows him." I stared ahead, thinking out loud. "Anyway, if we bring up the idea of an auction and the benefits of using us as an intermediary agent today, that will give them time to think it over before we present the appraisal. Giving them time to decide will make us come across as less pushy and more honest."

"You mean we aren't?" Tuck chuckled.

I shrugged. I was too lost in thought to argue the finer points. "It would give Nina time to talk with Frank, too. If we're lucky, we could go home today with a handshake promise and have the whole thing in black and white tomorrow."

The *brrring* of my phone came from where it sat in its cradle.

"I hope Kala hasn't hit a snag," Tuck said.

I answered, using the hands-free control. "Everything okay?"

"Um—shouldn't it be?" Shane's voice filled the van.

Oops. "Shane!" My face heated. "Hi. Sorry, I thought you were Kala." I backpedaled some more. "She's a great employee, but she phones when even the tiniest thing goes wrong." A total lie.

Shane's voice lowered. "I was thinking about you . . ."

Silence hung in the air and a nervous feeling pinged in my stomach. Shane's voice sounded sexy. Not that it didn't always sound that way to me, but if he was building up to saying something personal, I preferred Tuck didn't hear it.

Tuck made a soft chortling noise, then pulled a finger across his lips, zipping them shut. Still, his eyes glistened with amusement.

I scowled a warning.

"How's the appraisal going?" Shane asked.

"Fine." I shot another look Tuck's way. "Tuck and I are on the way there now. We're planning on finishing up today."

"Is the collection as nice as you thought?"

I bit my lip. "Definitely. It's been a real treat to handle the pieces."

Tuck frowned and made a cutting motion across his neck with a finger. Then he relented and shrugged as if Shane knowing wasn't an issue. He was right, though. The appraisal was private business between us and the Bouchards—and Shane knew that. I didn't ask him questions about his probationers, did I?

We reached the Bouchards' mailbox. I slowed and turned into their driveway. The familiar ferns scraped the sides of the van.

Shane's voice once again reverberated, deep and sincere. "I should let you get back to work. You still up for pizza? Tomorrow night's looking good for me."

"That would be great. I'll—"

Up ahead, bright red lights strobed through the trees, illuminating the sky and reflecting off the beaver pond. Emergency lights.

"I've got to go," I said, ending the call with Shane. I couldn't see exactly where or what kind of vehicle the light was coming from, just the pulse of hot red, over and over.

"Is that a fire truck?" Tuck craned forward, staring out the windshield.

Sheer terror beat inside me. "I can't see yet. Do you see any smoke?"

"No. There might not be any, if the place went up last night."

I lowered my window. "I don't smell anything. We'd smell something, right?"

The van heaved as I sped over the rickety bridge. I stepped harder on the accelerator. To hell with the pig. It would just have to get out of the way.

The Bouchards' yard came into view. An ambulance was pulled up next to the dumpster, red lights strobing. The attendants were loading a gurney into it.

"Sweet Jesus," Tuck muttered.

My thoughts flew in a thousand directions. Claude? Smoking weed. The chainsaw. Working while stoned was really stupid. Or Mudder, maybe it was him? Gracie? Dear Lord, not Gracie.

I parked the van out of the way. In a second, Tuck and I were sprinting across the yard. My pulse slammed in my ears. My breaths came in short bursts. We weren't family. We shouldn't interfere. But maybe we could help.

As we neared the ambulance, it started to pull away. I caught a glimpse of an attendant riding shotgun. Nothing about them revealed how desperate the situation was.

The ambulance's lights went off as it turned down the driveway and silently cruised toward the main road. Fear gripped me. No siren. No lights. That couldn't be a good sign.

Nina rushed from the front door, pulling on a cardigan. One of its arms was tangled inside out. She yanked the cardigan off, then struggled to right it.

Gracie pushed past her and onto the porch. She stared after the ambulance, tears streaking her face.

"What happened?" I asked, hurrying to the steps.

"It's Claude. They're taking him to the hospital."

"Is it bad?" Tuck asked.

"He had a seizure. Gracie found him. She called 911."

"Oh, my God," I said. It was surreal how fast things could change. The genuine panic on Nina's face seemed equally surreal. She was beside herself. It was clear she really cared about Claude.

"I was so scared," Gracie sobbed.

"You did the right thing." Nina managed to get her cardigan on, then put her arms around Gracie, snugging her close. "Don't worry. Pepe's going to be fine."

My gaze went past them to the open front door as I wondered what kind of seizure he'd had. A stroke, maybe. A heart attack. My chest squeezed. I truly hoped for their sake that he was going to be okay.

I quieted my tone. "I'm so sorry. This is a bad time. We can come back later and finish up."

Nina reached into her pocket and took out a key ring. She shoved it at me as she came down the steps. "I don't want you to do that. I want the appraisal finished, right away. The sooner the better."

The key ring was heavy, lots of keys and a decorative fob in the shape of a chainsaw. I met Nina's eyes. "Be sure to let us know how Claude is. I feel horrible about this."

She nodded. "I'll call from the hospital. If you leave for any reason, lock up. Claude's barn coat is on the back porch. Put the keys in one of its pockets."

"Let us know if we can do anything else to help," Tuck added.

"Don't let any cats inside—and for God's sake don't let Frank in if the bastard shows up."

As she took Gracie by the hand and towed her toward their car, I glanced at Tuck and whispered, "It's nice she trusts us, but how the heck are we supposed to keep Frank out?"

"Besides barricading ourselves inside and calling the police?" Tuck shrugged.

I thought back. "I don't remember anyone mentioning a restraining order against him."

"I don't either."

As we went up the steps and onto the porch, a black cat streaked out of nowhere, past us and through the still-open front door.

"Just what we don't need," I said.

Tuck raised an eyebrow. "I'm going to pretend I didn't see it."

I hooked my arm with his and leaned close. "Then I won't mention what color it was." I released him and met his eyes. "Do you think it was a good or a bad sign that the ambulance didn't have its lights or siren on?"

"It means they weren't in a hurry."

"That doesn't really answer my question," I said.

"We'll have to wait and see, right?"

"I guess." I rubbed my hands over my face. "This really stinks. Just when everything was going our way. I hope Claude's going to be okay."

It felt wrong to even think about Tuck's and my futures, the appraisal, or the auction. However, if Claude didn't make it or if he'd died already, things would only get more complicated for everyone. Thank God, they'd all signed the contract. Still, lawyers would get involved, drawing things out. I couldn't see Frank and Nina not fighting tooth and nail over everything, including the decoy collection.

Tuck touched my arm. "Since we're staying, I'm going to run back to the car and get the gear. You want the camera, right?"

"That would be great," I said.

I rolled my shoulders, working out a knot of tension. The farm seemed oddly silent without Claude around. No hum of his chainsaw. No distant voices. Not even the chime of frogs down in the swamp, or the snuffling of the pig. In reality, the quiet should have excited me. There was no one to disturb or watch us. No one to see if we snooped or explored, or to wind annoying alarm clocks. Utter freedom, finally.

But the silence only made me uneasy. It was as if the entire property—the house and barns, even the beaver swamp, every box of junk, every decoy—was holding its breath, waiting in suspended animation for life to return to normal. Until then, trespassers beware.

"Earth to Edie?" Tuck's voice broke through my thoughts as he came back from the van.

I took a quick breath. "What do you think will happen to this place if Claude doesn't make it?"

He handed me the camera bag. "A developer like Rene St. Marie will snap up the property. It'll be broken into lots in no time flat. There'll be streets with cul-de-sacs and white picket fences."

"I imagine you're right." That was my fear about what would happen to our home if we didn't get an infusion of cash in the not-so-distant future. Not that our historic house would get torn down like this place. Still, the land would be subdivided, and the home would be a relic of yesterday surrounded by a village of look-alike cottages and vacation condos. Even with the long-term lease, the airstrip land would eventually go. That was, if we didn't pay the property taxes and get caught up on the bills.

Tuck took me by the elbow, propelling me inside. "Come on. Let's get to work."

After we closed the door and latched the deadbolt for good measure, we went into the so-called parlor, a living room to most people. Yesterday, I'd only been in the room long enough to take the questionable photographs of *The Hunting Blind*.

"Holy cow," said as I looked around. Most of the decrepit furniture and every inch of the smelly wall-to-wall carpet was gone.

Tuck sniffed the air. "Doesn't smell half bad."

I wrinkled my nose. It was better, comparatively speaking.

I went to where the painting had been rehung over the fireplace. "What do you think?"

Tuck studied the piece. "It's a bit yellowed from smoke and dust. Nothing a professional cleaning wouldn't take care of. I think the photos you have are fine."

I took it down and carried it to a window. In the good light, I could see he was probably right. Most likely I'd just been overly critical of my work.

Thunk! The sound of something toppling over echoed from a doorway behind us.

My heart launched into my throat but settled in an instant. The kitchen. Whatever it was had sounded heavy and plastic. Perhaps a wastebasket hitting the floor.

"Want to bet that was the cat's doing?" I said.

Tuck hotfooted toward the kitchen. "I'll get the monster."

As he disappeared, I took a couple of new photos of the painting to err on the safe side.

"Yowch!" Tuck shrieked. More crashes followed. "You little vermin."

I hung the painting back up and rushed to see what was going on.

Sure enough, a kitchen wastebasket had toppled over. Garbage was strewn across the floor—a meat tray, tea bags, butter wrappers, and what looked like brown sugar, probably left over from making the *sucre a la crème*. The cat certainly had gone for the gold.

Tuck swore again, his voice reaching out from somewhere just beyond my sight.

"Where are you?" I called.

"Pantry. Open the back door and get ready to shut it fast."

I picked my way around the trash, careful not to make the mess any worse.

"Is it open yet?" Tuck's voice pitched upward, tinged with pain.

Something hissed, then yowled.

"One second." I swung the back door open, revealing a small porch, piled with firewood. Claude's barn coat hung on the back of a wooden chair. "All set!"

A nearby door flung open. Tuck emerged, holding the black cat by its scruff. It wriggled and growled as he tossed it outside. I slammed the door shut, then watched as the cat recovered from its flight, glowered at me, and took off across the lawn.

"Not exactly friendly," I said.

Tuck blew out a long breath. "Remind me never to do a stupid thing like that again."

"Did it bite you?"

"No. Just scratched the bejesus out of my hands."

While he went to the sink to wash off blood, I righted the wastebasket and swept up the strewn garbage. I was putting the broom back in its corner when my gaze was drawn to a pair of framed lithographs hanging on a wall beside a padlocked door, likely the door to the cellar, judging by how farmhouses were normally laid out.

I took another step closer and glanced again at the lithographs. They were medium size, no more than a foot or fifteen inches across. One featured an elegant pair of trumpeter swans flying over a swamp. The other was of Canada geese. However, the lithographs weren't the only things contained within the frames. Small, matching images were also included, and I didn't need to get any closer to know what they were. Duck stamps.

Duck stamps framed with corresponding lithographs were the first thing I'd ever collected, thanks to Grandma gifting me with a set for my sixth birthday. I'd treasured them and individual stamps until just over four years ago, when they'd been at the center of my arrest for selling stolen property.

I closed my eyes, trying to block out the unwelcome memory. It came nonetheless:

Mom and I had set up a booth at a small antique show. On Saturday afternoon, a guy appeared: middle-aged, redneck. Mom chatted with him like he was a good friend. She'd supposedly met him at Fisher's auction. They'd also shared a drink or two at the Jumping Café's pub. I didn't recognize him—but pickers come and go, and I hadn't spent much time at home since I'd started working toward my master's degree.

"I have some stuff to get rid of," he said, totally casual. "I'm helping out a buddy . . ."

I tucked my hands in my pockets and listened as he and Mom talked. It seemed his buddy ended up with a shed full of his dead uncle's stuff. The story sounded plausible. Still, something about the guy sent up a small red flag. Maybe it was his shoes. Not work boots that would have matched with his flannel shirt and generic carpenter jeans. Not sneakers. His shoes were high-end loafers with pointy toes and tassels, brand-new, very expensive.

While Mom continued to chat with him, I went to the other side of the booth and waited on a customer. As I remembered, I sold them a set of camel-shaped bookends—1920s, an attractive set. When the customer left, Mom walked over. She nodded at the guy with the stuff for sale and whispered, "He has some of the things from the shed in his car. You should take a look. Why not? Could be a good deal."

I shook my head, no. I had extra money and had always done some dealing on my own, but something about the guy made me uneasy.

Mom murmured something about me being ridiculous and that she'd buy the pieces from him for the shop, except the house insurance was due and she didn't have any cash to spare.

I hesitated. Something was off. But what could it hurt to look? Mom knew him. Other than an unsubstantiated feeling and his incongruous choice in footwear, I couldn't justify my apprehension.

I talked to the guy for a few minutes. Turned out his buddy's uncle had collected lithographs and duck stamps. A sentimental favorite I could value quickly.

"If you're not interested," he said. "I'll ask another dealer."

While Mom watched the booth, I went with him. He drove a black BMW, not new but fancy, like his shoes. He caught me eyeing the car. "It's my buddy's," he said. "He lost his driver's license, so he loaned it to me."

More red flags went up. Like an idiot, I focused on Mom's words. "*Why not? Could be a good deal.*"

There were several boxes, framed lithographs, an album full of loose duck stamps—and another album of stamps attached to old hunting licenses, my personal preference, since they went beyond the pure collecting value by adding a sense of personal history to the stamp. The guy seemed to know the collection's value. Down came one red flag. If anything, the price he wanted was on the high side. Another flag lowered, but so did my enthusiasm.

As I turned to head back to the booth empty-handed, he relented. "Alright, I'll take a thousand. Cash money. My buddy's not going to be happy with me, but that's his tough luck."

Even though my gut said something was fishy, I didn't get his name, or his buddy's name or contact information. I didn't check online to make sure similar items hadn't been stolen in the area, not even in the recent past. Essentially, I was lazy and stupid, and that isn't a good excuse in the eyes of the law.

Two weeks later, I was at an antique show in Stowe when a well-spoken woman in an L.L. Bean jacket asked me if I had any duck stamps. Yeah, concern about the origin of the lithographs and stamps still lingered—one reason I hadn't unboxed them yet. Nevertheless, I took her to the van, dickered a price, took her cash—and then watched as she pulled out her badge. Thank you, Mom, for the worst day of my life.

Chapter Eleven

Several hours later, Tuck and I were in the Bouchards' attic going over the decoys one last time when Nina texted.

Claude's going to be okay.

I exhaled a long breath. *Glad to hear that.*

There was a pause.

He has to stay in the hospital overnight. I'm staying with him.

Before I could type my answer, my phone rang. Nina calling. That was weird.

"Hi," she said timidly. "Um . . . I should tell you—"

I covered the phone with my hand and gave a low whistle to catch Tuck's attention, then waved him over so he could listen in. I'd be lying if I didn't say I was worried.

"Yes?" I urged her to go on.

"When you see Claude, it would be better if you didn't ask him about his *accident.*"

"Accident?" That was a long way from the seizure we'd been told about before.

"Umm . . . There's no easy way to put this. Claude's had it in his head that he's dying of kidney cancer. That's what his father died from."

I thought back to how I'd previously wondered if there was an underlying reason for Claude's brusqueness and marijuana smoking. Still, I didn't get where Nina was going with this. I looked at Tuck. He shook his head to say he was as confused as I was. I shifted the phone to my other hand and asked, "But Claude doesn't have cancer, right?"

"Not according to his doctor. It was lucky Gracie found him when she did."

"Definitely, though it must have been horribly scary for her."

Her voice choked. "He overdosed. It was intentional."

It was as if all the strength had drained from my body. Abrasive old Claude had tried to kill himself? It was hard to believe. "I'm so sorry. Is there anything we can do for you?" I wasn't sure why she was telling me all this. Perhaps it was easier to make sense of the situation by saying it aloud to someone who was essentially a stranger. Still, the less shaken part of my brain wondered why Claude had chosen drugs rather than a gun. It didn't fit his personality, and I'd spotted plenty of weapons around the house.

"Please don't say anything to anyone," Nina whispered.

"We won't."

"He was convinced backaches and his having to go to the bathroom all the time were cancer symptoms, not from all the beer he drinks and overworking himself." Her voice intensified as she abruptly shifted topics. "Do you think you'll have the appraisal done soon?"

It took me a second to accept that I'd heard her right. "We're about to leave for today. I'm planning on going over the final figures this evening. Then I'll print off a copy of the appraisal for you. We can go over it whenever you're ready."

"Tomorrow," she said. "I can meet you at the house in the morning. Would eleven o'clock work for you?"

"Sure." I glanced at Tuck. He nodded, clearly as surprised but eager to have things wrapped up as I was, even more so now, with Claude's mental health becoming an issue we hadn't foreseen.

"Thank you. And again, please don't mention what happened to Claude. It's . . . embarrassing."

Embarrassing? I pressed my hand against my throat, breath stalling as I let the word she'd chosen replay in my head. It shouldn't have surprised me that Nina had reacted this way. She'd hired us because she knew I could relate to her fears of public embarrassment and I understood discretion. I understood the stigma of mental health issues too. After my grandparents died, my mom had forced me to go to therapy. I'd hated every second of it. Still, in this instance, Nina's response felt cold.

I steadied my voice. "Don't worry," I said. "I'll see you at eleven."

* * *

Claude remained in the forefront of my mind as we finished going over the decoys, then locked the attic and left by way of the front door. While Tuck secured that lock, I walked around to the rear of the house, padlocked the kitchen door, and stashed the key ring in the pocket of Claude's barn coat, as instructed.

As I walked away, the scent of his coat clung in the air around me: chainsaw exhaust, beer, and marijuana. A chill raised the hair on my arms, and the silence of Claude's absence struck me once more. I hadn't known Claude that long. I certainly didn't know anything about his medical or mental history, but it was hard to believe he'd attempted suicide.

I looked across the backyard to where the pig now rooted next to a woodpile. Claude's chainsaw and a gas can sat on the ground as if he intended to return to them. Nearby, the freshly turned earth of a vegetable garden stretched.

No. I couldn't believe Claude had attempted to kill himself.

And definitely not when there was a chance of Gracie finding him.

Chapter Twelve

Even a full night of sleep didn't lessen my belief that Claude hadn't attempted suicide. Tuck agreed and so did Kala. But none of us were psychiatrists or privy to the same details as Claude's doctors.

"I think it would be better if Edie met with Nina alone today," Kala said over breakfast. Surprisingly enough, we'd all gathered for a sit-down meal at the kitchen table, now clear of junk thanks to Kala's organizational skills. The only thing more surprising was how her statement came out of the clear blue, like the bark of a command sergeant.

Tuck frowned at Kala. "That doesn't make sense. It would be faster and easier if Edie and I both went."

"Maybe, except—" Her voice caught in her throat, her bossy demeanor fading.

I cradled my mug, letting the scent of coffee seep into my brain as I studied Kala. Her chin was trembling now. A hint of tears dampened the corners of her eyes.

"What is it?" I asked softly. She was way more than a little upset.

She glanced down, wiped the tears away with her fingers. Finally, she looked up. "Even if we suspect it wasn't a suicide attempt, that doesn't mean Nina feels the same way." She hesitated, as if she was unsure about sharing more. This was so different from the Kala I'd gotten to know over the last few days, always bubbly and quick to speak her mind. Her eyes met mine. "One of my college roommates committed suicide. Afterwards, everyone kept crowding in around me, wanting to talk, wanting me to do stuff . . . I know they were trying to be nice, but I couldn't stand it. It felt like I couldn't breathe."

I knew that suffocating feeling and the pressure from too many people. My grandparents hadn't died from suicide, but the cause of the crash had been questionable at first. For days afterward people had stopped at our house: neighbors asking if we needed anything, friends piling casseroles into our fridge . . . investigators talking to me and Mom, over and over. Mom doing her usual histrionics. It had been too much at the time.

I pressed my hands over my eyes, took a deep breath. I totally got how Kala must have felt. It had to have been rough. I offered a sympathetic smile. "I'm so sorry you had to go through that."

Kala shrugged. "There were three of us stuck in the same tiny dorm room." Her voice choked. She waved off the memory. "I know Claude's alive. Still, I think it would be kinder to keep it low key for Nina's sake. One-on-one. No extra people hanging around, talking. She's probably embarrassed that she didn't see it coming."

I nodded. "I'll present the appraisal, then take off—let Nina have her privacy."

Tuck glanced my way. "Maybe you and Kala are right. And I hate to say it, but today might not be the best day to pitch the auction idea either."

"I agree with that," I said. "I'd like Claude to be there when that happens, and I can't see him being released this soon."

As Kala got up and headed for the coffee maker with her empty mug, Tuck reached across the table toward me, a comforting gesture. "Don't worry. Everything will work out. It's just going to take more time than we counted on."

"I suppose," I said.

One thing was for certain—we wouldn't get anywhere if I kept putting all my energy into obsessing over Claude and what had happened. I needed to shove that onto the back burner and concentrate on the impending appraisal presentation. All three of us had worked hard and done an excellent job with research and documentation. Nina was going to be impressed, hopefully by the competence of our work—and definitely by the values we'd come up with.

* * *

The rest of the meal was more upbeat. Tuck wasn't impressed by the breakfast quiche Kala had created. He grimaced. "A little greasy, don't you think?"

"It's the bacon," Kala announced proudly. She winked. "Razorback."

Tuck stabbed at the quiche with his fork. "Fattened on human flesh, I'm assuming?"

I nearly snorted coffee out my nose.

By the time I arrived at the farm later on, I felt energized thanks to the joking around—and to the iced latte I'd bought on my way there, along with an extra-loud dose of mood-boosting music. I'd also taken time to curl my hair and worn a new blouse. New clothes always made me feel up.

Nina, on the other hand, arrived only a second ahead of me, and she looked horrible. Well, her clothes weren't rumpled, and her hair formed a soft halo around her face, freshly washed and styled, by the looks. But even her foundation couldn't hide the dark circles under her eyes. Clearly, she hadn't gotten much sleep at the hospital. It was a good thing we'd decided to keep the presentation low key as Kala had urged.

"Is Claude doing better today?" I asked as we started around toward the back porch to get the key. Even if I was trying not to obsess over his welfare, it would have been rude not to ask, and I did want to know.

"He should be able to come home tomorrow. Thank goodness," she said quietly.

"I'm glad to hear that." I retrieved Claude's key ring and unlocked the padlock on the back door. "Is Gracie handling everything okay?"

"She's worried about her pepe, of course. Her dance teacher dropped her off at school today—that's who she stayed with last night. Other than that, I'm hoping to keep things as normal as possible."

"Sounds like a good idea to me," I said. I wasn't so sure whether that was true or not. If I were Gracie, I wouldn't have wanted to leave my grandfather's side. Either way, not having Gracie around for the appraisal presentation would lessen the chance for interruptions.

Nina set her bag on the kitchen counter. "How about I make us coffee? If it's okay with you, we can talk in here."

"That would be perfect." I put the key ring on the table and took out a bound hard copy of the appraisal. I was about to sit down when I spotted a piece of grimy plastic wrap on the floor. I glanced to make sure Nina wasn't looking, then scooped it up and dropped it into the wastebasket. No need for her to discover that a cat had snuck in on our watch and rampaged through the kitchen.

With that done, I made myself comfortable at the table. Claude was coming home tomorrow. Things were moving along. Maybe it wouldn't be as long as I'd feared before we could all gather and discuss the auction idea.

"Here you go." Nina brought coffees, spoons, and some sweetened creamer over.

Once she settled into a chair across from me, I opened the appraisal and slid it over for her to look at. As I went over the various decoys and values, her tired gaze remained downcast, looking only at the pages. The expression on her face didn't waver, an odd combination of self-control and exhaustion, I assumed. But, as I neared the end, her eyes brightened, and her hand went to her mouth as if to stifle excitement. When I flipped to the final page and pointed out the seven-figure estimated value for the collection as a whole, she gasped.

"You said valuable. I never . . ." Her voice trailed off as she looked at the total again and blinked as if unable to believe her eyes.

"That's insurance value," I said firmly.

She shook her head. "Are you sure it's right?"

"Yes, very much so." I took out the invoice for our services and pushed it toward her.

The pleased expression fell from her face. Her voice faltered. "We can still trade for this, right? I know you gave us a general cost estimate before, but I can't afford . . . especially not now with Claude's trip to the hospital."

"We totally understand," I said.

I hesitated. Sure, the easiest next step was to ask for the drake mallard or the pair of teal in lieu of payment and be done with it. Once we owned them, we could sell them to a collector for a nice but discreetly undisclosed amount. I could probably even negotiate the trade with her here and now, though we'd still need to get Claude and Frank's consent. Until this moment, I'd supported the idea of not discussing an auction today, but this opening was too perfect to miss.

"What are you thinking?" she asked.

I spoke slowly, choosing my words with care. "Tuck and I discussed your situation at length. We have an alternate proposal that you might like even better. That's what the appraisal costs in cash or trade value. But, of course, *if* you were planning on auctioning the collection with us acting as your intermediary agent, we could discuss wrapping the value of the appraisal into the commission." I looked her in the eyes. "The amount you could get at auction would be life changing."

Nina flipped to the last page of the appraisal again, rereading the summary as if she expected to find that the decimal point had shifted in the wrong direction. Seven figures is hard to believe at first glance. She looked up. "How would that work, exactly? What do you have in mind?"

I explained how an intermediary agent worked, commission rates, and how we could arrange an auction for all or most of the decoys, paintings, and books. I stressed the benefits of using us. Expertise. Expediency. Discretion. A reasonable commission. Claude would end up with enough money to fix up the farm and with plenty left over to make everyone's lives easier, including Gracie's.

For the most part, I did all the talking. She sipped her coffee and nodded. I finished my pitch by essentially repeating the reasons she'd given when I asked her why she'd hired us to start with: "Your name will be kept out of the limelight. Out of the tabloids. No one will discover your current situation."

Nina closed her eyes and took a deep breath. "We'll need to discuss this option with Claude, of course—and Frank, and our lawyers. Personally, I think disposing of the entire collection at auction would be best for everyone concerned, and I'd prefer to continue to work with you."

I wanted to leap to my feet and do a happy dance. Instead, I swallowed my joy and nodded professionally. Besides, somewhere deep inside me a heavy sense of worry tumbled. This was all great, but I hated to leave with only a handshake. Granted, it was a foolish way to feel. This was a no-lose situation for us. We'd made as solid a connection with her and Claude as possible. Even if they backed out of the auction idea, they still owed us for the appraisal—either as cash or trade, and there were any number of pieces I was dying to get my hands on.

"Once Claude gets home—and if he agrees," I said, "we'll need to do additional paperwork and discuss things in detail. You don't think Claude's situation—his stability—will be an issue?" It had to be said.

Nina laughed; good humor tempered by a note of frustration. "He'll probably try to check himself out of the hospital today, knowing Claude. He's insisting it was something he ate."

"Food poisoning?" I asked.

She scoffed. "Leftover macaroni and cheese doesn't send anyone into convulsions, no matter how old it is."

I smiled and nodded. I had to agree with her there. Though, to my mind, food poisoning made more sense than a suicide attempt. "I'm just glad he got to the hospital in time."

Nina scooched her chair back and got to her feet. "Before you leave, would you mind if we went up to the attic? The appraisal is very clear, but I'd love to go over it one more time with the decoys in front of me. I want to make sure I have everything right before I talk to Claude."

"Of course." I was pleased that she'd asked. I was proud of our work and eager to elaborate.

Nina picked up the key ring from the table, then we headed to the second floor. By the time we reached the attic door, the glitter of excitement had returned to her eyes. In fact, her cheeks were flushed, and her hands shook as she undid the padlock.

"Do you think we should store the decoys somewhere safer?" she said, leading me up the stairwell to the attic. "I confess I'm more than a little worried."

"I definitely think that's a good idea. Does Claude have a gun safe? You could use it temporarily," I suggested, then added, "You also should talk to your insurance provider. You can have them call me if there are any questions."

"I already upped that some a while ago, after Claude kept insisting they were valuable."

"Oh," I said, surprised. "I'm assuming you mean your general homeowner's policy. I thought Frank was unhappy with it."

"Nothing makes Frank happy. But now that we have the appraisal and I know just how much the collection is worth, we'll have to add on separate policy for—"

Nina stopped dead in her tracks, so fast I nearly ran into her.

She stood immobilized for a long, cold second, then she began to tremble.

"What's wrong?" I asked.

She raised a shaking hand and pointed toward the far end of the attic. Her voice drew tight, a strangled cry of horror. "Where—where are they?"

Terror seized me. Cold sweat iced my spine. I didn't want to look. But like a child drawn into a nightmare, I lifted my head and followed her line of sight.

At the far end of the attic, sunlight slanted in through the window. Dust motes danced in the brightness. The light illuminated the table below. For an overpowering second, my eyes refused to register what they saw.

There was nothing on the table.

Not one single decoy.

Chapter Thirteen

Nina's voice spiraled toward panic. "What did you do with them?"

"Nothing," I said. "They were right there when we left."

I couldn't breathe. Couldn't think. I rushed to the table. They had to be here somewhere.

Pulse hammering, I dropped to my knees, digging through the newspaper-filled boxes, desperately searching the trunk. There wasn't a trace of the decoys. Not even one.

Stolen. Taken. The words rang in my head like a death knell. I leaped up and wheeled to stare at Nina. "Did you see any broken windows downstairs?"

She glared. "No. You forgot to lock the door, didn't you?"

"Of course not." I took a quick breath. "Who else knows you hide the keys in that coat?"

"I've never left them there before."

I licked my lips. "Who else has keys? How about Mudder?"

"Are you kidding? Mudder'd lose his own head if it wasn't nailed on." Nina's hands fisted at her sides. "Claude's the only other person. And if you think I'm going to swallow that Claude snuck out of the hospital and stole his own collection, you're crazier than I think." She planted her feet, standing squarely between me and the path to the stairwell. "And don't bother to ask about Frank. That's the set of keys I gave you—the only ones I have."

I shook my head, trying to make sense of what she'd said. "You didn't have your own keys before?"

"No," she wailed. "Frank, the idiot, didn't even let me have a car. Claude bought me the car. Claude got the keys from Frank and gave them to me."

"Frank could've had duplicates made."

For a beat, she fell still. Then she shook her head violently. "No! The bastard knows that Claude—that I'd kill him if he ever tried something like this."

My mind whirled. Clearly, Frank was even more of a jerk than I'd thought. But he'd warned me to watch out for Nina. There had to be a logical answer. Nina couldn't have taken the collection. She was at the hospital. "Someone could've used a screwdriver to remove the padlock hasps from the doorframes, then put them back."

She pointed a finger at me, shaking it in my face. "Or you took them—you and that uncle of yours, and that black girl. I should have known better than to trust you."

I wanted to jump down her throat for the ridiculous accusation, and her referring to Kala like that only made me angrier. I clamped my hands over my ears, head spinning as I scanned the attic for answers. None of this made sense. We'd locked all the doors. I hadn't noticed any signs of burglary when we'd walked into the house or on the way up to the attic. Nothing in the attic looked out of place. Nothing.

My gaze spotted a faint trail of footprints leading to the armoire. Most likely our tracks—but maybe not.

I dashed to the armoire, snatched Claude's hidden key off the top, and unlocked the door. Relief flooded through me when I saw the contents were still there. I swiveled toward Nina. "The songbirds are here. So are the books." My voice choked. "You have to believe me, I have no idea what happened to the rest."

Bright patches of red blotched her face. She hurled the written appraisal to the floor and snarled, "I should have known better than to hire you. I read about your mother. I was told about you—slimy, underhanded—"

"The decoys were here when we left," I shrieked.

She stalked toward me. "Don't think we didn't realize you picked the lock to get into the armoire. We aren't stupid. What else did you break into? My jewelry? Claude's gun safe?"

Heat boiled up inside me. I clenched my teeth. I couldn't let my temper get the best of me. I wanted to scream at her, but I had to stay cool. Stand my ground. "I'm telling you the truth."

"I'm calling the cops," she growled.

"No, please."

Terror gripped me. What if the real thieves hadn't left any evidence? *People are innocent until proven guilty*, I reminded myself. That was the law. But Nina would swear I was the only one with access. I knew what the birds were worth. I knew where they were kept. Add in my and Mom's pasts, and I'd be at the top of the police suspect list. The only people who'd seen me last night were Tuck and Kala, and they'd be accused of being accomplices. We could end up in prison, and even if we avoided that, just a whiff of us being connected to a robbery would make us a pariah in the industry. It would be the final nail in Scandal Mountain Antiques' coffin. We'd lose the house. We'd lose our land and collections . . . There had to be a way out of this. There had to be a way to convince Nina that someone else stole the birds.

I took a sharp gulp, trying to steady myself and regain control. *The appraisal event.*

I looked Nina in the eyes. "Someone must have seen the plover on the *Morning Show*. They guessed who you were. Figured out where you lived. A professional thief."

"Do you think I'm that gullible? No one in their right mind would risk breaking in here after seeing that beat-up decoy. You said yourself it wasn't worth much. No one, except you, knew about the collection."

"Listen to me," I said.

She folded her arms across her chest. "For all I know, *you're* a professional thief. How can I be certain you and your little crew weren't the ones who robbed that museum in Canada? Bouchard things were taken at that robbery too. Was that just a coincidence? I'm not so sure anymore."

"What?" I gaped at her. "Are you nuts? I told you. We didn't take the decoys—and we certainly weren't involved in any museum heist. You were the one who came to the appraisal event. You phoned us and asked me to look at the collection."

The red-hot patches on Nina's face burned impossibly brighter. I realized something then—she hadn't actually made a move to call the police. She'd only threatened. She hadn't even insisted we be careful about not contaminating the crime scene, not that my fingerprints weren't already on everything. There was something off here.

Two things slipped into my mind simultaneously. When we'd walked into the house, she'd left her bag on the kitchen counter. She didn't have her phone on her. More importantly, there was the reason she'd hired us to start with. Embarrassment. Privacy. She didn't want her family to know about her living situation. She wanted the valuable collection back, but she wanted to keep this quiet. And that gave me a reason to hope.

I pressed my hand against my chest, relieved for a heartbeat, and put on a soothing tone, soft and sympathetic. "I'm not a thief and I don't know who took the decoys, but I want to figure it out as badly as you do." I wet my dry lips. "When thieves take valuable art and antiques, they generally don't sell them right away. They'll hide the decoys and wait for things to cool down. The plover might not have looked like much to you, but there are people out there who would have recognized it as a Bouchard decoy when the episode aired on TV. A greedy collector might have hired a professional to do this—a theft for hire. The collection is legendary."

Nina's eyes narrowed to slits. "What are you suggesting?"

"I'm suggesting you hold off calling the police. As soon as you contact them, the FBI's Art Crime Team will be notified because of the Bouchard name and its connection to the Canadian robbery. Just the mention of FBI involvement will make a lot of collectors and dealers uncomfortable. Even if they don't know anything—or think they don't—they'll shut their mouths and stay as far away as possible from this situation. People in the industry don't like to get involved with things like this." I swept my hands over my head, working up my nerve. I lowered my voice. "We should do our own investigating. Right away, before the police and all their red tape make finding the decoys impossible."

She sneered. "You'd like that, wouldn't you? You are a slick one."

"If I'm so slick, then why would I steal the collection knowing full well that I'd be the most obvious suspect? You said it yourself—I'm one of the few people who knew about the decoys, I had the keys and the opportunity. Stealing them like this would make me the dumbest thief in the world."

Tilting her head, she paused, then glared. "If not you, then who? Answer that one for me."

I raised my arms in surrender. "I can't tell you. I don't know, at least not yet." I let my arms fall limp to my sides. I pulled in a breath. "First we need to go downstairs and make sure the paintings are still here. We should check all the windows on every floor. Look for footprints, any clues. This could be more straightforward than we think. Does Claude have any enemies? Would Mudder have told anyone about the decoys?"

"It wasn't Mudder. If his friends were going to steal anything, it would have been Claude's ATV or hunting rifles. He knew about the paintings stolen in Canada, but he didn't grasp the decoys were worth more than sentimental value." She pressed her fingers over her eyes. "Claude's never going to forgive me when he finds out the cops were climbing all over this place without him being here."

"Then don't call the cops yet. Give me a week. I'll figure out who did this and get the decoys back." It sounded like an impossible promise even to my own ears. But I had to give her something and I was out of other options.

She turned, looking toward the empty table. For a long moment she stood that way, unmoving. Finally, she wheeled back to me. Sweat gleamed on her forehead. "Okay, maybe you're right." Her expression went fierce, eyes as sharp and dangerous as her voice. "You have three days. After that, I'm calling the police."

Three days? Terror shifted my pulse into overdrive. I could never find them that fast.

I rested my hands on my hips and bluffed for all I was worth. My gut said the dangerous look in her eyes was rooted in fear. Fear of her family finding out she was destitute and abandoned by her husband. Fear of the decoys vanishing underground as I'd suggested. I countered her offer. "Five days. Seriously, if the police get involved, you might never see the decoys again. There are thieves out there who would destroy the collection before they'd let the cops discover it."

At that, she paled, impossibly white. She closed her eyes, then opened them, her gaze now unyielding. "Alright, five days. By next Wednesday at noon, not one hour more. I want every last decoy back." She glanced to where the bound appraisal lay sprawled on the floor. "I'll know if you don't return all of them. In the meantime, if word leaks out or the police or FBI show up here, I'll deny we had a deal and you'll go down for this."

I nodded. "Don't worry. I'll find them."

Chapter Fourteen

"Get out of there," Tuck said, when I phoned him from the privacy of the Bouchards' upstairs bathroom. I'd already taken a ton of photos of the attic, the second floor, and the first—anything I thought might help, and even things I just suspected might matter.

"I'm leaving soon. I want to look around outside before I go." I gripped the phone tighter. "I managed to talk Nina into not calling the police, but it's hard to believe she went along with it."

"You're damn right. It's strange. This whole thing could be a setup, Edie. Remember your mom's arrest? Get out of there now."

"Fine," I whispered, even though I didn't like the comparison to Mom's situation and couldn't see how not calling the police could be a setup. I hesitated, then added, "The songbirds are still here, and the paintings. I can't believe the thieves didn't take them."

Tuck's voice cracked. "Get going, Edie. We'll talk later."

"See you soon." I hung up.

In truth, I could barely think, and what clarity I had was torn. One part wanted to run, and the other was determined to stay and take in even the smallest detail. But no matter how carefully I scoured for clues in the mountains of junk, I found nothing. Not even a chip of wood off the end of a decoy's beak. Not a flake of paint or a fragment of cloth from the yellow-legs' thighs. The thief or thieves had taken their time and been careful.

Outside, I took a few more photos. No broken windows. Not even any trampled weeds around the sheds or the barn. Nothing fresh, at least. Not even new pig tracks.

It wasn't until I gave in to my need to escape and hurried to the van that I spotted something interesting. In the driveway, close to my and Nina's cars, there was a set of tire tracks in a patch of soft dirt. They were wide enough to have come from a larger-size pickup and just old enough that a trace of pollen from the nearby willow tree had coated them. Not Claude's truck with the wooden tailgate. It was at the garage being repaired. Not Mudder's vehicle. He drove a small hatchback. And Frank drove a restored Corvette.

I snapped a bunch of photos. In some of the shots, I included my hand for size comparison. For a second, I thought about showing Nina what I'd found, but it seemed smarter to keep it to myself. Even with the addition of this possible clue, her willingness not to call the cops raised a red flag next to her name for me, even though I had previously managed to justify her reluctance. All she'd have needed was an accomplice who drove a larger vehicle.

After that I took off, heading for home. But by the time I reached the village of Franklin, a risky alternate plan had formed in my mind. No matter if Nina was involved or not, she would need to tell Claude what had happened. It sounded like he wouldn't be home from the hospital until tomorrow, but I couldn't see her waiting that long to tell him. I also couldn't see her telling him over the phone. She might have another coffee and look over the appraisal again, but soon she'd lock the house and head back to the hospital—with or without stopping to pick up Gracie at school.

Cautiously, I glanced in my rearview mirror to make sure Nina's car wasn't behind mine. The timeline for her actions was only a guess, after all.

There was no one behind me, just the rural road stretching and twisting out of sight.

I stepped on the accelerator. The medical center in St. Albans was the closest hospital, the only one in the county. On the small side but modern, it was where the ambulance would have taken Claude. If I got to him before Nina, I could make sure he heard the truth about the decoys' disappearance.

When I reached the hospital, I parked in the visitors' lot. I marched in through the front entrance's automatic glass doors and straight past the reception area, like I knew where I was going. Maybe I'd never been inside the hospital before, but I wasn't about to ask what room Claude was in and be turned away.

Ahead, a smiling gray lady stood in the middle of the hallway, greeting people and asking if they needed help, also known as monitoring who did and didn't belong beyond that point.

I glanced past her to an array of signs: surgical services, radiology . . . *restrooms.*

Slowing my steps, I let a middle-aged man with a young boy holding a bouquet of flowers move ahead of me. As the gray lady greeted them, I scooted past and zoomed into a rest-room. No one would question that.

I waited a minute, then glanced out. The gray lady was facing away from me, once again waiting to greet the next person. I scanned in the opposite direction. The man and boy were farther down the hallway. Probably on their way to visit someone.

Adrenaline pushed into my veins as I slipped out and followed them around a corner and into a different hall. One glimpse through an open doorway told me I'd found the patients' rooms.

I smiled. My guess had paid off.

However, the hall was busier than I'd expected, nurses and visitors coming and going. I shouldn't have been surprised. This wasn't a normal Friday. It was the beginning of Memorial Day weekend. With all the upcoming celebrations and Monday being a day off for many, some people were probably eager to get their visiting done so they could kick back or head out for the holiday.

I spotted a waiting area, nothing more than a dozen chairs gathered in an alcove. All the seats were taken, except for the one closest to the hall. I dropped into it to get out of the way while I figured out my next step. I could only go on the assumption that Claude had spent time in the ICU last night and was in a normal room by now. Finding that room wouldn't be easy. It wasn't like I could wander down the hall and do a bed check without drawing attention.

Thoughts of the confrontation I'd had with Nina in the attic began to replay in my mind. Nina had said she should have known better than to hire us. It wasn't a surprise she was aware of our tarnished reputation. That had been clear since the first day when I asked why she'd invited us to look at the collection rather than a different appraiser. However, this time, Nina hadn't said she learned about the offenses online or in the newspaper. She specifically said someone *told* her about me. Nina didn't care for antiques, so she probably didn't go to auctions or hang out at antique shops. If she hadn't heard the gossip in those places, then who had she been talking to?

Martina Fortuni? She spent time at their house checking out jewelry. It could have been her.

Or perhaps Nina had heard it at the appraisal event. As much as I disliked Graham, it wasn't him. He sent Nina to our table in the first place. It didn't make sense for him to badmouth us and then do that. There was the man at the appraiser check-in, *Jules Ramone*, according to his nametag. Plaid trousers. Yellow pullover. Face like he'd sucked on a sour pickle. He certainly hadn't hidden his disdainful feelings toward my family.

"Excuse me?" A woman's raised voice echoed up the hallway, pulling me from my thoughts.

"*Je m'en tabarnak!*" a man snapped back at her. Claude.

A gray-haired nurse dashed out from a nurse's station, shoes squeaking against the tiles as she streaked toward the ruckus.

I jumped to my feet and stared after her to see what was going on. The nurse sprinted toward where a larger nurse had Claude corralled between a dinner cart and a wall. Claude was dressed in work pants, belted high on his waist. His shirt was half unbuttoned.

The gray-haired nurse slowed her strides, approaching with her hand held out. "*Calme-toi.* Calm down. No one's saying you can't leave—"

"*Va chier!*" He shoved the cart aside, bulled past the nurses, and took off down a side hallway, out of my line of sight.

I hurried, walking as fast as I dared toward the nurses and where Claude had disappeared.

"What happened?" the gray-haired nurse asked the other as I passed.

"He just started swearing and saying he was going home," the large nurse answered.

Heck with it. I started to run, rushing down the side hall. Who cared about discretion? I needed to talk to Claude now.

Claude was a couple dozen yards ahead of me, zigzagging around nurses and doctors. He dodged visitors, less careful and more willing to plow them over than I was. In no time flat, we were down one hall and up the next. I couldn't believe an old man who'd been in ICU so recently could move so fast.

I lost sight of him for a second. When I spotted him again, he was zinging out the automatic front doors. As he stopped on the curb, I ran for all I was worth and finally caught up with him.

"Claude," I said, panting.

He grinned. "*Mon rusé carcajou.* Come to pay me a visit, eh?"

"I wanted to see how you were doing."

"Doctors are fools," he snarled. "Don't believe what they're saying. I'd never try to kill myself."

"I don't—"

He cut me off. "One good thing came out of this, the *maudit* doctor says I have a kidney infection, not cancer." A taxi pulled up to the curb and he brightened. "Got to go before those crazy nurses handcuff me to a bed. Lots to do. My truck needs picking up at the garage. Things need planting. The pig needs feeding . . . A man's got to take care of business, don't you know."

"Wait, there's something I have to tell you," I said, too late. He'd already jumped inside and was shutting the door.

"No," I groaned, as the taxi pulled away.

Chapter Fifteen

Tuck met me at the door when I got home.

"I sure didn't see this coming," he said, shoving a cold bottle of beer into my hand.

I took the beer and downed a long sip. It soothed the dryness in my throat but did nothing for the fear twisting in my stomach. "I can't believe Claude got away before I could tell him I didn't take the decoys. What if he calls the police?"

"I was going to suggest we do exactly that, except—" Tuck left the sentence hanging as he steered me away from the kitchen door. Once we were in the downstairs hall, he continued—"Kala uncovered something."

I stopped and turned toward him. "What are you talking about? What is it? When did she have time to find anything out?"

"It's probably better if she tells you herself." He gripped my elbow, propelling me into the formal dining room.

As I took in the room, I could only stare. The desktop computer that belonged in the carriage barn office now occupied the sideboard where Grandma's silver candlesticks usually sat. Next to the computer, a printer thumped and droned, spewing out paper. Two landline phones rested on the marble fireplace mantel. By the window, one of Mom's painting easels held a whiteboard with a timeline scribbled in neon green. The place looked like a scene from a Hallmark mystery.

"Is that a murder board?" I asked, waving my hand at the whiteboard.

Kala looked up from where she sat at the head of the mahogany dining table with a laptop open in front of her and a notepad beside it. She grinned. "Welcome to our command center."

I stared at it all, mouth open. They must have started setting it up as soon as I called and told Tuck about the robbery.

Kala's eyes glistened with enthusiasm. "What do you think?"

"Uh, I—" Confusion and frustration twisted inside me. I clenched my teeth to keep my feelings to myself, but they refused to be contained. "This isn't a game," I snapped. "If this goes public, the gossip alone about us being connected to another crime will destroy the business."

The glisten in Kala's eyes went icy. "Of course I know it's not a game. I'm not an idiot. I was just joking to relieve some stress."

Regret tightened in my chest. I set my beer on the table, then rubbed my hands over my face. "I'm sorry. I'm not upset with you. I'm mad at myself. I should have known the appraisal was too good to be true, that it was going to lead to trouble. For God's sake, Frank warned me to be careful."

Tuck spoke up. "Kala, tell her what you discovered."

Ignoring Tuck's comment, I slumped into a chair and continued my apology. "Really, I feel awful. About yelling at you—and for getting you involved in this to begin with." I hushed my voice. "There isn't any reason for you to get in any deeper. You can leave, stay clear of this whole mess. I'll give you what we owe you, plus a bonus."

"No way. I came here to learn the business, the good and the bad. Besides, I don't think you have the skills to get through this on your own."

I frowned at her. "What are you talking about?"

She glanced at the laptop, then cleared her throat. "I'm good—*real* good—at doing stuff on the internet. More than just appraisal research and selling on eBay." She looked at me, then pushed her hair back in an unmissably dramatic gesture. "I'm not saying I'd turn down a bonus. You can call it hazard pay if you want."

"If we get out of this with a whole skin, I'll give you double your normal salary."

Kala winked. "Cash, not check?"

"Definitely cash," I said. "Now tell me—what's Tuck talking about? What did you find?"

"The other day, I noticed a profile pic in passing when I was doing research for the appraisal. I got busy and it went out of my mind until Tuck told me the collection was stolen, then I started wondering and double-checked." Her attention went back to the laptop, fingers flying across the keys. When she finished, she turned the laptop around so I could see the screen. "Look at the third comment down from the top."

The comments were on a blog post about Canadian folk art. I scanned to the third one. At first the profile picture simply looked like a rustic front door. I could see how Kala might have skimmed over it while researching something else. But I also knew why it had stuck in her mind. It looked exactly like Scandal Mountain Antiques' logo.

As I enlarged the image, my mouth went dry. It *was* our logo. "I'm assuming you or Tuck didn't make the comment?"

"Unfortunately, no. Check out the bio," she said.

As I read the bio, I pressed my hands over my mouth. It was the description we used on our social media accounts. Same contact information. Same everything, word for word.

"It's an imposter account," Kala clarified.

"Why would anyone do that?" Goose bumps peppered my skin. On top of the theft, this was more than disturbing.

"It could be some troll's idea of a joke," Tuck suggested. His voice lowered, gravely serious. "It also could be that someone's been setting us up to take the fall for the robbery."

Kala looked at me steadily. "If I wanted to plant evidence to make it look like you—or all of us—stole the Bouchard collection, I might start with impersonating Scandal Mountain on social media. For it to really come across as damning, I'd have other fake profiles plant insinuations in more obscure places, including the darknet."

"The darknet?" I asked, not that I'd never heard of it, but it had always seemed surreal, a galaxy beyond the one I traveled in.

"You know, the dark web where they sell illegal things—stolen stuff," Kala said. "Where you can't go without special software and authorization. Where the police would have to work to uncover the evidence."

"You really think someone could be framing us?" I wanted to ask how she knew so much about these things, especially the dark web. I mean, there are your usual super-good computer nerds, and then there are people with more dubious *skills*.

She shrugged. "I'd have to do more digging before I could say for sure. It would take someone a lot of time to make the evidence look natural. But the collection is worth millions—and that's one big stack of enticing motives."

I picked up my beer, holding it a moment before taking a long sip. "If the police find out the Bouchards' decoys have gone missing, and then they discover evidence against us online—"

Kala finished my train of thought. "It wouldn't matter if you were the one who called them or not—you, Tuck, me, the business—all our reputations would go down the drain before their cyber team got everything untangled to their satisfaction." Her voice toughened. "We can't risk getting the police involved yet. We need to find the decoys and figure out who did this first."

"Agreed," I said. "But we can't forget that Nina only gave me five days."

Tuck rubbed his beard. "Do you think we could get Nina to loosen up on the time frame by showing her evidence as we uncover it, like the fake accounts?"

I sat back in my chair, shook my head. "What if Nina's involved in setting us up?"

Tuck frowned. "If that were the case, then why didn't she just call the police and accuse you on the spot? I can't see her being afraid that you'd physically try to stop her."

"I don't know. But I don't think it's smart to rule out any person or motive—or to tip our hand by sharing our discoveries, giving whoever a chance to cover up evidence against them. The thief could be Nina—or it could be a total stranger for all we know."

"Then we better get to work," Tuck said. "Where do you want to start?"

Another thought pushed into my mind. Though it was horrifying, it had to be said. "I've got the feeling the thief or thieves knew no one would be home last night."

Kala's eyes widened. "You mean, they knew Claude would overdose and end up in the hospital?"

"That's a frightening thought," Tuck said.

Kala scrambled to her feet and went to the whiteboard. "Okay, time to get this down in black and white." She wrote Nina's name in capital letters. "Nina has an alibi for last night. But she knew where the keys were. She had access to Claude's food."

I piped up. "Put *'Why didn't she call police?'* on there. Not wanting her parents and childhood friends to find out she's fallen on hard times could be part of her motive, but there's got to be more to it."

"There's lots of reasons people don't want cops around," Kala said.

Tuck nodded. "That's true. If Nina's working with a partner, she might be buying time for them to get the collection out of the area or for a buyer to pick the decoys up. As you said, several million dollars is a lot of motivation."

Kala turned toward the board, neatly adding the bullet points beneath Nina's name. When she was done, she turned back. "Who's next on the list?"

"We can't forget Mudder," I said. "He said his grandmother thinks she should have inherited some of the collection. Maybe he feels like Claude cheated his family."

Tuck shook his head. "I think that's a reach. If you were talking about stealing a six-pack of beer from the back of someone's truck, I'd believe Mudder did it. He's no master thief or computer whiz."

"I'll put Mudder on a lower tier." Kala quickly added his name in bold, precise letters.

"We also can't forget that the plover was on TV," I said. "A dealer or collector might have recognized it as a Bouchard piece."

Kala wrote: "*Unknown dealer/collector.*" Then she took a fresh grip on the marker and wrote "*Frank*" in extra-large letters. "There's no love lost between him and Claude. It's no big deal to have spare keys cut. He had a set until recently."

She was right about that. I sat up straighter. "I actually think we should talk to Frank in person. I want to know why he warned me about Nina. I'd also love to be the first to tell him about the robbery before he hears about it from Nina or Claude—or even Gracie. Face-to-face, so I can see his reaction. That is, if Nina hasn't told him already."

"Do you know where he lives?" Tuck asked. "If Frank is hiding something, it might be smarter to surprise him rather than emailing first. You don't have his phone number, right?"

"No. Just his email. Besides that, all I know is that he drives a vintage red Corvette."

Kala snagged her phone from where it lay on the table. "Do you remember if it had Vermont license plates?"

"Yes, I'm sure of it. I noticed them when he drove in."

She headed toward the door. "I've got to make a call. Don't worry, I'll find Frank—or at least his Corvette."

As she vanished into the hallway, Tuck chuckled. "Why do I feel like we just unleashed a cyber-razorback on Frank's ass?"

"I'm just grateful she's on our side," I said.

* * *

While we waited for Kala to return from making her call, I went to the whiteboard and added a few more details—along with Graham's name. He knew folk art. He'd seen the plover and sent Nina to our table at the event. We already suspected him of not being aboveboard. Then I removed Tuck's Christmas cactus from the stand under the window and used the spot to set up a second board.

I stepped back, staring at the puzzle of names and minutiae. "We're never going to figure this out."

Tuck's voice grew taut. "I hate to say it, but there is someone else we need to consider."

"Who?" I couldn't imagine who he meant, but I didn't like the sound of it.

"Shane knows about the collection, right?"

I gaped at him, stunned. "You can't be serious."

"You said we needed to include everyone."

"Everyone that makes sense." The mention of Shane reminded me of something I'd forgotten. "Damn. I'm supposed to get together with him later."

I whipped out my phone and shot off a text. *Have to cancel tonight. I'm not feeling well. Upset stomach.*

Shane answered instantly. *That doesn't sound good. Flu?*

Lunch. Bad mac and cheese. I silently thanked Claude for the inspiration.

Food poisoning?

Probably just a 24-hour thing.

He responded a bit slower. *I'm definitely going to Fisher's auction tomorrow. Are you?*

Though I hadn't taken time to preview the auction online, Fisher's Memorial Day Extravaganza was always one of their best. A good auction would draw a lot of dealers, and dealers like to gossip. We might be able to learn something important there.

I texted back. *For sure. If I'm feeling better.*

Shane sent another message. *Did you finish the appraisal?*

I pressed my lips into a hard line. I'd have preferred to stay as far away from that topic as possible. *Almost done.*

You'll feel better once that's behind you. A lot of decoys?

My stomach gave a flip-flop for real this time. *I'll tell you about it when I see you.*

You take care of yourself, he texted back.

I will.

A bead of cold sweat traced down my spine. Shane was pretty intuitive. Texting was one thing. It wouldn't be as easy to hide my fears from him when we saw each other in person. But I'd have to do it, if for no other reason than to keep him from guessing what had happened. If he figured out that the collection had been stolen, he'd feel obliged to report the theft—and that was the last thing we needed.

Chapter Sixteen

L ess than half an hour later, Kala swaggered back into the dining room with an enormous grin on her face.

"You found the Corvette's registration?" I asked, totally impressed.

"Better than that." She sat down at the head of the table and slid the laptop back in front of herself. Her fingers danced on its keyboard. "I was going to go the registration route, then one of my ex-girlfriends suggested something else."

Tuck stiffened. "You told someone?"

"Of course not—just generalities. Mostly I humiliated myself. The solution was embarrassingly obvious." She swiveled the laptop around so Tuck and I could see. "Sometimes Google is the only friend you need."

Frank Bouchard's LinkedIn profile spanned the screen.

His headshot was recent: deep tan, hair slick and styled, perfect teeth. He worked in Stowe in the tourism industry. An executive coordinator at a resort. There were photos of him on a ski slope, rubbing elbows at an art show in Stowe, and schmoozing someone up at a black-tie event.

I bent closer to the screen, studying the photos again. It was impossible to reconcile the lifestyle he was living in Stowe with how Nina and Gracie were struggling in Franklin, barely an hour away. "He certainly isn't suffering."

"That's only the tip of the Frank iceberg. There's also this—" Kala swiveled the laptop back to face her. She once again tapped a few keys, then revealed the next tidbit. "This is where he lives."

The screen now displayed a foreclosure auction listing with photos of a ski chalet and the word SOLD stamped across it. The address was 6 Snow Bunny Lane, Stowe, Vermont.

"Frank bought a chalet?" Tuck shook his head in disbelief.

"Yup, no question about it," she said.

I swiped my finger across the laptop's screen, bringing up pre-auction photos of the chalet's interior. A basic story-and-a-half house. Wall-to-wall carpet. Stucco fireplace. Vinyl flooring in the kitchen.

"Before you ask," Kala said. "This is all public record. Nothing that's going to alert anyone." She reclaimed the laptop and brought up yet another image: a property tax bill for the chalet, complete with assessed value, address, and date of purchase: last summer, several months before Nina claimed he'd left her.

"Frank really is a sneaky bastard, isn't he," I said. "I'm willing to bet none of his new friends know he's technically still married."

Kala nudged the laptop aside. "Speaking of new friends and hobnobbing. According to Beau Bouchard's social media— that's the nickname Frank is currently using—he's going to be at a benefit tonight. Wine tasting. Sampling dishes from Stowe chefs. Dancing under the stars . . . After a night like that, he'll probably sleep in tomorrow morning."

I smirked. "Sounds like the perfect time to catch him at home. A lot better than getting caught sneaking into a high-profile party to catch up with him."

"It'll also give us time to do some more research," Tuck added.

* * *

We set to work digging deeper into Frank's background. Before he and Nina moved in with Claude, they had lived in Lake George, New York. He'd majored in travel and tourism in college. He and Nina met around that time. Currently, he had a low credit rating. Nina's was even lower. Her parents lived in an affluent suburb just outside Washington, D.C.

"Wow, this is interesting," Kala's said. "Nina has a degree from Cornell in computer science."

Tuck chuckled. "Well, now. Looks like we found someone with *skills*."

"I'd never have guessed that one," I said.

Kala scoffed. "It doesn't mean anything. You can't get into Cornell without excellent high school grades, but a degree from a Richie Rich college doesn't guarantee she's got talent. It's just a piece of paper."

I waved that off. "Whatever. We need to add that to the whiteboard: '*Nina possibly the impersonator*.' Could have skills to create fake accounts and digital trail leading back to us."

Kala blew a raspberry. "I'm writing it in teeny-weeny print. I bet if I got a look at her college records, I'd find a 6.5 GPA."

I let that go. Kala was right about degrees not always equaling talent. Plus, I'd never seen Nina exhibit any great interest in computers. That said, her life had changed dramatically since college—from affluent parents and Ivy League to being left broke and living in a rundown farmhouse with Gracie and Claude.

After that important morsel, we didn't uncover much more about Nina. She wasn't on social media. She didn't even pop up or get tagged in photographs, except around the time of Gracie's birth and on cruises she and Frank took to the Bahamas years ago.

On the other hand, Frank—or, more currently, Beau Bouchard—was all over the net. He belonged to a variety of charity organizations. He was a member of the Vermont Chamber of Commerce and Toastmasters . . . Nothing shocking or anything that raised a red flag.

While Kala and Tuck continued to look into Frank, I moved on to scanning the FBI's National Stolen Art File, a public database that lists stolen art and cultural property, taken in the U.S. as well as abroad. I was looking for missing folk art with similarities to the Bouchard collection. What was taken and where might help clarify whether the theft of the Bouchard collection was an isolated incident or not. I agreed with Tuck that we couldn't afford to simply make assumptions about the thief's motives or identity. We needed to check out all possible angles.

Obviously, the FBI listed an inventory from the Canadian Museum of History robbery, including the pieces I'd read about online as well as others: a William Hart merganser decoy, an exceptional Quebec rooster weathervane, Ozama Martin's hooked rug, *Le Velo Jaune* (*The Yellow Bicycle*) . . .

When Nina had accused me of being involved with the Canadian robbery, I'd been beyond furious. She did have a point, though. The two events could be connected, especially if someone involved with the Canadian robbery had seen the plover at the appraisal event or on TV. Either way, the more I dug into the FBI's list the more it became clear that there had been a noticeable uptick in the theft of decoys and hunting-related art. Folk art in general. Another Ozama Martin piece had vanished from a Boston gallery, a brilliant wall hanging titled *The Great Race*. That was interesting. Two of her pieces. Other than being folk art, I couldn't begin to think how the pieces tied in with hunting-related items, but that didn't mean there wasn't a link.

Around midnight, we all surrendered and went upstairs to get some sleep. I took a hot shower to help me relax, then crawled into bed. But as soon as my head hit the pillow, my mind started humming even faster than before, swirling with images of the stolen Canadian Museum pieces and the Bouchard decoys. Other pieces of missing folk art from throughout New England and Canada mixed in, things I'd come across in my research and pieces I'd seen over the years. The images tossed and turned, and finally blurred into a dream.

I was riding the canary yellow bicycle from Ozama Martin's hook rug through the Canadian Museum of History, balancing decoys and paintings in my arms. I pedaled faster and faster, flying down hallways, careening around corners, searching for a way to escape from the building. I was moving so fast that the paintings on the walls blurred into ribbons of color. At one point, my mom's harping voice echoed. *"I told you I didn't do it. Edie, you never listen. You think it's been easy for me . . . ?"*

Sculptures whipped by. I rocketed into the Grand Hall. Totem poles closed in, their faces taking on the appearance of Claude and Nina. A Canadian Mountie appeared ahead. Blood seeped out from a shotgun wound in his chest. He stumbled toward me with arms outstretched like a zombie. I stomped on the brakes, but the bike wouldn't stop. I kept flying toward him—

I turned in my sleep, half awake for a second. Bloody chest. A shotgun wound. Was that right? Had the news ever reported how the officer was killed? *No.* Maybe stabbed? Maybe run over? The security guard had died recently in the hospital.

Sleep came back over me, the zombie Mountie fading into the ribbons of colors. My disturbed sleep deepened into oblivion, troubled only by a whisper of thoughts: I hadn't stolen the Bouchard pieces. Yet I was having to defend myself by finding them. In a way, it was like Mom, claiming she was innocent of the forgery.

But that wasn't right. The two things weren't comparable. I'd seen Mom practicing Maxfield Parrish's signature. I'd seen it. She was guilty.

Chapter Seventeen

On the trips to and from the Bouchard farm, I'd barely paid any attention to the Jumping Café. This morning as we passed it on the way to confront Frank in Stowe, it called to me like a siren's song.

The café itself wasn't the problem, it was the flea market tents that glistened seductively in the field beside it. I'd been so focused on the appraisal and then the theft that I'd all but forgotten about the upcoming market, not to mention Monday's barbecue and fireworks.

I tapped the brakes, slowing and then stopping as a group of people dashed across the road, hurrying for the cluster of tents. A bunch of kids in ladybug costumes barreled out of an SUV, swarming toward the café's reception hall. Two scruffy guys were draping bunting on the café's deck. Other people were installing security fencing along the edge of the parking areas. When I was a kid, the days leading up to the festival felt as exciting as the wait for Christmas morning.

Tuck swiveled in the passenger seat, looking at me. "Hurts not to stop, doesn't it?"

"Mostly it reminds me how simple things were before this whole mess. I barely slept last night. I kept thinking about the Canadian robbery and the decoys."

"I had a nightmare about Frank Bouchard." Kala's voice came from where she sat in the back. She leaned forward and whispered ominously, "When we got to Frank's house, he'd been murdered. Guts and blood splattered all over, Freddy Krueger style."

I cringed. "Yeah. I think we can rule that out. Along with razorbacks ripping open his Corvette and eating him alive."

"You never know," she said. "Just look at the news. Creepy stuff happens all the time."

I pushed the whole idea out of my mind. The last thing we needed was for Frank to turn up murdered. Then there would be no keeping the police out of it.

Once we got a mile or so past the café, the traffic grew lighter and I picked up the pace, cruising along, only slowing as we went around Dead Man's Curve, zipping past farms and fields.

In no time at all, I was driving up Smuggler's Notch Road. As we headed into the wilderness, the last of the houses disappeared. The road turned steep. Waterfalls spilled down the roadside ledges. At the top of the mountain, the trees grew stunted and the road tapered to a single lane as it snaked between boulders and naked rock face.

Normally, the twisty Notch Road was one of my favorite drives, wild and a challenge to navigate. Today it made the muscles along the back of my neck knot with tension, releasing only after we started down past the ski areas and my GPS announced we should take the next road on the left.

When we reached it, I turned as instructed after a small group of shops, including a bakery that Kala enthusiastically pointed out. We passed a tennis court. Snow Bunny Lane was directly beyond it, flanked on one side by the court and on the other by a line of dense cedar hedges.

"There it is." Tuck pointed at the second driveway.

I could see at a glance he was right. At the end of the drive, the number 6 was painted on a post. Unfortunately, the hedge obscured the view of anything other than the driveway's mouth. There was no way to get a preview of what we were driving into.

"Here goes nothing." I winged into the driveway. No sense delaying the inevitable.

We went by a bed of spent daffodils. There was an island of birch trees, then the small chalet. It was nicer than it had appeared online. Still, it was basic, especially compared to the flashy Corvette Frank drove.

Kala leaned forward. "What are we going to do if Frank doesn't answer the door?"

"I don't think that's going to happen," I said. "His curiosity will get the better of him."

I turned around in front of the chalet's single-car garage and parked facing out the way we'd come.

Tuck chuckled. "Preparing for a fast getaway?"

"You never know." I certainly wasn't ruling out the possibility. Nina could've told Frank about the robbery. He might call the police as soon as he saw us. I took a deep breath. "Everyone ready?"

"I am if you two are," Tuck said.

We all got out and hiked to the front door. Next to it, a pair of crisscrossed 1960s skis decorated the wall. The name

"Bouchard" was calligraphed across them. On their own, the skis were worth maybe ten bucks. Done up as wall art, they were worth an easy hundred. Mom had created similar pieces and sold them at shows.

As I went to push the doorbell, I noticed something strange. The screen door was ajar, and the inside door was halfway open.

Uneasiness gathered in my stomach. I glanced at Tuck and Kala. "What do you make of that?"

Tuck pressed the doorbell. Its chime echoed inside, and we all stood still, listening.

Nothing. No one shouted they'd be right there. No tap of approaching footsteps. The only sound was the faint mumble of a TV set coming from somewhere deep within the chalet.

Tuck knocked on the door frame. "Hello! Anybody home?"

"Maybe he's not here." Kala stepped back a few yards and looked up toward the second-floor windows. "There's a light on upstairs, but I don't see any movement."

The uneasiness inside me transformed into a slow burn. I pulled the screen door open, then nudged the inside door with the toe of my shoe. It swung open, thumping as it hit against a wall.

I stepped over the threshold, taking one tentative step inside and then another. No need to worry about alarms or cameras—I hadn't noticed any. Besides, it wasn't like we were breaking in.

"Anyone home?" I called out.

To my left, a carpeted staircase led to the second floor. Straight ahead was a living room with cream-colored furniture, a white stucco fireplace, and a sliding glass door that led out onto a deck. To the right of the living room, I could make out the shape of a kitchen island. The rest of the kitchen, no doubt, was just out of view.

"Frank, are you here?" Tuck shouted.

No response.

The lights were on in the living room, but the air didn't smell of coffee or bacon, nothing reminiscent of breakfast. Just a hint of bleach.

"I'll check upstairs," Tuck said. "You two look around down here. Be careful. Something doesn't feel right."

Kala moved in close to me, clutching my arm. "I really don't want to see blood-spattered walls."

"Neither do I." My pulse hammered as I edged my way into the living room.

Tuck's voice echoed upstairs. "Frank! Are you here? We want to talk to you about Nina and Claude."

"Seriously, this is creepy," Kala whispered.

Holding my breath, I inched forward. Logic said there was a simple answer to why the door was open. Still, I fully expected to discover Frank's mutilated body sprawled on the wall-to-wall carpet.

But there was nothing on the floor, not even a speck of dirt or a stray potato chip. If there was such a thing as the mirror opposite of Claude's farmhouse, this was it.

Tuck's footfalls reverberated as he came back downstairs. "Frank was here at some point. The bed's slept in. The TV's on."

"Maybe he went to the corner bakery for coffee?" Kala suggested.

"Could be." I freed myself from her grip. "While we've got the place to ourselves, we should snoop around. Look for things connected to Nina or Claude, paperwork from a divorce lawyer, anything about Claude's estate—or decoys."

"Are you sure that's a good idea? Frank could show up any second," Tuck said.

"We can always say we came in because we were worried about him. That wouldn't be a lie. Just don't touch anything with your bare hands. You know, don't leave any fingerprints, just in case."

"Sounds smart to me." Tuck headed for a desk that sat on the far side of the living room.

"Do you want me to keep watch out the front door?" Kala asked.

"Great idea," I said. "Whistle if you see anyone coming."

I turned toward the kitchen. The island and the white countertops sparkled as if scoured clean. The sink was empty of dishes. The coffee machine was pristine, not a single smudge or trace of grounds. It reminded me of the kitchenette in my New York apartment. I'd spent all my time at the auction house, eaten out, and never invited guests over. Essentially, the kitchen was never used. I hadn't even taken time to hang a curtain in its lone window, much like Frank had also failed to do.

I pulled my sleeve down to cover my fingers—the best replacement for gloves I could manage on short notice. Then I opened the refrigerator door. A lot of people hid important items in weird places. One time, I bought a superb eighteenth-century snuff box that a woman stored in her fridge's vegetable drawer, along with a mayonnaise jar full of silver half dollars.

Unfortunately, this vegetable drawer contained potatoes and nothing else. The rest of the fridge held equally normal items: milk, cream, butter, eggs, a large package of hamburger, and some Canadian bacon . . . Definitely not empty like my apartment refrigerator.

With my sleeve still covering my hand, I checked the kitchen cupboards. Spaghetti sauce, a jumbo box of dried macaroni, Ritz crackers. All the usual things, right down to a full selection of baking supplies, spices, and a roll of extra-large vacuum sealer bags.

I glanced at Tuck. "Either Frank takes his cooking seriously or he's not living alone."

Tuck shook his head. "There weren't any signs of anyone else upstairs, and I did look in the closets."

"So Frank's a neat freak who likes to cook," I said. I didn't fully believe the cooking part. Frank seemed more like the kind of guy who preferred to be waited on rather than doing for others. Still, I did recall Nina saying that Frank's mother had been an amazing cook. Maybe he picked up the interest from watching her.

I moved from the kitchen into a mudroom that connected the rest of the house to the garage. There was a closet inside. Across from it a door led into a bathroom.

Instinct drew me to the closet. I pushed its sliding door open. Coats, sweaters, jackets, all neatly hung on matching wooden hangers. I studied a lavender sweater: women's size medium, cashmere with wildflowers embroidered on the collar, very expensive. Not the sort of clothing a woman left behind unless she intended to return.

Beneath the hanging clothes a footstool-size cardboard box rested on the floor. It was too small to contain any more than a couple of decoys. But it was sturdy looking and clean, the sort of box Kala might have used for shipping an eBay item. Even if I only found one decoy inside, then we'd know we were on the right track.

Hands trembling, I crouched and pulled back the box's flaps. Inside, a pair of nineteenth-century brass candlesticks lay tangled in bright-white newspaper. I growled under my breath. Not a decoy.

I crossed my fingers and pushed the candlesticks aside. There was a bulge of something buried deeper in the box. Maybe I'd still get lucky.

Holding my breath, I pulled away more newspaper. My fingers tingled as they brushed a hard surface, but as I removed the paper, my excitement sank. It was an antique stoneware storage jar. Salt glazed. Decorated with a simple floral design. A. K. Ballard/Burlington, Vermont. Beautiful, but valueless thanks to a crack. Not a decoy. Not even remotely connected to one, and there was nothing else in the box.

I picked up the jar, feeling its orange-peel textured glaze as I studied it more closely. I wasn't sure why, but it seemed oddly familiar. Then again, it wasn't exactly an uncommon maker or style of stoneware.

Tuck walked over. "What did you find?"

"A stoneware jar and some candlesticks. You haven't seen any other antiques around, have you?"

"Not one piece," Tuck said. "I wonder why he kept those things?"

"Who knows?" I wrapped the jar and the candlesticks back up and returned the box to the closet. It wasn't like we had time to stand around dreaming up hypotheses. "You want to look in the bathroom, while I check out the garage?"

"Fine, but we really should get out of here soon."

I shut the closet door, but I left the door to the garage open as I went out into it.

The single-bay garage was tiny and as immaculate as the house. An extra set of tires sat in a corner wrapped in plastic. Tennis rackets hung on a wall. Signs for a walk-a-thon were piled by a door that led outside. The Corvette wasn't there.

Tuck's voice came from the bathroom, listing off what were most likely the contents of a medicine cabinet. "CBD oil. Two toothbrushes. Mouthwash. Lubricant—strawberry flavored."

I wrinkled my nose at an image of middle-aged Frank frolicking with a woman dressed only in a lavender sweater.

He continued, "Two bottles of prescription medicine on the window ledge. High blood pressure, I'm guessing."

As I stepped further into the garage, something crunched under my heel. Dried mud. Pieces of a tire track. Scattered and desiccated almost to powder.

I knelt down, comparing its width to that of my hand. It was hard to tell by what little was left, but the imprint might have originally been as wide as the tracks at the farm—which was odd since logic said this was where Frank would have parked his Corvette.

Straightening back up, I studied the pieces of tire track. I didn't know much about Corvettes, but it seemed like they might have special tires. Were they wider than the ones on normal cars?

I hurried to the tire pile—most likely winter ones taken off the Corvette last month. I peeled back the plastic. One look answered my question. They were notably wide, enough so that their track might resemble a truck's.

"Hey!" I called to Tuck. "Come here."

I took out my phone and started snapping photos of the tires.

"That's interesting," Tuck said, as he joined me. One thing I loved about Tuck was that I didn't have to continuously explain myself; ninety percent of the time we were on the same wavelength.

"Do you think those came off the Corvette?" I asked.

"It's a good possibility, unless Frank has another vehicle."

Kala's voice came from the mudroom door. "I'm getting really nervous. Can we get out of here?"

"I'm ready to go, too," Tuck said.

"All right," I said. We might have not found any paperwork of interest or the decoys themselves, but if the tires matched the tracks at the farm, then risking a look around had more than paid off.

Chapter Eighteen

After I wrapped the plastic back over the tires, we slipped out the garage's side door. In a minute we were in the van headed out of Frank's driveway.

I drummed on the steering wheel. "I still wish we could've talked to Frank. I really think if we could see his reaction to the robbery, we'd have a better idea if he's guilty or not."

Tuck gestured toward the bakery just beyond the tennis court. "If I lived in the neighborhood, I'd be there for coffee every morning like clockwork."

"I would too," Kala said. "Except I'd walk, not drive."

"Frank probably likes to show off his car, though," I said.

I cruised out of Snow Bunny Lane, then into the parking lot the bakery shared with the other shops. The place over-flowed with cars, but no Corvettes, let alone a fully restored and bright red older model. So much for that idea.

I pulled into an open parking space, blew out a frustrated breath, then glowered through the windshield. The tennis court was directly in front of us, but I could still see the mouth of Frank's driveway on the other side. Why couldn't he have just been home?

"While we're here," Tuck said, hand already on the door latch, "I'm going to run into the bakery and use their restroom. You know us older men, we need to go every five minutes."

I glanced at Kala. "I'll make you a deal. I'll buy something for all of us to eat if you wait here and keep an eye on Frank's driveway. If he comes home, we can go back and talk with him."

"Fine by me," Kala said. "Just bring me back something big and sugary—raspberry turnovers, maple cream donuts with bacon crumbles."

I narrowed my eyes at her. "Definitely no bacon. I don't need any more jokes about razorbacks or serial killers feeding people to pigs."

She laughed. "You're the one that brought up razorbacks the last time."

I cringed. "Yeah, I guess you're right."

Tuck and I walked across the parking lot to the bakery. Gigantic pots of petunias flanked its front door. Inside, people clustered around small tables and waited at the display counter. The place was warm and bright, and smelled of homemade bread, cookies, and something spicy.

Tuck beelined for the men's room. As I walked toward the display case, I scanned the crowd. There were older and younger people, bicyclists, and a local guy in worn jeans and a Red Sox T-shirt. Not that I expected to see Frank, but it didn't cost anything to look.

I selected a dozen assorted turnovers and donuts, paid for them, then waited by the door. I wanted to pretend Frank and his Corvette would simply materialize any second, but down deep I had a really bad feeling. Whether he'd gone out last evening and spent the night elsewhere or he'd left the chalet early this morning, it didn't make sense for him to not shut and lock the door.

Tuck reappeared and we headed outside.

Once the bakery's door was firmly closed behind us, I turned to him. "Do you think something happened to Frank . . ."

My voice trailed off as I noticed the shop next door. It wasn't open yet, but the front window held a display of stoneware, neatly arranged and spotlit. The shop's name swept across the glass in a sophisticated font. *Ramone's Art and Antiques.*

Ramone's. Jules Ramone was the name of the sour pickle-faced guy who had manned the sign-in table at the appraisal event. Just last night I'd wondered if he might be the one who told Nina about my expunged charge for selling stolen property. He'd also been gossiping about me with Felix Graham just before I arrived at the appraisal.

I nudged Tuck's arm. "Does that store belong to Jules Ramone?"

"I believe so. Him and his wife, Rosetta. She and your mom locked horns over authentication of a painting about a year ago or so. Cost the Ramones a large sale. Since then, Rosetta's made a habit of bad-mouthing her."

"I don't remember them at all." I folded my arms over my chest. So Jules did have a reason to dislike me, bad blood between his wife and my mom. Thanks again, Mom, for leaving me to deal with your fallout.

Tuck stroked his beard. "As I recall, they moved up from New Jersey not long after you left."

I walked over, cupped my hands against the glass and peered inside. Mostly paintings, professionally displayed. A few high-end pieces of furniture. Some custom European stuff. Silver. More top-notch stoneware. A sleek marble statue of a nude. Lots of expensive items, but no decoys whose presence might have indicated the Ramones had an interest and at least some expertise in at area. Still, I couldn't let the lack mislead me.

I looked back at the coffee shop, only a few yards away. It seemed likely Frank might have met the Ramones. After all, this was home territory for both of them. Over the last few months, if Frank had become curious about the value of Claude's decoys, he might have struck up a conversation with the Ramones at the coffee shop or paid a visit to the store. There was another distant possibility as well.

I glanced at Tuck. "Have you ever heard rumors about the Ramones being shady?"

"Not particularly. I'm assuming you're thinking about the decoys?"

"If Frank stole them, he's going to need someone discreet and knowledgeable to help him market them. With his ego, I can't see Frank selling the decoys himself for little or nothing, or flagrantly risking getting caught."

"I don't know. You could be right, though I've never thought of the Ramones as that connected, or even as knowledgeable as they act."

I gazed through the shop window again, my mind whirring. Hunting for any link between Frank and the Ramones could be a dead end. But other than their proximity to one another and the tire tracks, we didn't have any other possible leads.

I turned to Tuck. "Come on. I've got an idea."

"I'm not sure I like that look in your eyes. What are you thinking?"

"Fisher's auction. I told Shane I was probably going to stop by. Can you think of a better place to find out who's in bed with who?"

He chuckled. "We're not talking literally, are we?"

"I'm not ruling anything out."

We left the Ramones' window, walking quickly back to the van. As I got in, I held the bakery bag over the back of the seat to Kala—

She shoved the bag aside and waved frantically toward Frank's driveway. "Someone just drove in. An SUV. I'm not sure what kind. It was gray. It had a bike rack."

I jumped into my seat, tossing the bakery bag on the console. "Did you see the driver? Was it Frank?"

"It looked like a woman, but I could be mistaken. There was someone in the passenger seat."

Tuck leaned close to the windshield, eyes straining as he looked toward the tennis court and Frank's driveway beyond. "He could have been out all night. A little wine tasting. A little hanky-panky. He might have left his Corvette at work or someplace."

I rubbed my hands down my pant legs. Maybe it was Frank's mystery woman—a possible co-conspirator I hadn't considered. "We should give them time to settle in, then knock on the door again."

"You sure?" Tuck said. "If we hold tight and follow the leads we have, they'll never know we're nosing around."

I nodded. He was right. "Okay, we'll stay put. If the SUV comes back out, we might catch a glimpse of the driver."

Kala snatched the bakery bag off the console. "No need to starve while we wait." She took out a maple donut without even teasing about the lack of bacon, then held the open bag out to me.

"Thanks." I grabbed a turnover. It was plump and sticky, with granulated sugar on the outside. My stomach grumbled in anticipation. But before I could take a bite, an SUV flew out of Frank's driveway and down the lane. It was silver in color. There was a driver and someone else in the passenger seat.

I tossed the turnover onto the console and snagged my phone.

"Get down," I shouted to Tuck and Kala as I pointed the camera toward the van's side windows, readying to catch a shot when the SUV drove by the bakery parking lot.

A dump truck pulled in beside us, blocking my view.

Desperate, I swiveled all the way around and aimed the camera toward the rear window. Maybe I could get a shot after it turned onto the main road.

People walked past. Cars obscured my view. An evergreen tree was in the way—

My gaze stalled on a dark-colored Land Rover parked on the edge of the main road. For a disorienting second, I was certain it was Shane's vehicle. But Land Rovers weren't uncommon in Stowe. It could be anyone.

The Rover pulled into traffic and vanished, along with the silver SUV.

Chapter Nineteen

"**D**amn it," I snarled. I was ticked at the dump truck for blocking my view and equally mad at myself for getting distracted by the Land Rover.

Tuck gave my arm a comforting squeeze. "They might have had an innocent reason for going to Frank's house. A friend from work. Someone with the wrong address."

I pressed my fingers over my eyes. The fact that he was right only made me more angry with myself.

Kala spoke up. "Or Frank could've been sitting in the back of the car when they drove in. I might not have noticed."

I glared at her. "Are you serious?"

She shrugged. "I only saw the driver and the person riding shotgun for a second. There could've been a third or even a fourth person."

I thought back to what I'd seen. "I'm sure there were only two people in the car when it came out." I started the van. "We have to go back and see if Frank's home now."

I shifted into reverse, then pulled out and sped toward the chalet. By the time we were partway down the driveway, I could see the front door was still ajar—just the way we'd left it.

I pulled up and parked.

"Wait here," I said to Tuck and Kala.

I jogged to the door and rang the bell.

No one answered. Not a big surprise.

I crept inside and called out, "Frank? Are you home?"

The place was as silent as before. I tiptoed to the living room. The only difference was that the carpet appeared slightly more disturbed, as if the other people had also done a walk through, but that could have been my imagination. Just like it could've been my imagination that the driver of the SUV had been in a hurry when they left.

Disappointed, I returned to the van. "What do you say we give up on Stowe and head to Fisher's auction—see if we can dig up dirt there?"

"Sounds smart," Tuck said.

* * *

Fisher's Auction House was a long, low concrete building located in what had once been Scandal Mountain's railroad yard. The building was used as a feedstore for most of its life, then briefly as a community recreation hall until the Fisher family bought it and converted it into the auction house just over a decade ago.

I threaded my way through the parking lot, driving slowly. The place was packed with cars and trucks from Quebec, New York, Massachusetts . . . and Vermont, of course. Eventually, I found an open spot near the base of the old granary. The size of the crowd didn't surprise me. Fisher's auction extravaganzas always drew more people than their biweekly junk sales. True, some dealers preferred the convenience and anonymity of bidding by phone or online, but others liked to see things in person. Besides, as much business went on in the parking lot as on the auction floor.

"Once we get inside," Tuck said, "I'll talk to my friends. You and Kala stick together if you want."

Kala smugly gave her hair a toss. "That's silly. If anyone should be on their own, it's me. There are benefits to being the new girl in town. I can get away with asking anything."

I laughed and opened the van door. I couldn't argue with her. "Hopefully, it includes questions about the Ramones."

"Yup, among other things, like rumors about rare decoys surfacing," she said.

The air reverberated with the intoxicating sound of the auctioneer's chant, echoing from inside the building. "I've got five hundred dolllaars. Six anyone? Will anyone make it six . . . ?"

Even at a distance, the chant and lure of so many antiques tugged at me, very much the way the Ramones' shop and the Jumping Café's flea market had done earlier. I lengthened my stride, marching toward the auction with the unmitigated fervor of an alcoholic headed for a liquor store.

But as we went inside, I forced myself to resist the distraction of the antiques and focused instead on the job at hand. I had to figure out what was going on and locate the decoys or I wouldn't enjoy any auctions or flea markets for a very long time—not if the police arrested me as a prime robbery suspect.

Tuck stepped close to Kala and me. "Meet back here in an hour?"

"Perfect," I said.

Kala nodded, then she took off into the crowd, making her way toward the back alcove and the auction house's concession stand. Good move. Hanging around the coffee pot was the perfect way to insinuate yourself into a conversation.

"Sold!" The auctioneer rapped his hammer on the podium.

I took advantage of the pause in the bidding to scan the crowd. Most people sat in the audience. Others stood along the walls and in the back. I spotted a lot of familiar faces—notably Jules Ramone in the front row, perched on the edge of his seat like he was ready to buy up a storm. Felix Graham sat next to him. Interesting to see two thorns in my side rubbing elbows, but not proof they were close friends.

A conspicuous absence also struck me. Shane wasn't anywhere to be seen.

The Land Rover in Stowe pushed into my mind. I hadn't noticed any Land Rovers here in the parking lot, but that didn't mean anything. If Shane had parked on the other side of the building, I wouldn't have seen his car.

"Hey, Edie." I jumped at the sound of Shane's voice coming from beside me as if my thoughts summoned him from thin air.

I turned and there he was, sweet eyes smiling at me. Sandy brown hair, short but still long enough to run my fingers through. And—damn—the sleeves of his shirt were rolled up, showing off those forearms.

"Hey to you, too." I felt like an idiot for not being able to come up with something cleverer to say, but the sight of him weakened my legs and made my brain stagger. Those arms had felt so wonderful the other night, roped muscles pinning me close as lips grazed my neck.

"I take it you're feeling better?" he asked.

"Yeah, thank goodness," I said, a bit breathless.

He shifted his weight onto one leg. "How are things going at the Bouchards'?"

"Ah—" I reminded myself I couldn't risk saying anything to him, not with his connection to law enforcement. "Fine, I guess."

"The collection has to be amazing."

"I'm really not free to say anything. I wish I could show it to you, though." I swallowed dryly. *Or knew where it was, for that matter.*

His gaze met mine, warm and sincere. "When do you think you'll be finished?"

I shrugged as if unsure, then moved the conversation in a more desirable direction. It felt horrible to not answer his questions. "Do you happen to know Jules and Rosetta Ramone? Do they deal in a lot of folk art or mostly paintings?"

He frowned, his gaze studying me suspiciously. "Why?"

"I've been thinking about Mom. I guess . . . I can't help wondering about her situation. She and Rosetta were always at odds." It was a good cover for my questions and not a lie.

"Are you saying you think your mom was framed?"

"Are the Ramones aboveboard?" I pressed. The firm set of his lips made me think he was holding something back, but it could've been my imagination.

"That's the sort of thing you should bring up with your mother's lawyer. Relying on rumors and speculation is only asking for trouble," he said.

"I suppose you're right." Perhaps his comment should've made me angry again, but it was so Shane-like. Part of what attracted me to him was his practical answers and solutions. Of course, he would have refused to guess or share gossip about someone's honesty. That was why his belief in my innocence when I'd been on probation meant so much.

He glanced toward the office. "I should go register. I haven't gotten my bidding paddle yet and that Winchester Centennial is coming up soon."

"Oh—go on. Good luck. I hope you get it." I rested my hand on his forearm, enjoying the sensation of warmth against my fingertips. "Maybe next weekend we could try for that pizza?" I instantly wished I'd kept my mouth shut. Why was I even thinking about dates with Nina's threat hanging over my head like a time bomb?

"I'll give you a call," he said. "Honestly, I doubt I'll be able to. I'm pretty slammed right now."

"Ah, okay—" I was left speechless as relief and disappointment clashed inside me, an oil and water combination that left my thoughts racing. His schedule seemed genuinely odd compared to when I was on probation—and a little voice inside me worried he was reconsidering wanting anything to do with me. Still, his eyes and the kisses the other night argued against that theory. I offered a weak smile. "I guess we'll just have to play it by ear."

He touched my cheek, a light stroke. "Take care of yourself, Edie. Don't hesitate to call, about anything."

"Same to you," I murmured.

As he turned and walked away, I brushed my fingers along my cheek, reliving the sensation of his touch. I shook my head, took a cleansing breath. *Enough of this.* I had to forget about Shane for now. The whole "were we or weren't we" thing was too confusing, and I couldn't afford the distraction. Finding the collection and figuring out what was going on had to be my only priority.

I moved further into the auction gallery, putting more distance between Shane and myself. What I needed was to find someone who enjoyed gossiping. Someone who knew everyone, like one of the Fishers. The Fisher family made up a full third of the town, including cousins, spouses, ex-spouses, and assorted members of less-than-certain parentage. Even Shane was somehow related, though he hadn't grown up in Scandal Mountain.

I scanned the crowd and spotted a familiar spiky rooster-comb of blonde hair. *Perfect!* Pinkney Woods, strutting down the aisle with a side-by-side shotgun in her hands. She was a Fisher cousin. Sometimes she worked for them as a runner like she was doing today. Sometimes she bartended at the Jumping Café. Mostly, she was the queen of town gossip. Who was sleeping with whom. Whose husband got a vasectomy last week . . .

Pinky, as she preferred to be called, had gone to the same public schools as I had. Though she'd been a class behind me and surrounded herself with a rougher crowd, I'd always liked her. No one ever messed with Pinky or bullied her for waving her gay flag proudly. She was tough, outspoken, and someone who kept her finger on the pulse of Scandal Mountain, the good and the shady. I had, however, heard that Pinky'd taken to using extortion to get top prices for her various side ventures, including homegrown and even her nieces' Girl Scout cookies.

Pinky shoved the shotgun into the hands of a waiting bidder. Then she bulldozed to the end of the aisle, jogged a couple of steps, and finally disappeared into the ladies' room—also known as the perfect place to talk.

I wove through the crowd, reaching the restroom in time to see her disappear into a stall. At the speed she was moving, I didn't dare risk even attempting a fake pee.

Instead, I went straight to the sink and undid my ponytail. I ran my hands through my hair a few times, finger-brushing it to look busy. We were currently alone, but there was no telling how long that would last.

I messed with my hair again. The bathroom wasn't the most attractive place to hang out. Cracked tiles covered the walls. Rust formed circles where the faucets dripped nonstop into the sink—

The stall door flew open. Pinky emerged and strutted straight to the sink next to mine.

I turned to her and pushed surprise into my voice. "Pinky. It's been a long time. How are you doing?"

She sliced a look my way, then grinned. "Edie Brown. It's good to see you. Just home for a short visit or longer this time?"

"Depends on how things go, I guess." That was the honest truth now that the collection's disappearance had messed with my plans to leave soon after the appraisal.

"Must be lonely for Tuck without you or your mom at home." She rested a hand on her hip. "Stinks what happened to her. Frickin' setup, if you ask me."

I looked down at the sink, taken aback to hear that she felt that way. Mostly, I was glad she didn't think less of my family. "I still can't believe how everything went down."

She cranked on the water and squirted soap over her hands. "You sounded great on TV—the appraisal thing. That plover was pretty cool, huh?"

"Yeah." I shifted my weight. It was now or never. "Speaking of decoys. Do you know the Ramones? Are they into folk art, hunting items, like decoys?"

Pinky held her hands under the running water, rinsing them. "Of course I know them. They're here all the time. Mostly they bid on paintings. I imagine they handle quality folk art."

"Not decoys specifically?"

She squinted. "I can't be positive off the top of my head. I suppose"—she turned off the water, then lowered her voice to a confidential whisper—"I could find out more. It depends on *just* how interested you are."

"Ah—" Pinky had never given me a reason to not trust her, but I could read between the lines. Charging for information along with extortion were now part of her repertoire. I nibbled my lip, thinking. Jules's store was across the street from Frank's chalet. Right now, Graham and Jules were sitting in the front row beside one another like best friends. Graham also knew Nina, or at least he'd been responsible for her coming to my table at the appraisal event. If I was going to pay for information, I might as well explore as many potential connections as possible. "I'm *very* interested. I know Graham deals in those sorts of pieces. Do he and the Ramones ever work together, like to buy larger collections?"

She rested back on her heels, arms folded over her chest. "I don't know off the top of my head, but I can ask around. As far as the Ramones' purchase history goes, that's as easy as a few keystrokes on the right computer."

"I don't want to get you in trouble," I said.

"Don't worry about me." She smiled slyly. "Someday I'll need something from you."

Sweat dampened my armpits. "Of course."

"Good. Just don't forget me when the time comes."

I held out my hand for her to shake, hoping sweat hadn't moistened my palms as well. "Deal?"

Pinky dried her hands on her pants. She reached for mine but stopped halfway. Wrinkles fanned her forehead, as if she was second guessing the agreement as much as I was. "Promise me one thing. This doesn't have anything to do with the FBI snooping around, right?"

I took a step back. "I don't even know what you're talking about."

"Agents from the FBI Art Crime Team. They were here last week, asking about pieces stolen from the Canadian Museum of History. You heard about that robbery?"

"Yeah. That was awful." Dear God. Please, don't let that really be connected to the robbery at the farm. If it was, then we were more over our heads than I already feared.

Pinky's voice hardened. "The agents acted like the case is heating up—and I don't want anything to do with it." She leaned closer. "Did you hear what happened last night?"

"No. What?" At this point, I wasn't sure I wanted to know.

"I overheard a couple of the dealers from Quebec talking about it. It's all over the news up there. On the internet too. They found one of the museum thieves in Stanstead."

I blinked, stunned. Stanstead, Quebec, was only a short drive from Scandal Mountain. "They caught one of the thieves? Did they get the stolen pieces back?"

"They didn't find the pieces, and they didn't exactly catch the guy. He's dead. Murdered."

"Murdered? When? Are they sure?"

"The Canadian police haven't released details. They only called the man a suspect in the robbery. There's a video of his body." She got out her phone, messed with it, then handed it to me and warned, "It's really disgusting."

I braced myself and hit play. The video was jittery and grainy, done in low light, a lot of the colors washed out. The camera panned across an abandoned warehouse. A car under a tarp. Crates. Old mattresses. Machinery of some sort. A man's naked body lay on the floor. A light blue strap bound his wrists together. The camera zoomed in on his head.

I gasped. His head was tightly covered by a clear plastic bag. Spittle and vapor from his dying breaths coated the plastic, obscuring all but his death-skimmed, bulging eyes. Bruises and a yellow nylon cord ringed his neck.

Pinky held out her hand for the phone "Gross, isn't it?"

The urge to puke crawled up my throat and my hands shook as I shoved the phone back at her. "That's horrible."

"It looks like an execution to me," she said. "I had this girlfriend once who was in a gang—"

She snapped her mouth shut as the restroom door opened and a fit middle-aged woman with a vibrant crossbody bag slung over one shoulder strolled in and went into a stall.

"I've got to get back to work." Pinky started for the door. "I'll have what you want tomorrow. Stop by the café in the afternoon, I'll be bartending."

"Thanks. See you then," I said.

I waited a heartbeat for Pinky to leave first, then I followed her back into the auction gallery. As I watched, she snaked through the crowd, hurrying toward an alleyway between the seated audience and a line of furniture waiting to come up for bid. I could only hope I'd done the right thing enlisting her help, and not just drawn unwanted attention to our search.

Pinky slowed, edging past a couple of people hanging out in the alley. When she reached where Shane stood with a super buff guy, she stopped and whispered something to them before continuing to the front of the auction.

She was talking about you. The possibility whisked through my mind. Logic said she'd more likely stopped to answer a question—or to tease Shane about trying to get an early look at the rifle the other day.

My gaze went back to the guy standing next to Shane. Short hair. Dark glasses. As muscular as a bodybuilder. I had the distinct feeling I'd seen him somewhere before. Maybe in New York or at some out-of-state flea market. My brain wanted to connect him to the antique business.

I sucked in a breath as I recalled where I knew him from. He'd been at the appraisal event, standing near the gazebo with another guy. I'd been certain he was security, or at least that's what I thought at the time. But what if I'd been wrong? A stranger. At the appraisal event. Watching carefully.

One way the thieves could've found out about the Bouchard collection was if they'd seen the plover on TV—or at the appraisal event, I reminded myself.

I raked my hands over my head and turned away. No, that was a ridiculous idea. I had absolutely zero reason to think the guy was a thief. For heaven's sake, he was a friend of Shane's. If anything, it was more likely he worked in law enforcement.

I felt my eyes widen. Pinky had said agents from the FBI Art Crime Team had been poking around. Was it possible the FBI had assigned an agent to hang out at the auction, someone

Shane knew through his work as a probation officer, college, or some sort of training? We'd come to the auction hoping to hear gossip. Why wouldn't the FBI do the same?

An FBI agent. I studied the buff guy again. Yeah. That totally fit.

Still, it was unsettling to think the FBI could be looking for the person responsible for the museum heist right here in the same room where I was standing. A thief, whose partner was murdered by someone last night in Stanstead, a town not that far away.

Chapter Twenty

"Sounds like an execution to me," Kala echoed Pinky's words.

It was midafternoon and we'd just walked into the house after leaving the auction. Kala had spent the entire drive home on her phone, searching for details about the Stanstead murder.

It seemed the disturbing video was posted online by a fame-seeking night watchman who happened upon the robber's body in a warehouse. The images had gone viral before the police even arrived on the scene. The watchman's video was now rapidly vanishing from the internet, replaced by blurry photos of a similar face caught on security and traffic cameras the night of the museum robbery, images the Canadian authorities had apparently just released.

"Maybe we should call the police and tell them about the decoys," I said.

Tuck took a pitcher of limeade from the fridge, then turned to me. "Because the FBI was at the auction house last week asking about the museum robbery or the Stanstead murder?"

"Both, I suppose." I rubbed my arms to ease a rising sense of apprehension. "The only trouble is that we still aren't sure if there's planted evidence against us online or not."

Kala looked up from her phone, her voice serious. "The FBI stopping in at Fisher's could mean absolutely nothing. They've probably questioned every auction house employee within hundreds of miles of the museum, especially if they think the museum robbery is tied to organized crime. And the murder in Stanstead? It looks to me like the sort of thing cartels do to make an example of someone. Maybe the thief double-crossed his boss."

I stopped rubbing my arms and eyed her. How the heck did Kala know so much about this kind of stuff—the darknet, organized crime? "You really think so?"

She shrugged. "Could be. There's bound to be chatter on the net."

Tuck set the limeade on the counter next to a trio of glasses. "Sounds like we should spend more time online before we call the police."

What they were saying made sense. Still, my intuition murmured things were going to get worse from here on out. Not that the murder made it any more likely that the museum heist was connected to the collection's disappearance, but its close proximity to Scandal Mountain was more than a little disturbing. Also, it would most likely increase the FBI's presence in our area—a complication we didn't need.

The *brrring* of my phone came from my pocket. I took it out. When I saw who was calling, my thoughts skidded to a halt.

"Someone you don't want to talk to?" Kala asked.

"It's Nina."

"Could be good news," Tuck said. The tension in his voice told me he didn't believe that for a second.

Kala flagged her fingers at the phone. "Put it on speaker. If you end up in court or something, we'll be able to swear we heard Nina threaten you, assuming she's about to do that again."

I scowled at her. "That's not exactly comforting." As the phone rang for a third time, I took a deep breath and answered. "Hello, Nina?"

"Since I haven't heard from you, I'm guessing you don't have them yet?"

I forced my voice to stay steady. "No."

"Then you better pick up the pace."

"We're working as fast as we can." I hesitated, not sure how much I should share. "At the moment, we're looking into some more likely scenarios, but there's an outside chance that you were right about the theft being connected to the robbery at the Canadian Museum of History."

"You don't know that for certain, though?"

"No. It just adds another layer to the mix." Like a layer that involves the FBI and a cartel-style murder.

"Sounds like a bullshit excuse to me." Her pitch rose. "You said the police's red tape would slow them down and make finding the decoys impossible. What guarantee do I have that *you're* not buying time to secret away the collection yourself?"

"We're not. Seriously." What had gotten into her? Why the sudden change of heart?

There was a long silence, except for the tap-tap of what I assumed was a fingernail against the mouthpiece of her phone. "You've got three days."

I gaped at the phone. She had to be kidding. "Three days! That wasn't our agreement. That's not enough time."

"I don't know why I'm even giving you that."

"You said you wanted to keep this quiet. That won't happen if the authorities get involved. It'll be in the papers. Everyone will know." She really was nuts.

"It won't just be my name in the headlines. *Yours* will be there too. Your mother can read all about her little girl's crimes while she waits for you to join her in prison."

The world seemed to tilt and pull in around me. "We had a deal—"

"Three days, that's it."

She hung up.

"That was horrible," Kala said.

"Are you alright?" Tuck asked. "You look pale."

My head throbbed. I felt sick to my stomach. "I need some fresh air. I feel—" I turned away. "I just need to be alone."

Unable to even breathe, I rushed across the kitchen and out the door. I staggered blindly up the walk, unsure where I was going other than away. I didn't want anyone to follow me. I needed privacy. Quiet. Space to think of a way out of this.

I hurried past the van and onto a path that led to the back of the carriage barn. The antique shop occupied the entire front of the building, but Mom's art studio was in the rear. Right outside the studio's atrium doors was what she called her secret garden. It was surrounded by a lilac hedge and filled with ferns and flowering plants.

I followed the path through an opening in the hedge and into the garden. It was flooded with afternoon sunshine. I collapsed onto a lawn chair and closed my eyes, struggling to block out an overwhelming sense of anguish, concentrating instead on the heat of the sunshine on my face. I took a deep breath, savoring the scent of the lilacs and the absence of human voices.

For a long moment, I resisted the urge to think about anything. I sank into the aromas, the stillness and warmth, relaxing, peaceful . . .

I pushed my mind to focus on pleasant memories. I vividly recalled Mom and me out here in the garden, standing at a makeshift table and finger-painting. I'd been in third, maybe fourth grade. I'd worn a one-piece bathing suit under a long artist's smock. She'd worn an identical long shirt, lavender with wildflowers embroidered on the collar. We must have looked ridiculous, splattered from head to toe with bright paint, even our faces and shirts. It had been easier to love Mom back then, back when my grandparents were at the helm of the family and Mom had just been my best friend.

A sad feeling pressed within the cage of my ribs. I smiled slightly, then forced that wistful memory aside and instead focused on what had happened today. I refused to believe that we'd totally wasted our time. There had to be a thread that connected everything, or at least some sort of answer in something I'd heard or seen, either to who had stolen the decoys or if we should risk involving the police.

Detail by detail, I pored over everything I could remember from our visit to Frank's chalet. Both the screen door and the inside door were ajar. The carpet was immaculate. TV and lights on. Food in the fridge and cupboards . . . I'd opened the hallway closet—

I sat bolt upright, eyes wide open:

The lavender sweater in Frank's closet was embroidered with wildflowers. Flowers like on my and Mom's matching artist smocks.

Sudden fear chilled me to the core. It couldn't be.

I rose from the chair, dazed by an appalling possibility. I retrieved the spare key from under a garden statue of Venus, walked numbly to the studio door and let myself in. Mom's favorite color was lavender. She loved clothes with artistic touches, like embroidery. Sure, those things alone weren't enough to condemn her, but there was something else: the cracked stoneware jar, an antique in a house with no others, except for the candlesticks.

The air inside the studio was hot, a million degrees by the feel of it. Sunlight razored through the doors and skylights. Without hesitating, I paced straight across the room to the supply cupboard. I pressed my hand against my chest, taking a deep breath while I gathered my nerve, then I swung the door open and scanned the shelves. Old tin coffee cans. A box of chalk . . .

My eyes homed in on a brand-new wooden holder filled with Mom's favorite paint brushes. I'd never seen it there before. For as long as I remembered, the brushes had been stored in this cupboard, in a stoneware jar with a simple floral design on it. Salt glazed. A. K. Ballard/Burlington, Vermont. Undamaged.

Back when I was maybe twelve, I'd questioned her about that choice. It had seemed to me the jar was too old and valuable to use as a storage container. She'd pooh-poohed that idea and told me to quit making a big deal over nothing. Sure, it was entirely possible a number of similar jars existed—just like other women loved lavender-colored clothes embroidered with folksy flowers. Still, the *what if* possibility of the jar and sweater I'd seen at Frank's belonging to Mom was unsettling to say the least.

Time stood still as I stared at the new wooden holder, brushes all cleaned and neatly arranged by size and bristle type. *No.* Mom buying a new holder didn't mean anything. It didn't mean the jar she'd cherished for years had gotten cracked and for some ungodly reason ended up in a closet in Stowe.

A voice inside me whispered, *Frank is a womanizer. Mom's weak when it comes to men like him. You saw photos online of Frank at an art show last winter. Mom likes to do art shows in Stowe. The Vermont Chamber of Commerce show, for one. They could've met there.*

My fingers clenched. I was creating connections where there weren't any. This suspicion was as ridiculous and unfounded as so many of the other threads we'd been trying to weave into sensible stories.

I turned on my heel, heading back for the door—

I stopped mid-stride.

An easel stood near the door. A half-finished watercolor rested on it, most likely the piece Mom had been working on before she went to prison.

In the watercolor, sunlight slanted through a curtainless kitchen window, brightening a white counter on which stood a pair of nineteenth-century brass candlesticks. Next to the candlesticks was a stoneware storage jar decorated with a simple floral design. A. K. Ballard/Burlington, Vermont. A crack ran down one side of the jar. It was filled with daffodils, fading and slightly wilted.

We'd passed a bed of spent daffodils when we'd driven up to Frank's chalet.

Chapter
Twenty-One

I snatched the painting from the easel. Mom and Frank Bouchard? It couldn't be. Still, there was more than just daffodils and a stoneware jar for evidence. There were the candlesticks and the sweater—Mom's size and style. When Frank confronted me at the house and warned me to back off, he'd mentioned our messy kitchen table. Was it possible he hadn't simply seen it through the open door, that instead he'd been in the kitchen before? Had Mom once again been so self-absorbed that she failed to see the sort of person and situation she'd gotten tangled up with? Frank. Nina. The Bouchard collection. Mom. Had our family been targeted because Mom was already in trouble with the law—or because of her and Frank's affair? Was all of it a setup or just part of it? Maybe I was wrong, but it seemed like there were too many links for a mere coincidence.

I stumbled back to the house with the painting under my arm.

Kala was in the dining room, typing on her laptop. She glanced up. "I'm doing some more digging for decoy buyers and planted evidence. I figured I'd work on comparing the Corvette tires and the tracks from the farm later."

"Whatever," I snapped. "Do you know where Tuck is?"

She frowned, her concerned gaze going from my face down to the painting. "He went up to his room a few minutes ago. Is something wrong?"

"I'm not sure." I turned away, rushed back into the hall and up the staircase to the second floor. My fingers cramped from the death grip I had on the painting. A headache pulsed in my skull. Mom was involved with Frank Bouchard. Nina's husband. Not decades ago. Or years ago. Recently, very recently, if not still today. This was bad, very bad.

When I reached the landing, I turned in the opposite direction from my room. I dashed down the hallway, through an open door, and into a small library.

The library was the largest room in what had been my grandparents' three-room suite. Tuck had moved into the rooms after Grandma and Grandpa died. Since then, the suite had changed very little. Bookshelves still lined all but one wall in the library. Club chairs still gathered beside the dark rolltop desk. The only new additions were Tuck's favorite rifle over the fireplace and a large encaustic painting of an angel by Celine St. Marie, the same Celine who gave us *sucre a la crème* at Christmas. Mom's best friend.

As I left the library and went into Tuck's bedroom, an earthy aroma caught my attention. I sniffed the air. Warm dirt, like the smell of a jungle—or Tuck's cardigan the other day.

Despite my angst, I couldn't help smiling. Not only did Tuck and Grandpa have similar taste in furnishings, they also shared the same way of relieving stress, namely horticulture. In Grandpa's case, his quirk took the form of a fascination with fern plants. Tuck's focus had recently narrowed in on the gesneriad family, specifically African violets. The moist jungle smell made me wonder if his hobby/business had expanded beyond the confines of the house's various windowsills.

Following my nose, I hurried across the bedroom to the closed door of his private bathroom. I listened for a second, waiting for the sound of a toilet flushing or a shower running. The room remained as silent as Frank's chalet, so much so that I became worried. What if something had happened? What if Tuck had suffered a heart attack and was laying on the floor?

I knocked lightly. "Tuck, are you alright?"

"Come in," his muffled voice answered.

As I opened the door, a burst of pink light joined the jungle smell. The bathroom's toilet and sink were unchanged. What had once been an enclosed shower as large as a lot of families' mudrooms was now a miniature greenhouse filled with plants and illuminated by intense lights.

Tuck's backlit outline came into view behind the shower's foggy door. He slid it open and stepped out.

I shook my head. "Holy cow. This really is something."

"Welcome to my violet nursery." He motioned with his hand, inviting me to look inside.

I scooched up next to him. Trays of baby violets, miniature and standard size, as well as various violet cousins, filled every inch of the space. Large pots of episcia and lipstick vines hung from the ceiling. An array of grow lights brightened everything. "I'm officially impressed."

He nudged the painting still gripped under my arm. "What's this? One of your mom's pieces?"

The weight of why I'd come to find him crashed over me. I turned the painting around so he could see it. My voice went harsh. "Look familiar?"

His jaw went slack. "Dear God. Those are the things from Frank's closet."

"I take it Mom was seeing someone from Stowe?"

"No—I mean, I don't know. She was dating a guy named Francis." He slapped his forehead and groaned. "Francis. Frank. Never in my wildest dreams had that possibility occurred to me. I mean, wasn't Frank going by the name of Beau Bouchard?"

"How long had she been seeing this Francis? Just recently or for months?"

Tuck took me by the elbow, leading me out of the bathroom. Letting go, he slumped down in a chair beside his bedroom window. "I have no idea. I never met him. You know how your mom is—love of her life today, forgotten tomorrow."

"Do you remember anything she said about him?"

"She said he was an art promoter, a muckety-muck with the Vermont Chamber of Commerce."

I leaned the painting against a wall, then crouched beside Tuck and took both his hands in mine. "Could Nina have known about my mom?"

He met my eyes, his worry clear to see. "That certainly would shine a new light on things."

"You can say that again." I hesitated. "Is it possible Mom started seeing Frank before she was arrested?"

"I don't believe so. You should ask her. She's scheduled to call tomorrow night. I don't see why she wouldn't tell you the truth."

I released his hands and got back onto my feet. Talking to Mom might clarify whether Nina could have had a motive for setting us up beyond insurance fraud. Now that I thought about it, when Frank came to the house, he'd specifically mentioned that Nina was vengeful. Was this what he'd been hinting at?

The muscles in my neck tightened and pinched. Had Nina shortened the timeline because she enjoyed making the daughter of her enemy squirm—or did she derive pleasure from the idea of my mom helplessly watching me flounder? More than likely, it was both.

I hooked my hands behind my head and stared out the window. Tuck was right; I should talk to Mom. But I could hear the useless conversation already: "Edie, sweetheart, you don't understand. Francis is a wonderful man. He loves me," she'd say. Then she'd sob. "You don't know what it's been like for me. Alone. With no one to help since your grandparents died."

My teeth clenched. I was seventeen when my grandparents were killed. First there'd been the stress of the crash investigation. Two weeks later, when the time came to plan their memorial service, Mom had claimed she was still too overwhelmed to go to the funeral home and help Tuck and me make the arrangements. Still, she managed to give us detailed instruction as to what the church and graveside services should be like, and she insisted on a catered reception at home.

The day of the service, Mom still didn't feel well enough to leave her bedroom. I sat alone in the front pew with Tuck. I held his hand at the graveside. When we finally got home, the driveway was already lined with cars and the spaces in front of the shop were full. Every room was packed with flowers and people. Caterers bustled about with drinks and trays of finger food. A quartet played in the background. To me, it felt more like a wedding reception than a memorial dinner.

But what I remember most vividly from that day is the music stopping and everyone turning to look as Mom appeared in the living room doorway, heavy mascara stains under her eyes, long flowing dress, a miniature calla lily tucked into her perfectly coiffed hair. I'd wanted a hug from her. But, in a second, she was pulled away and consumed with the crowd and their condolences.

I drew a long breath and released it slowly. Unfortunately, this wasn't just about me having to put up with Mom's self-pity and dramatics or even simply about finding the decoys so I wouldn't be accused of the theft. If Nina called the police, I wouldn't be the only one who'd end up accused. Tuck and Kala would be named as accessories to the crime. I had to talk to Mom, like it or not.

Except there was another major problem.

I looked at Tuck. "I can't ask Mom about Frank. None of us can. Aren't prison phone lines monitored? The last thing we need is for someone to overhear us and wonder what's going on."

"You're right. Damn it." Tuck pressed his lips together for a long moment. Then he grinned. "We could talk to Celine St. Marie."

Celine and Mom had been friends since grade school, cemented by a shared talent for art and a reputation for being "out there." However, unlike my mom, Celine was very conservative. She created pieces inspired by Christian scripture and angels who she claimed spoke to her. She wouldn't approve of anyone having an affair with a married man. Still, Mom would've spilled everything to her, and Celine would've listened and offered compassionate advice. On the downside, Celine was Rene St. Marie's sister. The same swaggering Rene St. Marie who lived next door to us and who I'd seen only the other day in the pub with Felix Graham.

I caught Tuck's eye. "Does Celine still live in town?"

"She's in St. Albans now. I have her phone number. She's one of my violet customers."

As he got out his phone and readied to call, I stopped him. "Wait. I should be the one to talk to her. There are details that she might feel more comfortable sharing woman to woman—like the adultery part."

"You're probably right." He brought up the number, then handed me the phone.

I put it to my ear, listening as it rang and rang. Eventually, it went to voice mail.

"You have reached Celine St. Marie. I can't come to the phone right now. Please leave a message. May the angels bless and watch over you."

I sweetened my tone. "Hi, Celine, this is Viki Tuckerman's daughter. Can you please give me a call when you get a chance? Thank you."

I hung up, then looked at Tuck. "Nothing to do now except wait."

Tuck scratched his beard. "When she calls back, you might be better off making arrangements to visit her in person. She's . . . well, over the last few years, she's gotten even more flaky. It's hard to hold a conversation with her on the phone."

My gaze once more went to the window. Dense clouds were rolling in, hiding the afternoon sunshine. Waiting for Celine and arranging a visit meant more delays, and time was slipping through our fingers. Still, talking to her about Mom and Frank might turn this whole thing on its head. "If you think it's smarter in person, it'll have to be."

I stopped talking as Kala breezed into the room.

"Having a party without me?" she teased, but the worry in her eyes said she knew full well that we weren't discussing something lighthearted.

"I discovered a rather unpleasant clue, but I wanted to get Tuck's reaction before I said anything." I picked the painting up and showed it to her.

She frowned. "I don't get it."

"Mom did this painting, and everything in it—the candlesticks, the stoneware jar, even the daffodils and the curtainless window—was all at Frank's house."

Her eyes grew wide. "Whoa. I didn't see the jar or the candlesticks while we were there, but that's definitely Frank's kitchen window. I can't believe it. Your mom—and Frank?"

"It seems so," I said.

"Wow. Just wow." She fell quiet. Then her throat bobbed as she swallowed hard. "Umm—I uncovered something too."

The pained look on her face worried me as much as the warning in her voice. "What is it? Did you find something bad online—planted evidence?"

"It's not that. But you're not going to like it. It's about Shane."

My chest tightened. "Shane?"

She hesitated, then talked faster as she explained. "I didn't intentionally go looking for him. I was checking out decoy stuff and Canadian folk art websites, forums, and other places, getting a handle on buyers and sellers, watching for someone impersonating Scandal Mountain. One username kept popping up. When I backtracked, it was Shane. I'm sure of it."

I let out a sigh of relief. "That's not a big deal. He's collected those sort of things for years. Guns, knives, decoys . . . I'm not surprised you came across him."

She cringed. "I'm not talking about just normal forums and sites—not even just the regular clearnet."

"Clearnet?" I'd heard the term in passing before, but I didn't like the implications. "What are you talking about?"

"Shane's spending time—a lot of time—on the darknet."

"That doesn't make sense. Shane's a total straight shooter. It's got to be another impersonator or some kind of mistake."

"I wouldn't be telling you unless I was certain," she said with full sincerity.

An icy wave of fear rolled over me. I turned away and closed my eyes. Illegal things happened on the dark web. It was the heart of the black market. It was where stolen things were sold and traded.

"I'm not accusing Shane of anything." Kala's voice came at a distance. "I'm just telling you the facts."

Tuck interrupted her. "Umm . . . Just to satisfy my curiosity. How are *you* getting on the dark web? Before you said it takes—"

"Special skills, software, and friends," Kala answered.

Skills. Software. Friends.

My mind went to the buff guy Shane had been with at the auction. His *friend*. At first, I'd wondered if the guy was involved in the theft. He'd been at the appraisal event. He'd seen the plover. Then I'd decided he was probably with the FBI Art Crime Team. An FBI agent might have access to the darknet. Was Shane working with him? Had Shane joined the FBI? It might explain why he'd been too slammed to find time to have pizza with me.

I shook my head. Shane would have told me if he'd changed jobs. Right?

Chapter Twenty-Two

Thick fog ghosted across the road and a cold drizzle smeared the windshield the next morning when I drove to St. Albans to talk to Celine. Each *slap* of the wipers only served to punctuate my conflicted thoughts. One slap reminded me how I'd have preferred to stay home and dig into Shane's online activities with Kala. The next slap would insist talking to Celine was more vital. I had to know for absolute certain if Mom was involved with Frank, and if Nina was aware of it.

Still, I couldn't get Shane off my mind, and the more I thought about him, the more likely it seemed that there was a side to him that I'd overlooked, like how Degas's famous *Portrait of a Woman* painting hides a second face beneath the top layers of paint.

I sat back against the seat, shoulders square. I nodded. Yeah. There was only one solution to this situation that made sense. When I got home from St. Albans, I'd phone Shane. Even if we couldn't get together, we could video chat. I'd tell him what Kala had discovered and straight-out ask for the truth about his activities. No matter what, I couldn't believe Shane would lie to my face.

Of course, the fact that Kala was surfing the dark web when she came across him was a bit of a stumbling block. I'd just have to deal with it when I reached that point.

*   *   *

By the time I got to Celine's house, which sat directly across from Holy Angels Church, the drizzle had transformed into rain, pounding harder by the second. I pulled past her driveway, then backed in so I could watch the church while I waited for her to come out. Celine had said the best time for us to meet was right after the service finished, and I'd arrived exactly on time.

A teenage girl in a rain slicker ran out of the church, retrieved an umbrella from a gold sedan, and then raced back inside. She reappeared, holding the umbrella over an elderly woman's head as they made for the sedan. Other people appeared, scurrying out from the church's front and side doors, rushing to their cars and trucks.

The rain picked up, sluicing down. Gusts of wind rattled the van's sides. I turned the defrost on high, vainly trying to keep the windows from fogging up. Had Celine forgotten we were meeting today? Tuck had said she'd gotten flakier.

Through the hazy windshield, I finally spotted her, holding a church program over her head as she dashed between the slicing raindrops. Dressed in an ivory cape and white dress, Celine appeared as ethereal as the angelic spirits she depicted in her artwork.

As she headed across the road toward her house, I got out of the van, hurried through the rain, up her front steps, and onto her home's wide porch. It was a cozy place, protected from the weather thanks to a wide roof and shingled half walls. An attractive set of wicker porch furniture was grouped near the front door. If this had been an antique-picking house call, I'd have asked if she wanted to sell the vintage set.

Celine breezed up the steps toward me. She halted, blinking through her pink-framed glasses with no hint of recognition.

"I'm Edie Brown. Viki's daughter. Remember, I left a message for you, then we talked on the phone last night?"

She took off her glasses, wiped them, then peered at me again. "Yes. Edie. I didn't recognize you. It's been a long time." She fluttered her fingers, indicating the wicker set. "Please, sit down."

I lowered myself into the closest chair before she could change her mind and invite me inside. I didn't need this to turn into an extended visit.

She glanced at the front door. "Would you like a cup of tea?"

"Thank you for offering, but I had a coffee on my way here." I lied.

"Oh, all right then." She sat down in the chair beside mine, cocooned in her wet cape, blinking blue eyes magnified by her glasses. "You're Tuck's niece, right? He's a lovely man."

I nodded, then got right to my point. "I wanted to talk to you about my mom."

She pressed her hand against her chest, where a gold cross hung. "I feel awful about what happened to her. Just awful."

My voice strained a little as I continued, "Do you know if my mom was seeing anyone special?"

"Oh—" She dropped her gaze to her lap and began twiddling her thumbs nervously.

"Who was it?" I pressed.

She peeked up. "She didn't tell you?"

"No. And it's very important." I leaned toward her, a hand on my knee. "Was she seeing a man from Stowe?"

She hesitated, then said, "His first name was Francis—like St. Francis. That's all I know."

"Was he married?"

A flush swept her cheeks, but the question seemed to open a floodgate. "I told her it was wrong. She said he didn't live with his wife—that their divorce was almost final."

"Did his wife know about my mom?"

"Why? His wife lives in California or somewhere on the West Coast. Is she harassing you and Tuck?"

"It's not that." I didn't correct her on the California lie Mom might have fed her, but I shifted uncomfortably at my own prolonged fib. "I've been wondering if the police missed something obvious to do with Mom's case, like someone who might have set her up."

"She never mentioned anyone." Celine touched her cross again. "I told your mother not to pay attention to that Francis's sweet talk. Sins are forgiven if we listen to our guardian angels and heed their advice."

I tried again. "Did his wife figure out who my mom was?"

"Yes."

For a long second, the gusting of the wind and the hammer of the rain on the porch roof reverberated like a hurricane. Not caring what she thought, I rocked forward, hugging myself. Dear God, or whoever's heavenly advice Mom should have listened to, help us all. Nina knew for sure. Everything we'd uncovered wasn't a pack of unfounded coincidences.

The Art of the Decoy

I glanced at the sheeting rain, all but obscuring the van. *Bitter and vengeful,* that's what Frank had called Nina. *Don't let her fool you into thinking she's a defenseless victim.*

There was no question Nina could have made the decoys vanish from the attic. She could also be responsible for Claude's far too convenient trip to the hospital. She might even be good enough on a computer to impersonate us online. She had a reason to hate my mom. But I didn't believe for a second that she had the knowledge necessary to sell millions of dollars worth of stolen folk art on the black market, any more than I believed Frank had that ability.

There was someone else involved here. Someone from the art and antiques world. Most likely someone who knew their way around the darknet.

Chapter Twenty-Three

Even before I got back to my van, I'd decided my next move should be to talk with Martina Fortuni. Sure, she was on the bottom of my suspect list, but I couldn't ignore the fact that she'd been to the Bouchard farm and purchased things from them. The truth was, even if Martina wasn't directly involved with the theft of the decoys, Nina might've approached her about selling them on the sly, and I had no idea if she was capable of doing that or not.

I pulled out of Celine St. Marie's driveway and drove toward Main Street. It also so happened that Martina's store was only a few blocks from Celine's house. The chance of her divulging anything was slim, but it was possible, and it made more sense to confront her while I was in St. Albans rather than later. Time was something I was rapidly running out of.

Ahead, a traffic light changed from green to yellow. I tapped the brakes and glanced in the rearview mirror. With the rain and all the puddles, it would be easy for a tailgater to hydroplane into the rear of the van. I really wasn't in the mood for a fender-bender.

No one was directly behind me, but there was a sedan a ways back, slowing, keeping its distance as if taking great care not to get too close. It was the size and shape of a Dodge Charger. Black. Shiny.

I rubbed my hand along the steering wheel. I might not have wanted to get rear-ended, but it was odd how the car kept such a consistent distance behind me.

My intuition fired a warning flare. *An unmarked police cruiser. Tailing me.* But the sedan was too far away to make out small details, like if it had a government license plate or blue lights hidden beneath its grille.

The muscles along my spine tensed as I noticed what appeared to be a spotlight set in front of the driver's side mirror. Maybe not a spotlight, but there was something there, something abnormal.

The sedan's turn signal came on. It slowed and then went down a side street, vanishing from sight.

I came to a full stop at the now-red traffic light and laughed at myself. My paranoia was certainly working overtime. Besides, why would it have mattered if a cop was behind me? I wasn't doing anything wrong.

The paranoia countered, *Maybe it's the FBI. Keeping tabs on you.*

I gripped the steering wheel harder and forced that thought from my head. Talking to Martina was going to be stressful enough without creating other reasons to be anxious.

The traffic light changed to green. I pulled onto Main Street and into an empty spot on the edge of the city park. Martina's storefront was directly across the street in the middle of a block of shops. *Fortuni Pawn and Treasures* was painted in gold across her front window. Beneath were the words: *Jewelry. Cash Paid. Antiques.*

Memories of Martina elbowing teenage me out of the way at lawn sales and church bazaars rushed into my mind. In truth, I'd been flattered at first that an adult dealer had noticed my existence and thought of me as competition, but the novelty of her less than desirable attention quickly wore off. There was no question about it, Martina would be shocked to see me step foot inside her store.

I considered texting Tuck to tell him what I was about to do and about my conversation with Celine. Problem was, he'd tell me to wait until we could visit Fortuni's together and that was an unnecessary waste of time. I just needed to play it cool, act trusting and not all that smart. Let Martina think she had the upper hand. What was the worst that could happen? It wasn't like Martina was going to shove my head in a plastic bag and smother me to death.

I shuddered as the blurry video of the dead thief on the warehouse floor replayed in my mind. It happened not that far from Fisher's Auction House—and even closer to where I stood right now.

I got out, crossed the street, and went up the curb and onto the sidewalk. A couple dashed between the raindrops and into a nearby restaurant. A woman waited under a bookstore's outstretched awning. But for the most part, there weren't many people around.

When I reached Fortuni's entrance, I took a second to study the front window. Fake diamonds the size of golf balls and gifts suitable for graduations and weddings rested on plexiglass boxes: gilded picture frames, sets of crystal champagne flutes, neckties, and vintage luggage. A meticulous display. Mediocre value.

I pushed the front door open and an electronic chime *ding-donged* as I walked inside.

The shop was arranged with brightly lit glass cases encircling the edges of the room. The center of the sales floor held a large display of coins and baseball cards. Off to one side, an open doorway revealed a second room that contained anniversary clocks, silver, and glassware. No hint of anything rustic, let alone folk art like decoys. Without even moving closer, I could tell the artwork on the walls was all low-end reproductions, cheaply framed. She probably sold them as "museum quality," perhaps online as well as here.

I made my way to the closest showcase. Vintage jewelry sparkled against a black velvet background. There was a ton, and it looked like good quality.

The click of high heels resounded. I glanced toward the sound in time to see Martina emerge from a curtained doorway. Her dark black hair had developed a Cruella de Vil streak since I'd last seen her, but she was no less bony. Her pointy elbows were still undoubtably capable of shoving their way through any crowd.

"Stopped by to give your sympathies like all the other dealers?" she snapped.

My mind went utterly blank. I had no idea what she was talking about.

Her gaze bored into mine. "Before you ask: *Yes*, I was robbed. *Yes*, everything was insured. And, *yes*, it's none of your business."

Robbed? "I didn't know about that. I stopped by to—" I struggled, searching for an excuse that would take her off the defensive, but my brain was caught on the idea of yet another robbery. "What did they take?"

Her glare narrowed, shooting a death ray at me. "Like I said, none of your business."

I toughened my voice. Why mess around? Might as well go into this head-on. If nothing else, I'd get to see her reaction. "I came here because I had a question about the Bouchards, Jean-Claude and his daughter-in-law. They live in Franklin."

"I know who they are," she said tartly. Her shrewish expression remained intact, and so did the rest of her surly body language. Not a single twitch or bead of sweat to indicate my mention of Nina and Claude had made her uncomfortable.

I stepped closer to her. "The Bouchards said you bought some jewelry from them."

She nodded. Her eyes narrowed even further, no more than slits now. "I saw you on TV with Nina Bouchard. You certainly overestimated the value of that horrible decoy."

All the tension in my body released. I'd totally forgotten she might have seen the show and there was no mistaking she honestly believed the decoy was valueless. "I didn't want to make her feel bad in front of all those people."

She sniffed derisively, then pushed sarcasm into her voice. "Of course that's what you were doing."

I pressed on, now feeding her white lies to gauge her reactions. "Speaking of the decoy. That's kind of why I'm here. The Bouchards offered to sell me some things. An old treadle sewing machine, wicker furniture . . . Nothing great. They have so much stuff." I shifted my weight from one leg to the other, as if uneasy about saying the rest.

Her hands went to her hips, one gold sandaled foot tapping the floor impatiently. "Spit it out. I don't have all day."

"I wondered where the Bouchards got all their things. They—they aren't selling stolen property, right?" The real question was, would Martina jump at the opportunity to scare me away from the Bouchard family?

"That junk? You've got to be kidding." She scoffed. "I certainly wouldn't have bought what little I did if there was any chance of it being hot."

I forced my face to remain neutral. If Martina had been trying to scare me off, she'd have agreed when I suggested some of the items might be stolen property, whether it was so she could buy things from the Bouchards in the future without the possibility of me interfering or because she feared her involvement with the theft might somehow be uncovered.

Martina's hands left her hips. She craned forward and her expression pinched as if she was growing more suspicious about my visit. "If that's all you want, I need to get back to work. I've got a necklace to restring for a paying customer."

I nodded. I'd gotten what I came for. "Sure. Thanks." I turned toward the door, but a tug of unwarranted sympathy made me swivel back. "I am sorry to hear about the robbery. I hope you get everything back."

She huffed. "Fat chance. The city police took fingerprints and my security tapes. The FBI even showed up, for all the good that did."

"The FBI?" I wasn't surprised they were notified. That was probably normal procedure. The question was, why had they shown up in person instead of leaving the investigation to the city police? "What did they say? Did they suspect anyone in particular? Was it connected to other robberies?"

She sneered. "All they did was take one look at the security video, ask what was missing, then leave. They weren't here more than ten minutes."

"That's awful." I glanced at the brimming showcase of vintage jewelry. I couldn't see where anything was missing. "How much did the robbers take?"

Her voice lowered to a growl. "Bastards took all my brand-new wedding rings and bands. The complete inventory. Gold. Diamonds. They knew what they were after. They didn't steal a single piece of vintage or costume jewelry." Her jaw worked. "I know who did it. Drug-dealing swine."

"I'm sorry," I said, and I meant it. But inside I was thankful. New jewelry and not folk art or even antiques all but eliminated the possibility she'd been robbed by the people I was looking for—probably the same conclusion that had dampened the FBI's interest.

As I left the shop and went back out into the rain, I erased Martina's name from the suspect list. Still, deep inside I couldn't totally banish my concern. *The FBI don't know Martina like you do*, I told myself. *They're looking at her as a victim of a crime, not a criminal.*

I put her name back on my mental list, one step below the bottom but bolded this time. There was a reason Fortuni's Pawn and Treasures had stayed in business for so long.

Martina was smart and slick, and she always had been.

Chapter
Twenty-Four

T he rain hadn't bothered me too much before, but the shivers hit me as I jogged back across the street toward the van. Between Martina's mention of the FBI and what I'd learned from Celine, I was now chilled to the bone.

When I reached the other side of the road, I'd only gone a few steps before a sedan on the far side of the city park drew my gaze. It was black and midsize like the one behind me on the way to Martina's shop. It was hard to tell at a distance and through the rain, but it looked like exhaust was rising from its tailpipe, as if it was idling.

My eyes went to the driver's side mirror. It was oddly large and lumpy, like something extra was attached there. It was the same sedan.

I looked away, pretending I hadn't seen it. Maybe the police were cruising downtown and watching the park for drug dealers, like the ones Martina believed had robbed her store.

Another chill went through me. It was also possible that Nina had already reported the robbery at the farm and the FBI were tailing me in hopes that I'd lead them to the collection.

I dropped my gaze to the pavement, forcing myself to not glance at the sedan as my legs carried me toward the van. I had to act casual. I couldn't let them know I'd spotted them.

I unlocked the van doors, got in, and instantly hit the locks again. Then I turned the heat on high and hugged myself against the shivers. Through the smear of haze and rain, I could still make out the sedan idling on the other side of the park. I focused all my attention on it, as if by sheer will I could compel it to drive away.

It didn't move.

The muscles along my shoulders tightened. My blood pressure rushed in my ears. There was only one way to know for sure if this was my imagination or not. It wasn't like I was in the habit of letting people intimidate me. It wasn't like I'd done anything wrong, either.

I put the van in gear, pulled out of the parking space, and drove up Main Street. One block. Two blocks . . . There were cars and trucks behind me, but I didn't see the sedan.

Without using my turn signal, I veered quickly into the parking lot of a small hardware store. I drove through the alleyway of cars, out the exit, and back onto the main street, going in the same direction as before. I glanced in the rearview mirror. The sedan was pulling out of the same hardware store exit. I clapped a hand over my mouth, holding back a gasp. Dear God, it sure looked like they were tailing me.

My thoughts spun. Who the heck was it? If not the cops, then maybe Nina? But why focus her anger solely on me? Stalking Frank made more sense. He wasn't simply the offspring of her perceived enemy. He'd cheated on her.

What I'd seen at Frank's house flashed into my head. The immaculately clean carpet. The bleached counters. The door left open as if to air the place out. Everything fresh and clean, like someone had sanitized the place. Granted it was just a theory, but could Frank have not been home because someone—like Nina, maybe—had just finished scrubbing away the last bloody traces of him?

I gripped the wheel harder, knuckles turning white. I forced myself to sit up taller. No matter who was following me, I'd be damned if I'd let them get away with it.

It was time to end this crazy hypothesizing.

Time to end this game.

Barely able to breathe, I flicked on my turn signal, then pulled slowly into a midsize shopping plaza. No matter who was back there, I wanted to make sure they saw where I went this time.

My muscles tensed in readiness as I wove through the parking lot to a space in front of the Wise Dollar Store. I grabbed my bag, slung it over my shoulder, and got out.

Overhead, the sky had lightened, dark clouds giving way to faint patches of brightness, but thankfully the rain was still steady. As much as I'd cursed it earlier, I now needed it to hang on for a few more minutes. Maybe more like fifteen.

I strolled into the Wise Dollar. It was busy, two registers open, customers milling around. As usual, it smelled strongly of floral air freshener and plastic doodads. My nose itched as I wandered down aisle three to the clothing department. Socks. Underwear. Umbrellas that wouldn't hold up against a light breeze.

"Damn it," I muttered when I saw the bin labeled rain-hats was empty, but a grin tugged at my lips when I spotted the bright yellow packets next to it—disposable rain ponchos, $2.49 each. Perfect.

I grabbed one and made for the checkout line.

The woman running the register wore a tag with a heart on it that said *Please be kind, I'm a trainee.* Just my luck, I'd picked the slowest cashier.

I took a deep breath. I needed to stay calm. This was going to work. I'd know for sure in a few minutes if the sedan was following me and—if so—who was driving.

Outside the store's front window, the rain had slowed to a drizzle. Finally, my turn to cash out arrived. I paid, then waved off the bag the cashier offered. "If you don't mind, I'm going to put it on right now."

She smiled. "You won't be the first person to do that. We've sold more rainhats and ponchos than anything else this morning."

My hands shook from nerves as I ripped open the packet and pulled out the vinyl poncho. Once I got it unfolded and wrestled it on over my head, I was pleased to find it draped to my thighs. Not a bad temporary disguise for less than three dollars.

I pulled the hood up and drew it close around my face, then wandered to a display of beachballs beside the front window. Using the display as a screen, I peered out at the parking lot. Hopefully, anyone looking in would think I was waiting for a ride to arrive. They certainly wouldn't expect someone dressed in bright yellow to be trying to hide.

I spotted the black sedan three rows behind the van. It had parked in the open away from most of the other cars, a place with a good view of anyone coming or going from the Wise Dollar. I couldn't see a ribbon of exhaust this time, but someone was in the driver's seat, as hidden behind the car's fogged glass as I was by my poncho.

Sweat dampened my armpits as I took my phone out. I couldn't hurry. I had to act nonchalant. I raised the phone, keeping it low enough to look as if I were texting, but pointing the camera at the window. I snapped a photo of the sedan, then another.

Then I turned from the window and strolled out the front door. I would have preferred a less obvious route, but using the store's delivery or emergency exits might have set off an alarm—and the last thing I wanted was to draw attention.

Head down, I jogged away from the store, diagonally across the parking lot in the direction of the black sedan. But I didn't aim directly at it. Instead, I aimed about a car's length behind. Hurrying along through the rain as if trying to stay dry and not interested in anything in particular, especially not that car. The photos might not be clear enough to reveal who the driver was, and I had to be sure. I had to see them. And I had to be careful.

My heart pounded hard against my ribs. I kept my path straight until I was about to pass behind the sedan, then I veered, speeding toward it, through the last of the rain, heading for the driver's side door.

The hazy reflection of a face appeared in the car's side mirror. The sedan shifted into gear and began creeping forward. They'd seen me, and I couldn't let them leave.

I sprinted, splashing through puddles.

The sedan pulled away, moving between the rows of cars. I pushed my legs, running faster. I had to see the driver.

A delivery truck backed out of a parking space less than a yard ahead of the sedan, forcing it to slow. That was all the time I needed. I skidded across the wet pavement and slammed my fist into the driver's door.

"Hey!" I shouted. "Stop!"

The delivery truck was totally in the way now, leaving the car no choice but to stay put. I glared through the glass at the driver.

My mouth dropped open. Shane.

Chapter
Twenty-Five

"Pull over!" I scowled at Shane and motioned sharply at the parking space the delivery truck had just left. Shane. Of all people. Following me.

He drove into the spot, then lowered the window. His voice was calm, only a touch worried. "We should get a hot coffee. Sit down some place comfortable and talk."

I yanked off the stupid poncho and flung it to the pavement. "I don't want coffee. I want to know why you were following me."

His tone remained even. His eyes were gentle. He rested a hand on the edge of the open window and leaned toward me. "Edie, I'm worried about you."

I planted my feet. No way was I going to let him twist this back on me. "You were worried, but instead of calling or stopping at the house to talk, you decided to stalk me?"

"It's not like that. I wasn't stalking you."

Anger simmering, I glared at the sedan. The last drops of rain beaded on its waxed and flawless surface, as spit-shine bright and polished as the shoes Shane wore to work. I'd stared at those shoes a million times in the probation office to avoid looking into his sweet eyes or at those damn sexy forearms. I pinned him with a hard look. "Why aren't you driving your Land Rover?"

Without answering, he opened the car door and got out. As he stepped close, I had to look up to keep my eyes on his. My breath stalled, a hundred conflicting emotions pulsing through me. Anger. Desire. Hope. Fury.

"What were you doing in Stowe yesterday?" he demanded.

The question caught me off guard and the truth blundered out. I wanted to hate him. But I trusted him. I wanted to be open with him. "I—We went to see Frank Bouchard, Nina Bouchard's husband. Why were you there?"

Shane took me by the upper arms, a firm grasp. "Edie, I don't know what you're up to, but you need to stay out of this. Stay away from the Bouchards—all of them."

"I can't. I—" I clenched my hands into fists. *Trust your heart*, Tuck would have said. Grandma would have told me the same thing. Still, I'd already told Shane too much, and I couldn't afford to be stupid, not until I knew what he was up to.

His eyes filled with an honesty I wanted to believe. "Don't worry about finishing the appraisal. Walk away. Please, for me."

I swallowed hard. I longed to tell him it wasn't that easy. That someone was impersonating us online. That I had to find the decoys and the thieves, solid proof of my innocence. That if I went down for this, I could lose everything I cared about. The business my grandparents had founded. My family home. My freedom. I'd destroy Tuck and Kala's reputations, never mind our chance to reconnect . . . But before I said a thing, I needed to get the truth from him.

I set my jaw. "Why were you following me?"

He let go of my arms and glanced at the sedan. The rain had stopped, but his hair was already damp, short curls clinging around his ears. "You asked why I wasn't driving my Land Rover. This is my work vehicle. I'm kind of on—"

"Yeah?" I said when he stalled. Dear Lord, I was pretty sure I knew the answer.

"You've been gone a long time, Edie."

He stopped talking as a compact car pulled into a parking space not far from us. A woman and a man got out. Once they walked toward the Wise Dollar, I narrowed my eyes. "You don't work for probation anymore, do you?"

"I changed jobs right after you left."

"And?" I needed to hear him say it. I was also angry at myself for assuming his life hadn't moved on while I was gone.

Shane closed his eyes, then opened them again. "I never intended to be a probation officer forever. It was a career layover while Mom was recovering. I had the right education. The right background. They were looking for someone who knew about local criminals."

"Exactly who do you mean by *they*?"

A gleam of pride shone in his eyes. "I joined the state police after you left. Rose up to detective. I'm technically a criminal investigator with them. That's been my goal for a long time. But now—"

"Now you're working for the FBI." I was sure I was right.

"More like I'm working in conjunction with their Art Crime Team. They needed a local expert, someone familiar with antiques and people in the industry—on both sides of the law."

"The guy you were with at the auction, the buff guy with the dark glasses? Is he FBI?"

"Um . . . I'm not at liberty to say. You're on the right track, though."

"Why didn't you tell me?"

"I was going to. Then you started talking about the decoy collection." His body was brittle with tension, his voice on edge. "You heard about the robbery at the Canadian Museum of History in Quebec?"

I glanced down at the asphalt. Shane was trying to do it again, switch the conversation away from him. My stomach tensed as a worrisome possibility occurred to me. I looked up and toughened my voice. "You told the FBI about the Bouchard collection, didn't you?"

He froze in place. "We think there's a chance the ringleaders might try to recruit you to steal the collection. There've been robberies similar to the Quebec one throughout New England and eastern Canada. They're dangerous people. Very dangerous."

"Are you talking organized crime? Like a cartel?"

"We believe so." His voice gentled. "Just so we're clear, I wasn't following you in Stowe. Today was the only time, and I'm not sorry."

My thoughts staggered. If it wasn't me he was following in Stowe, that didn't mean he wasn't watching someone: Frank, the Ramones, the people in the SUV that had pulled out of Frank's driveway, or all of them. No matter what, it was abundantly clear: the FBI Art Crime Team had no idea the Bouchard collection was already missing—which shouldn't have been surprising since it hadn't been reported.

His face became grave. "Did you see the video on the internet of the dead thief, the body they found in the warehouse in Stanstead?"

The taste of bile crept up my throat. *Wrists bound with a strap. The man's head. Suffocated in a plastic bag. Yellow nylon cord and bruises around his neck.* "It was horrible."

"It was real. Not fake. It was a brutal attack. An assassination." He stepped closer, resting his hands on my arms again. "We believe the thief double-crossed the ringleaders. These people are sadistic and ruthless, one reason you need to stay as far away from the Bouchards and their collection as you can."

"I can't do that." My voice was hushed, barely audible above the distant drone of traffic.

"You have to." He let go of me and thumped the side of his leg with a fist. "What about sadistic and dangerous don't you understand? If your family's that desperate for money, I have savings. I'll—"

"It's not the money. And no one's approached me about stealing the collection." My voice cracked. "I'm not a thief, and you know it."

"I'm not accusing you of anything. If you got in their way by mistake . . ."

I met his eyes. I didn't want to tell him, but Shane's mention of the dead thief had pinned that gruesome image back in the forefront of my brain. Sickening. Overwhelming. And real, as he'd said. The people behind this were involved with organized crime, and the danger didn't just involve me. Tuck and Kala's lives were on the line as well. They'd helped me. They'd been there every step of the way. Besides, if I told the truth, maybe any evidence trumped up against me wouldn't hold as much weight.

Shane reached out, his fingers brushing hair back from my cheek, a warm, kind touch.

"What's going on, Edie? Tell me, please."

I nodded, then surrendered. "I can't back out because the collection disappeared a couple of days ago. Before the auction. Before I saw you in Stowe. It happened Thursday night."

He stepped back, gaping at me. "The collection was stolen? All of it?"

"Most of it. Nina's given me until Tuesday morning to find the missing pieces or she's going to call the police and accuse me of taking them."

"Why didn't you tell me?"

"Because"—the underlying truth stuck in my throat, a lump I couldn't swallow around. Despite everything, I really liked Shane. I didn't want to hurt him, but I had to—"because you're the only person I told about the Bouchard collection. You even knew the collection was in the attic. I didn't really believe it—"

"You thought I stole them?"

"No. I—I just had the feeling you were keeping something from me. Turns out that was your new job, something I'm excited about for you." I looked up at the sky, patches of blue breaking through the clouds. Then I closed my eyes and told him our various theories. About how we initially thought Frank might have stolen the decoys, about Mom and Frank's affair, and how Nina could've taken them and set us up as part of a revenge scheme. I took a breath, then said the rest, "I also didn't tell you because I knew you'd feel obliged to report the theft."

"This isn't good," he said.

"Please, promise me you won't tell the FBI the collection is missing. Someone's been impersonating Scandal Mountain Antiques online. I'm worried they've planted evidence against us. Give me one more day to find the decoys. I'll turn them over to you, I promise." I scrubbed my hands over my face. There was another fear deep inside me, one I'd shared with Nina in the attic. "You know as well as I do that there are thieves out there who would destroy the collection before they'd let the police or FBI recover it and use it as evidence against them. The decoys are important. They're art. They're history. A record of a time, family, and culture. I can't stand the thought of them being lost forever."

His eyes filled with regret. "You know I can't keep this to myself, Edie."

I raised my chin and met those sad eyes. "Don't expect me to back off. I'm going to figure out who the thieves are and find the decoys. I have to—before they vanish underground or get run through a wood chipper, then burnt to nothing by some idiot who doesn't care about anything other than covering up their crime."

Chapter
Twenty-Six

Three years ago, when my weekend with Shane in the Adirondacks had come to an end, I'd left the cabin we stayed in and started back to Vermont ahead of him. I hadn't even gone a mile before I caught myself looking in the rearview mirror to see if I could spot his Land Rover coming up behind my van. Just thinking of the secret retreat we'd shared had swept excited tingles across my skin.

Today—as I left the strip mall parking lot and drove toward Scandal Mountain—my feelings were not so clear-cut. Logic said I'd put an end to Shane following me and it was a good thing. But a part of my crazy heart wanted to see him back there, trailing me at a distance, caring and keeping me safe. More than anything, I wanted to believe our personal connection wasn't broken forever. Either way, I wasn't done trying to rout out the thieves and find the decoys. My fears might have weighed even heavier now, thanks to Shane's worry that organized crime had the collection in their sights. We might have been working with a scarcity of evidence and an overabundance of speculation, but it was also possible I was about to shake something loose. That was, if Pinky had uncovered information that would help. One thing was for sure—I wasn't going to let us go down for the robbery or let those decoys get destroyed if I could prevent it.

As I approached the outskirts of Scandal Mountain, the now-dry roads became congested with traffic, not just cars but bicyclists as well. I slowed from my normal sixty down to fifty, then forty, ten freaking miles per hour below the speed limit. I passed two dozen bicyclists near Townline gas station and on the hills up to Dead Man's Curve.

I knew the source of my building impatience was frustration over everything that had happened today in St. Albans. Still, knowing that didn't do anything to relieve the tension in my shoulders and the headache taking root in my skull. Damn them all. Shane. Frank. Nina. Mom. The stupid bicyclists.

I stomped on the brakes as I neared the monstrous curve, slowing to twenty stinking miles per hour. Ahead, a pack of cyclists took up the entire lane, bent low, pedaling hard. Judging by the numbers on their backs, they were part of a race. Number 426. Number 500 . . . *Five hundred?* I'd never get past them all.

They bunched even closer together as they passed the spot where Mom had hit black ice one winter and nearly killed us both.

I slowed further, down to fifteen miles per hour. My fingers white-knuckled the steering wheel, and by the time I could speed up again, the Jumping Café had appeared ahead. The colorful bunting the guys hung yesterday now dangled limp along the deck railings. Next to the café, the flea market tents sagged under the weight of rainwater pooled in their canopies. The whole place looked as bedraggled as I felt.

I steered into the café's parking lot to a space by the front door. A vintage "It's 5:00 Somewhere" sign glowed in one window, removing any guilt I had about wanting a stiff drink. Hopefully, Pinky was here already and had come up with information beyond Jules and Rosetta Ramone's purchases at the auction house.

I got out, went into the café and from there to the pub. The same bartender was working as the other night. Today he sported a Hufflepuff T-shirt decorated with a multihued badger.

He grinned at me. "Nice to see you again."

"Same here," I said. "Is Pinky around?"

"She's on break right now."

When he hesitated, I widened my smile. "She's expecting me. I'm an old friend."

He gestured across the room, indicating a door to the reception hall. "I saw her heading that way with her lunch. I'd be happy to bring in something for you to eat or a drink, if you want."

"Thanks. How about just a citrus vodka on the rocks with a twist?"

"Coming right up," he said.

As I went into the hall, the brightness of the room blinded me for a second. Light shone down from a dozen chandeliers, gleaming off the polished floor and sparkling against a nearby wall covered with framed photos of brides who had gotten married in the room, square dancers from the '60s, line dancers, kids dressed like ladybugs and ballerinas.

"Edie," Pinky's voice echoed in the all but empty hall. "Grab a chair. Join me."

She was at a banquet table all by herself with a basket of chicken fingers and onion rings in front of her. In the glaring light her blonde rooster-comb hair gleamed like silver.

I snagged a chair and carried it over. I'd just gotten settled when the bartender appeared with my drink and a bowl of popcorn. He set them on the table, then flashed a broad smile.

"Think those pearly whites are going to get you a bigger tip?" Pinky teased.

He winked. "A man has to try."

I laughed and reached for my bag to get out my debit card, but Pinky waved me off. "This one's on me."

"Thanks," I said, though I wasn't sure I wanted to get any more in debt to Scandal Mountain's kingpin of small-time extortion.

She waited until the bartender left, then scooted her chair closer to mine. "I looked at the auction records but didn't find what you were hoping for. The Ramones haven't purchased any decoys or hunting-related items from what I could see—nothing, nada, zilch. I asked around too, just some of the pickers at the auction. They haven't sold them anything like that. They don't think the Ramones have any real knowledge in that area."

I took a long sip of my drink, savoring the lemony tang. If the Ramones had no interest in decoys, it seemed less likely they'd be involved with Frank or the theft, especially not as ringleaders.

I smiled at Pinky. "Actually, that helps a lot. You said before you don't think the Ramones are especially close with Graham?"

"Not any more than most dealers." A devious sparkle glistened in her eyes, like she was holding back a juicy tidbit. She plucked an onion ring from the basket, took a bite, chewed slowly. "Man, these are good. You want one?"

"I'm fine." I tried hard to not sound irritated, but I wasn't in the mood for being toyed with.

She wiped her mouth on a napkin. "Now, where were we?"

"The Ramones and Graham."

"Now I remember. It doesn't have anything to do with the Ramones," she said.

"Yeah?"

"I'm guessing your current interest is connected to that plover decoy. Jack—the other bartender—and I rewatched your appraisal on TV."

I sat up straighter, totally curious, didn't give her a yes or no. I needed to be careful how much I said. Pinky was more than living up to her reputation for being the queen of hearing, seeing, and knowing all.

She took a chicken finger from the basket and bit off a hunk. Thankfully, she downed it faster than the onion ring. "I've seen that woman you were talking to before—the one with the plover. Is she married?"

"Sort of. Why?"

"She comes in here sometimes."

My mouth started to fly open, but I managed to clamp it shut. *Nina? Here?* "Are you sure?"

"I didn't see her myself. Jack remembered her. According to him, she and Graham are getting it on."

"She's seeing Graham?" I couldn't believe it. I'd known Nina and Graham had at least met at the appraisal event.

Graham had told me himself he was responsible for Nina bringing the plover to our table, but this went way beyond a passing acquaintance.

"I can't say it's true for certain. Jack's the one who's seen them." Pinky scarfed down the rest of her chicken finger. "That woman's husband drives a restored Corvette, right? He's friends with Graham, too. I've seen them riding around in that car."

I felt myself pale. Graham was friends with Frank—and with Nina?

My head whirred from the information.

Pinky dabbed the corners of her mouth with her napkin. "Last Thursday night, Jack and I figured Corvette guy had something going on. He never came into the pub, but his car was parked outside most of the night, even after we closed."

"That is strange." I picked up my glass, feeling its chill before taking a sip. Last Thursday, the night Claude was in the hospital and the collection was stolen. "You sure it wasn't someone else's car?"

She rolled her eyes. "A red C5 Corvette? How many of those do you think stop by this place?"

"You're positive it was Thursday night?"

"Totally." She made a face. "That whole night was a flipping monkey show."

I leaned forward, pulse hammering harder by the second. "Why? What happened?"

"It was really busy—Board Game Night—and we were running out of bottled beer. I drove down to Quickie's to snag a couple of emergency cases. On the way back, a town cop nailed me."

"Sobriety check?"

"That's what I thought it was. But, *nooooo*. Someone stole the license plates off my car. Can you believe it?"

"Really?" I bent even closer. I didn't want to miss a single detail.

"That isn't the weirdest part. When I went out to the parking lot after work, the plates were back on." She squished her napkin into a ball, hand fisting. "I've got a good idea who did it. One of these days . . ."

"You caught them on the café security cameras?" I guessed.

"Unfortunately, no. I threw some guys out earlier in the night, teenagers from the campground across the street. Underage sleazebags. I bet their mommies made them put the plates back on."

"Did you call the police?"

"Damn straight I did. The cop ripped up the ticket she'd given me earlier, but she acted like I was trying to pull a fast one on her. What would I have to gain by driving around without plates on?"

I took another sip of my drink, buying myself a moment. Missing plates. Returned plates. Thursday. "You said the Corvette was here all night?"

"It was gone Friday morning when I stopped by for coffee." She scooched closer to me, her tone sweetening as she abruptly shifted the conversation. "I noticed you've got a new employee—cute black girl, into vintage stuff?"

"Kala? Mom hired her. She's great," I said.

"There's Game Night again this Thursday. You should come—*and* bring her. Pizzas. Local beer tasting. Some of the old gang from school usually show up."

"Maybe." I wasn't all that into seeing the so-called old gang—hers and mine weren't the same anyhow. Also, I wasn't wild about the idea of playing matchmaker between her and Kala, if that's what she was hinting at. Still, it felt good to be invited—normal, like maybe things were going to be okay.

I laughed at myself. Yeah. Maybe they'd be okay, if we didn't all end up arrested or assassinated by some crime boss.

As Pinky's attention went back to her food, I got up. "Sorry to take off so fast, but I should have been home hours ago. Thanks for everything."

She stopped mid-bite. "Before you go, there is a little something—something I need to hit you up for. I wouldn't want to shirk my duties as a good citizen of Scandal Mountain."

An uneasy feeling fluttered in my stomach as she popped to her feet and headed for a pile of cardboard boxes stacked against a wall. What was she up to? Whatever it was, I got the distinct feeling saying *no* to it wasn't an option. I'd gotten my information. Now it was time to pay.

Pinky opened the top box. She reached inside and pulled out a gaudy toy flamingo in a sparkly tutu. "Nice, huh?"

"I guess," I said, totally confused.

She dangled the toy enticingly in the air. "Only forty bucks will get you this limited-edition ballerina bird. It's a fundraiser for the dance class."

For a second, pure shock stole my breath. *Ballerina bird? Dance class?*

As I gawked at the flamingo, my mind raced back to the Bouchards' attic and to Gracie. She'd rushed past me toward the table, her small arms straining as they reached for the yellowlegs decoy. She'd screeched, "Ballerina bird!"

At the time, I'd assumed ballerina bird was simply a cute moniker, something any child might make up for a bird with long dancer-like legs. Now I realized it wasn't a one-off thing. This was where Gracie had picked up the name, a sparkly flamingo, a fundraiser for her dance class.

The rest of a likely scenario came together in a rush. While Gracie had her dance class in this room, Nina waited in the pub. Graham met her there and introduced himself, buying her a drink. Graham had a reputation for being charming when he wanted something, just like Frank. People have a habit of being attracted to the same kind of jerk over and over.

Pinky shoved her hand into the box again. "The money from the fundraiser goes toward costumes for the dance class. If pink flamingos don't light your fire, there's always this—" She pulled out a blue flamingo wearing a boy's dance top and shiny leggings. She flicked at a paper tag hanging from the bird's wing. "It sucks that they're gender specific, Ms. Pink Tutu Bird and Mr. Boy Blue."

Mr. Blue? This time my heart sank. Unlike the mention of the ballerina bird, this made a bit of my hope unravel. Even if everything else fell apart for me and the stolen decoys never resurfaced, I'd hoped for Gracie's sake the mysterious Mr. Blue was a priceless blue heron decoy, a masterpiece Claude had squirreled away and could sell for a large sum of money if need be. Now it seemed like Mr. Blue, probably on Gracie's closet floor by now, was nothing more than an overpriced stuffed animal, not a priceless piece of folk art.

Pinky waved the blue flamingo back and forth like a hypnotist's watch. "You can have both for seventy-five bucks. All the money goes to the kids. Or—" She reached back into the box.

I raised a hand to stop her before she could fish out an even more expensive option. "I'll take the pair. How about I give you eighty for both?"

Pinky grinned. "Make it a hundred and the extra will go toward a parade costume and chicken barbecue for a needy child."

I scowled. "Okay. A hundred. But that's it."

Chapter Twenty-Seven

I gave Pinky the hundred bucks and told her to keep the flamingos. I'd gotten a lot of information, but I didn't need a physical reminder of what I'd paid for it. Still, I did want one more thing. Before I left I checked out the framed photos. I'd come this far; there was no reason to go home with a supposition when proof was close at hand.

Sure enough, right there in the middle of a photo of kids in ladybug outfits and glittery costumes, Gracie stood looking cute as anything in a sparkling blue tutu. Proof positive. Gracie had dance classes here. I couldn't be as positive Nina and Graham were hooking up, and I had absolutely no idea how Graham and Frank had met, but the puzzle pieces were coming together.

* * *

With all I'd learned replaying in my head, I drove home. As I pulled the van into its parking spot, I noticed the shop lights were on in the carriage barn. Through the windows, I saw Tuck and Kala carrying a piece of furniture toward the storage room.

I hopped out and sped to the shop. What was going on? Why were they messing around out here? The plan had been for them to keep searching online.

As I hurried inside, they set the piece of furniture down, a vintage dental cabinet, as ugly as sin thanks to someone's careless refinishing. Tuck glanced toward me. "We were wondering if you were ever coming home."

"You'll be proud of us." Kala grinned.

I must have looked irritated because Tuck instantly clarified. "Don't worry. We haven't been out here long. In fact, we uncovered some very interesting things earlier. Then a couple of dealers from Boston showed up. We are in business to sell things, right?"

"Yeah, of course," I said. I gave the cabinet a closer look. Five years ago, I'd thought Mom had lost her mind when she way overpaid for it at an estate sale. She'd insisted I was the one who didn't know a good buy when I saw it. I shook my head. "I can't believe they want that piece."

"We weren't going to argue with them." Tuck stopped talking, then frowned and asked, "What took you so long? Why didn't you call?"

I pressed my hands over my face and sank down on a high-backed church pew. "Everything happened so fast. I talked to Celine, then stopped by Fortuni's pawnshop."

Tuck pulled a stool up and sat down directly in front of me. He rested a hand on my knee. "Slow down. Start at the beginning."

"Did you find out if Nina knew about your mother's affair with Frank?" Kala asked.

I nodded heavily. "No question about it."

"Yikes," Kala said.

"You can say that again." I took a long breath. "For a few minutes I even convinced myself Nina might've murdered Frank because of it. I was pretty upset at the time, overthinking everything. It's not like we found a body at the chalet. Frank was probably just off somewhere in his Corvette. If he left by way of the garage, he might not have realized the front door was open."

Tuck gave my knee a squeeze. "Honestly, that makes sense. How about Martina? Was she at the shop?"

"She was. She's either an unbelievably good liar or she's not involved. However, I learned something totally unexpected. Her shop was robbed recently, and it wasn't just the police that showed up to investigate."

He withdrew his hand and sat back, clearly shocked. "Not the FBI again?"

"Exactly." I ran my fingers along the church pew's smooth wood, breathing deep and taking in the subtle scent of beeswax and lemon polish. I wasn't ready to tell them about Shane. Not quite yet. "I'll get back to the FBI part in a minute."

Kala came up to stand behind Tuck. "There's more?"

I nodded. "After I left St. Albans, I stopped at the café to talk with Pinky, and I swear she knows more about what's going on than God. Frank and Mom weren't the only ones having an affair. Nina's hooking up with Graham, or at least that's the rumor."

Kala's eyes grew so wide I thought they might pop out of their sockets. "What? Felix Graham and Nina? You're kidding me."

Tuck got up from the stool, shaking his head. "How do they even know each other?"

"On the way to Stowe the other day, did either of you notice the kids in the café parking lot dressed like ladybugs?"

Kala smiled. "Red tutus. Sweet as hell."

Tuck's voice lowered. "Let me take a wild guess. You think that's where Gracie goes for dance classes."

"Better. I'm certain of it. I'm also certain that's where Nina met Graham, assuming the rumors about them being a couple are true." I bit my lip, holding back the part I'd dreaded. I pushed up from the bench and paced to the sales counter. Finally, I turned back to look at them both. "Remember I mentioned the FBI?"

Worry lines fanned outward from the corners of Tuck's eyes. "You said they showed up when Martina's shop was robbed."

"I had a run-in with them too, sort of. Someone was tailing me, but I turned the table on them."

Tuck gawked at me. "The FBI?"

"Not exactly. It was Shane. Seems he's not a probation officer anymore." I looked down at the counter, embarrassed and distressed. Even without Shane saying anything, it should have occurred to me he might have a different job. I'd been ready to jump in bed with him, but not ready to ask questions. I raised my chin and looked at them. "Seems Shane's a state police detective."

"Whoa," Kala said. Then she shrugged. "At least it explains his walk on the dark side of the internet—probably undercover work, investigating."

"I imagine so . . ." I made my way behind the sales counter, then rested my hands on its surface as I divulged the entire conversation I'd had with Shane—about how he was working with the FBI Art Crime Team, and that I'd told him the

Bouchard collection was missing and that we suspected someone was planting evidence against us online.

Tuck came over to the end of the counter. He opened his arms wide, offering a hug. "I'm sorry, kiddo. That must have been a shock."

I went to him, squeezed my eyes shut, and leaned my head against his shoulder as he hugged me close. "Everything feels so unreal."

"It sounds scary real to me," Kala said. Then her voice lifted. "I came across something super interesting while you were gone. It totally ties in with what you just told us. I'd say it's vital."

I slipped from Tuck's hug. "Really? What is it?"

"How about Graham, Frank Bouchard, and your neighbor Rene St. Marie?"

"You found a connection between all three of them?" I couldn't believe it. "Pinky said she saw Graham riding around with Frank in his Corvette. I was about to tell you."

"They're all members of the Vermont Chamber of Commerce," Kala said. "There are photos on the Chamber website of the three of them sitting together at a harvest dinner last November. Then some from February of just Graham and Frank at a Chamber art show in Stowe."

A sour taste crawled up my throat. "You're about to tell me that's where Mom met Frank, aren't you? That show has always been one of her favorites."

Tuck nodded. "There's a photo of your mom dancing with Frank. They were both on an awards committee."

I ran my hands over my head. *Mom.* Why did she have to get tangled up with Frank of all men? Why couldn't she see he was nothing but a lying scumbag?

"There is good news," Tuck said. "We can't find any evidence Rene St. Marie is involved with this. He's on the Vermont Chamber's board of directors, so it makes sense for him to know Graham and Frank." He hesitated. "We just thought you should know about it, since you mentioned seeing Rene and Graham together at the pub the other night."

I smiled. That was good, though not a surprise. Art and antiques weren't anything I'd known Rene to care about—other than buying them because it was something you did when you were rich. Real estate was his thing. "So, if we leave Rene out of the picture, then we're left with Graham cozying up to both Frank and Nina."

Tuck and Kala agreed with that possibility. We went on, comparing theories about how Frank, Graham, and Mom fit into the puzzle. We all saw the events unfolding in a similar way:

Graham was always on the lookout for art and antiques. If Frank had mentioned at a Chamber meeting that he was co-trustee of an estate along with his estranged wife, it would have grabbed Graham's attention. Even if Graham didn't realize Claude's decoys were *the* Bouchard collection, he would have wanted to get his hands on them. Frank meeting Mom could've been pure coincidence, or a bit of slippery finagling on Graham's part. Graham could've wanted Mom and Frank to date as part of setting her up to take the fall for the robbery, a scheme that included online impersonation. Unfortunately for Graham, the plan started to unravel when Mom took the plea agreement and went to prison sooner than expected. Then I stepped into Mom's shoes at the appraisal event, providing them with a new fall guy.

"It all sounds logical," Kala said. "But let me play devil's advocate. Why would Graham get tangled up in something illegal? Why not simply talk to Claude and buy the decoys?"

I frowned at Kala. With her darknet knowledge, it seemed like this was something she'd already know. "Claude technically owns the decoys, but if Graham could cut him out of the picture, there'd be a bigger pot for everyone who was left. On top of that, if Graham sold the collection on the black market himself, there'd be no easy way for Frank or Nina to find out how much he'd sold it for. Graham could hand Frank or Nina a pile of cash and claim he'd taken only the commission he'd agreed to. In reality he could skim a million off the top and they'd never know."

"That still doesn't answer my question. No matter what the plan was—whether it was Graham convincing Nina to commit insurance fraud or Frank straight-out stealing the decoys and handing them over to Graham to sell on the black market—it's still illegal. Why would Graham risk that?"

Tuck's gaze went icy. "It wouldn't be the first time Graham did something shady."

I shuddered. I knew Tuck didn't have proof of what he was saying, but I also knew he firmly believed Graham was the one who talked Mom into forging the signature on the replica Parrish painting.

Kala grinned as if satisfied. "So Graham's just got a crooked streak. Makes sense, especially with Shane saying organized crime might be involved."

The assassinated thief in Stanstead passed through my head. "That possibility is something we can't afford to forget.

When we first started this, I knew there were risks. Frankly, I was mostly worried we'd end up in jail."

"Are you afraid someone might try to kill us?" Kala asked.

I looked at the dental cabinet they'd sold, once beautiful, now a piece of nothing thanks to a previous owner's abuse. "I think we need to find the collection fast, before something happens to it or us. So far all we have is speculation backed by a few photos. We need proof."

Tuck walked closer to me and rested a hand on my arm. "What are you thinking?"

"Like it or not, we need to pay Graham a visit and find out if he's seeing Nina. Right now, their relationship is nothing more than barroom gossip. If we confront Graham and he is involved with her or any of this, his denial won't be subtle."

Tuck chuckled. "You can say that again. More like kicking a hornet's nest."

"When were you planning on talking to him?" Kala asked. "It's almost four o'clock. Won't his store be closing soon?" She paused. "You aren't thinking of going to his house, are you? Wouldn't a public place be safer?"

"I totally agree, public is our best bet. Besides, it's not like Graham would let us in if we showed up on his doorstep. If we wait until tomorrow and go to the shop, there'll be employees and customers around. Graham won't want to make a scene." I met her gaze. "I also think only Tuck and I should go. I need you to stay here and watch over command central."

"Sure, if that's what you want. Those people are also picking up the dental cabinet tomorrow, early afternoon."

"There's something else," I said. "It's more important now than ever that you keep looking for evidence against us online. It's impossible to counteract something if you don't know what's coming."

She saluted me. "Yes, boss."

"Don't just look for Scandal Mountain Antiques," I said. "See if there's anything specifically pointing at my mom—or me."

Chapter
Twenty-Eight

I t was the next morning and we were hiking across the parking lot toward Graham's store, Golden Stag Antiques & Gallery in Burlington, about an hour from our place. All the way there we'd been rehashing theories.

"Then why did Nina bring the decoy to the appraisal?" Tuck asked. "It wasn't like Graham knew for sure that you'd be there."

I fell silent as we walked past a group of people getting out of a BMW from Quebec. The parking lot was amazingly full, especially considering it was only a few minutes after ten. There were fancy cars from Connecticut and New York, a gray Ford Explorer from Massachusetts with two identical bikes in a rack—and, most importantly, a Mercedes SUV with the shop's golden stag logo on the door and "Graham" on its license plate.

I fiddled with the strap of my bag as I considered Tuck's question. I shrugged. "Maybe Nina decided to bring the plover without mentioning it to Graham ahead of time?"

"That's possible." He opened the Golden Stag's front door and held it to let me go first.

The light from dozens of chandeliers and Tiffany-style lamps brightened the shop's interior. I tingled from the nearness of all the amazing pieces: country furniture, folk art . . . My nose delighted in the scent of leather-bound books, old wood, and a spicy fragrance that emanated from a bowl of clove-studded oranges by the register. Graham might have been a self-aggrandizing jerk and perhaps played a role in Mom's situation, but he did have an amazing store.

"Janet, how are you?" Tuck said to a Miss Marple look-alike who was smiling at us from behind the front counter with powder-pink lips, upswept gray hair, and a high-collared blouse. "I was surprised not to see you at the garden club meeting last week."

"I was trapped here all day." Her gaze shifted onto me. "It was wonderful to see your segment on TV. You're as smart and photogenic as your mother."

Warmth spread across my face. I resisted the urge to wave off the compliment and got right to the point. "Does Graham happen to be in today? We wanted to speak with him."

"He's with a couple of book dealers right now. If you want to browse around the shop, I'll let you know when he's free."

Janet glanced toward where Graham's office lay beyond a partition made of antique stained-glass windows. By and large, the wall of old glass was hard to see through, but a wide strip of transparent panels down the middle allowed me to catch a glimpse of Graham half-sitting on his desk, talking to a middle-aged man and woman. Even from the back, the woman looked vaguely familiar.

Tuck nudged my elbow. "That's the couple from Boston who visited our shop yesterday."

I studied them again. The woman was fit and tall, dressed in a loose top over patterned bicycle shorts. A vibrant, cylindrical-shaped crossbody bag was slung over her shoulder. It was an unmissable bag, very trendy, with a turquoise strap and geometric stripes in pink and yellow set off by a black background. It came to me. "I saw her at Fisher's auction. She walked into the bathroom while I was talking to Pinky." I looked at Janet. "You said they're book dealers?"

She nodded. "Very much so. They're great friends of Graham's."

"Huh, interesting," I said. "The other night, Graham mentioned a client who might like to purchase some of Grandpa's books. I wonder if he meant them."

"That's likely. They purchase a lot from us."

Tuck frowned. "They didn't mention books when they stopped by our place."

She laughed. "You know dealers. You people are always being sneaky. Pretending to want one thing when it's really something else you're after."

She was right. It was an old, rather see-through trick. "You don't happen to know their names?"

Her lips puckered, holding back a smile. She leaned toward Tuck and stage-whispered, "Your niece is a slick one." Her voice hushed further. "I can't remember their names off the top of my head, but I'll ask later. I'd rather have you sell them your books directly than have Graham get a slice of the action. He's on my naughty list right now."

I smiled at that. "We'd appreciate it, but I don't want you to get in trouble."

"Pish posh. I've had enough of Graham. He made me miss garden club because he would've had to pay another employee overtime to cover for me." She sniffed. "He thinks I don't know what he's up to with all his games. No sick days. No paid holidays."

Tuck shook his head. "That's no way to keep a good employee."

On the other side of the glass partition, the couple were getting up from their chairs as if readying to leave. I stepped closer to the front counter. If Janet was more than willing to talk about her boss behind his back, maybe we could get our information without confronting Graham. "You said you saw the TV show with the appraisal. The woman I was talking to, the one with the plover, is she dating Graham?"

She thought for a second. "I don't remember what that woman looked like very well. But"—patches of bright red bloomed on her face. She bit down on her bottom lip and smiled devilishly—"I did get an eyeful of Graham's latest *friend* when I went to his house to deliver flowering baskets. He always orders petunias from the garden club fundraiser. He should have been expecting me . . ."

"And?" Tuck encouraged her to go on.

"It was last Thursday, right after supper. Almost dark. Graham didn't answer the door, so I tiptoed around the side of the house to leave the baskets on his terrace. He was in the hot tub—naked—with a woman."

"Thursday night?" I stood up straighter. Nina had told me she left Gracie with a babysitter and spent the night in the hospital with Claude. But it sounded like she might've bold-faced lied. I bent closer. "Are you sure?"

"It was Thursday, all right. Oh my gosh, I'll never forget it. They were fighting. More like she was screaming at Graham for being friends with her husband. Graham claimed he only knew the guy from the Chamber of Commerce."

Adrenaline pumped into my veins. *Thursday night. Chamber of Commerce.* This was way more than I'd ever dreamed of finding out.

She went on. "Graham's quite the bigwig in the state Chamber, you know." She glanced toward the glass partition, making sure Graham was staying put.

"But you didn't recognize the woman he was with?" Tuck asked.

"No. But I saw more of her than I wanted to. She kept screeching about Graham lying to her and cheating her. I have to give Graham credit, he stayed calm, just kept calling her sweetie and offering her Dom Perignon—horribly expensive stuff."

"I can't imagine Graham putting up with that," I said. "I would have thought he'd send her packing."

"I thought the same thing. Even if she was too drunk to drive, he could've called a taxi." The pink in her cheeks deepened. "After that, things started to go the other way—the sexy way. That's when I left, before someone saw me. With Graham, you never know who the woman might be, a customer, an employee, a married someone from the city council."

I took out my phone, fingers moving fast as I found the TV station's website and brought up a recording of the appraisal with Nina. "Now you've made me even more curious," I said, as if I were only after gossip. I held the phone out for her to see. "Is that the woman you saw in the hot tub?"

Janet giggled. "She didn't have clothes on. But, *yes.*"

"I thought it might be." I said it lightly, but my heart was racing with the news. Nina had definitely lied. She hadn't been at the hospital with Claude. She'd been with Graham, at least early in the evening.

Tuck chuckled. "It's lucky you didn't drop his hanging baskets right there and then."

"I almost did," she said. "I left them on the front porch, then put my car in neutral and coasted out of his driveway. I was so embarrassed."

I glanced toward the office. It seemed like Graham and the couple should have come out by now.

The office was empty.

"Where did they go?" I frantically scanned the shop, looking down the closest aisles and off toward the art gallery rooms, then in the opposite direction to the oriental rug area and to where cases full of crystal and silver shimmered.

Janet tsked. "That slippery eel. He must have gone out his private exit again. He does it all the time, leaving me alone to tend the shop without so much as a word."

I glared at the empty office. Had he noticed us waiting? Was that why he took off?

"How long do you think he'll be gone?" Tuck asked.

"It's hard to say with Graham. He could be gone an hour or all day. Then he has the gall to get upset with me when a customer makes an offer and I can't get hold of him for approval."

"What does Graham do? Take off to spend the afternoon with his women friends?" I asked, unable to hide my annoyance—though we had gotten an answer about Nina, which was a relief.

Janet laughed. "In this case, probably a business lunch."

Tuck touched my elbow again. "The couple was supposed to go back to our store around noontime. They have a cabinet to pick up."

"Oh, that's right." I'd totally forgotten. My thought shifted from Graham to the book dealers. I couldn't help wondering if they'd bring up Grandpa's library to Kala and try to score not-for-sale books while Tuck and I were away. "We should probably get back home, then."

Tuck smiled a Janet. "Speaking of hanging flower baskets. I have some stunning lipstick vines. I'd be happy to give you one."

"I'd love that. I've always wanted one," she said, glowing.

"I'll drop a pot off at your house." He winked. "I'll phone first, so I don't catch you *au naturel.*"

"Ha, ha . . . Don't worry. If I knew you were coming, I'd put on my best negligee."

* * *

A few moments later, we were out of the shop and in the parking lot. The place was still crowded with cars, but the Golden Stag Mercedes and the Ford Explorer with Massachusetts plates were both gone. Made sense—Graham and the couple from Boston, most likely.

"Janet certainly got an eye and an earful," Tuck said.

I laughed. "That must have been priceless. I'm also willing to bet Graham was a lot angrier with Nina than he let on. I'm guessing he had a reason not to throw her out of his house."

"Like a million dollars' worth of decoy-shaped reasons?"

"Exactly. If Nina was with him, she wasn't at the farm. Which left it open for someone else—like Frank—to leave his Corvette at the café, hop in a different vehicle and take the collection while the farm was unoccupied."

"Does that mean you think there was someone else driving a second vehicle?"

I nodded. "It's the only thing that makes logistical sense. If Frank had done it on his own, he'd have had to jockey two vehicles to and from the café—which we know was the case since the Corvette was in the parking lot all night and then gone in the morning. Plus, there's the robbery itself. It wasn't quick or easy to carry that many decoys down from the attic and out to a vehicle. It would've taken a ton of trips."

"I couldn't have done it on my own," Tuck said.

I rubbed the back of my neck, piecing together what we'd learned. "So we're thinking Graham manipulated Nina into assuming they were going to steal the decoys as a team, collect the insurance money, then sell them on the black market and sail off into the sunset together several million dollars richer. But Graham double-crossed her and had Frank take the collection before she got the chance."

Tuck chuckled. "I don't know as I blame Graham for not wanting to get in any deeper with Nina." He hesitated for a heartbeat. "The question is—assuming we're right—who was driving the second vehicle, since we know for a fact that Graham was keeping Nina busy in his hot tub?"

"Mudder?" I suggested.

"I don't know. Him or maybe someone else—like the person who's currently storing the decoys, perhaps." Tuck stopped talking as we reached the van.

Once we got in, I turned toward him and hardened my voice, leaving no room for argument. "We're finally making headway and we don't have any time to spare. I think we need to keep the ball rolling, but I'm not comfortable with Kala being alone when those people from Boston pick up the cabinet."

"Me neither," he said. "I didn't get a weasel vibe off them yesterday, but them not mentioning books when it's their specialty doesn't sit right with me. We need to get home before they arrive."

I braced myself. He wasn't going to like my next suggestion. "Once I drop you off, I'm going to head to the farm, talk to Claude, and see what he remembers about Thursday night. I'll ask him straight out who he thinks took the collection."

Tuck narrowed his eyes. "I'm not sure I like that. I'm willing to bet Nina's tried to convince him you stole the decoys. Even if she suspected Frank did it, the pleasure of attempting to destroy you and things your mom cared about while keeping her own reputation intact might be as sweet to Nina as a million dollars."

"I totally agree, but that doesn't mean Claude believed her. He's not a pushover. He's smart as they come. Do you remember Bucky Sanders—tobacco juice–stained beard, the sharpest dealer in Vermont? That's who Claude reminds me of."

Tuck laughed, then smiled wistfully. "Who could forget Bucky, swaggering into auctions in those torn snowmobile suits, looking like he just crawled out from under a rock? Aren't many dealers as brilliant as old Bucky was."

"I think Claude knows more than he's letting on," I said.

"You're probably right about that."

Still thinking about Claude and Bucky, I shoved the key in the ignition. I glanced in my rearview to check before backing out of the parking place—

A plastic bag was taped to our back window.

I stared in confusion at what looked like a bread bag with something the size and shape of a grapefruit inside it. The grapefruit thing had a human face. In a plastic bag.

The murdered thief jolted into my mind. *His head was tightly covered by a clear bag. Spittle and vapor from his dying breaths coated the plastic, obscuring all but his death-skimmed and bulging eyes. Bruises and a yellow nylon cord ringed his neck.*

I swiveled around to get a better look. "Is that a doll?"

Tuck glanced over his shoulder at the window. Then he reached for his door latch. "Wait here. I'll get it."

The worry in his voice didn't soothe my rising fear. A head. In a bag. Staring blindly. It wasn't a good luck troll, that was for sure.

My pulse banged in my chest as Tuck ripped the bag off the window. I wanted him back in the van. Back behind a locked door where it was safe. Trash didn't just blow in from nowhere and tape itself to a window. Someone had done this. On purpose. They knew who we were. What we drove.

Tuck climbed back in. He locked his door, then handed the bag to me. "This is more than creepy. Are you thinking the same thing I am? Stanstead?"

I nodded. There wasn't a whole doll inside the bag. Just a head. Blue eyes. Two buck teeth. Curly hair. Midcentury might not have been my jam like it was for Kala, but I knew who this was.

"There wasn't a note with it," Tuck said.

"We don't need one. It's a Chatty Cathy head. I think between that and the plastic bag, they're getting their point across. People who talk too much die."

"We need to show this to the police."

I looked at the head, blank eyes staring back at me. "It also means we're getting close enough to the truth to worry someone."

"Like me?" he said. "Organized crime plus threats equals call Shane in my book."

"I'm with you," I said, and I was, to a degree. I pulled out my phone, took a photo and added a short explanation, then hit send.

Tuck glowered. "That's not what I meant by 'call' Shane."

I started the van and backed out of the parking space. "I'm not waiting around here for the police. We need to get home. Kala's there by herself."

He studied me for a moment. "And after that?"

I kept my gaze straight ahead, trained on the traffic. "Like I said, we can't afford to wait."

Chapter
Twenty-Nine

When we got home, the couple from Boston thankfully still hadn't appeared at the shop to pick up the dental cabinet. I had faith Tuck and Kala could handle them. I also suspected the doll was essentially a warning shot over our heads. Whoever had left it wasn't going to attempt anything worse, at least not until they knew if they'd scared us into backing off or not. Still, this had definitely upped the stakes, and only made the need to talk to Claude more pressing.

With that in mind, I left the house and headed for the Bouchards'. I took a roundabout route and kept an eye on my rearview mirror. No one was going to get away with following me this time. I was done making it easy for anyone—Shane, the police, organized crime bosses, thieves . . . Tuck and Kala might not have liked the idea of my going alone, but they agreed with my reasoning.

The thing was, this afternoon was the Memorial Day celebration at the café. The parade was going on right now. Scandal Mountain's fire and police departments would be in it, the school bands, lots of other groups, and most importantly—as far as my plan was concerned—the kids from the dance class, including Gracie. After the parade, all participating kids and their parents would be treated to free barbecue, followed by front-row seats at the parade award ceremony where trophies would be handed out for best float, best marching band . . . and best dance group. Next came live music and fireworks. Claude was still recovering from his trip to the hospital. I couldn't see him spending hours running around, playing the role of supervising parent. Which left Nina stuck at the celebration at least until the award ceremony was over.

As I sped along, I rehearsed the questions I was going to ask. I'd apologize and declare my innocence first, of course. Mostly I needed to get right to what he remembered from the night of the robbery. Was Nina at the hospital at all? When did she leave? Did she come back? Who did he think committed the robbery? Frank was currently at the top of my suspect list, but it didn't seem smart to give anyone a free pass just yet.

I took an extra-long look in the rearview as I went by the Quebec *frontière* sign, then turned onto the road to the Bouchards'. Not a soul behind me. Still, it wasn't until I'd turned into the farm's driveway and was out of sight of the road that I dared to let my guard down. No more worries about people following. Now it was just me and Claude. Sure, Mudder might be around, but he didn't worry me much. He'd always been easy to deal with.

The van thumped through the potholes and over the makeshift bridge. I watched closely for the pig. The last thing I needed was to run into it and put the van out of commission.

The farmhouse and yard came into view.

In the deep shade of the maples, the dumpster sat with the lid closed. No one was near it or hanging out on the porch. A large padlock secured the front door. There wasn't a car or truck to be seen.

A sinking feeling unfolded in my chest. It didn't look like anyone was home.

I shook my head, refusing to believe it. I couldn't think of another way or time to catch up with Claude alone, and I couldn't spend the whole afternoon making round trips out here for nothing. I eyed where the driveway looped around to the rear of the house. That was it. Claude's truck was simply out back. It had to be.

I turned the van around and parked in front of the house as I'd done in the past, better to act like everything was normal, as well as make sure I could get out in a hurry if things went sideways.

I shut off the van, lowered the window and listened for a second. A wood thrush called from the maples. Crickets chimed in the rising heat. There weren't any human sounds, no distant drone of a radio or TV, no buzz of a chainsaw . . . However, I didn't sense Claude's absence as acutely as I had when he'd been taken to the hospital.

Gathering my nerve, I got out and strode up the rest of the driveway toward the rear of the house, arms swinging, pretending I was as confident as could be. But with each step it grew harder and harder to convince myself that Claude was home. It became impossible when I rounded the last corner and saw his truck wasn't there.

I cursed under my breath. Why couldn't he have just been home?

The little voice in the back of my mind whispered, *Claude's truck might not have been ready to pick up from the garage like he'd thought at the hospital. Nina could've left him here without wheels.*

I glanced up at the back of the house, hoping to spot him looking out.

The attic window that had provided light while we'd worked on the appraisal was dark, totally blackened by shadow. I lowered my gaze to the second-floor bathroom where I'd faked a pee before going to see the painting in Claude's room. I'd been so full of hope back then.

I clenched my teeth. *No*, I couldn't give up this easy. There was still a chance he was here. Even if he wasn't, if I could get inside the house, there was a chance I might find something important that I'd overlooked before.

Determination pounded inside me as I hurried onto the back porch. I edged between the piles of firewood and to the kitchen door. It was padlocked shut. So much for my theory that Claude might still be home.

My gaze went to his barn coat, hanging on the back of the chair like before. I rushed to it and shoved my hands in its pockets, searching for the key ring. Nothing. What had I expected? Nina had told me they didn't normally stash them there.

I turned on my heel and hurried off the back porch, circling toward the front of the house. There had to be a way to get inside.

Folding my arms across my chest, I glanced past the dumpster and down toward where the driveway ran alongside the black alder swamp. My thoughts rushed back to the first time I'd driven in and seen the farm. Mudder had been tossing things in the dumpster. When we parked and started for the house, he'd shambled away and vanished down the bulkhead, like a woodchuck fleeing into his hole.

The bulkhead! That was it. Another possible way in.

Heart in my throat, I hurried beyond the front porch and the rusty freezer to the equally rusty bulkhead—

I blinked and blinked again.

The bulkhead doors were closed, but the hasp that would have held the padlock was open, and the lock itself lay on the ground nearby, tossed aside as if someone had been in the cellar but left in such a hurry they'd forgotten to secure it.

The sense of hopelessness that had been closing in around me released its grip. The day I'd discovered the decoys missing, it never occurred to me to search the cellar for evidence or even for the birds themselves.

Nerves pinged in my stomach as I sprinted forward and grabbed hold of the bulkhead door's handle. The heavy door groaned as I heaved it open. I took out my phone, turned on the flashlight app and fanned the beam downward. The light's muted brightness illuminated the worn cellar stairs, but it didn't reach into the darkness beyond.

One careful step at a time, I worked my way downward. The musty odor of dirt and moist cardboard surrounded me. Darkness closed in. I covered my nose with my empty hand, blocking the mildew stench and the encroaching reek of cat urine.

At the bottom, I fanned the light into the darkness. On my left was the outline of a workbench, tools hanging above and below it. A large kitchen knife lay beside a whetstone. Rakes, shovels, and a hoe leaned against a wall. A stack of gas cans materialized under the watery flood of my light.

To my right, early canning jars packed the shelves of a wooden cupboard, a seriously old Quebec piece with traces of original paint. Under normal circumstances, it was the sort of antique I'd have died to get my hands on—though dying in any form wasn't currently on my to-do list.

I wiped my sweaty palms on my jeans. I needed to relax. Focus.

Moving methodically, I made my way toward the workbench. One step, then another. I fanned the flashlight beam slowly, deeper into the cellar. The outline of a pile of broken chairs. A wheelbarrow—

Thump! Thump!

I swung toward the sound, heart racing.

It was the noise of a sump pump starting up. I let my breath out. That's all it had been. A normal basement sound. Nothing to worry about.

My intuition whispered, *Just a little farther. Keep going.*

I crept past a hip-high bin filled with shriveled potatoes, so old they were hard to recognize. A wooden barrel. Some half-rotted firewood . . . The gray outline of a staircase appeared ahead. When Tuck and I had chased the cat in the kitchen, I'd noticed a padlocked door. I thought it had been a door to the cellar. Most likely that was where these steps led to.

Swallowing hard, I moved closer. I swept the light up the wooden steps. At the top, it shimmered off a doorknob. Should I check to see if it was still locked?

I studied the steps again. They weren't just coated with dirt and cobwebs. Some of the treads were missing, others looked punky.

I turned away. *No*, the last thing I needed was to break a leg and end up down here screaming until someone—like Nina—came and found me.

My hand shook as I pointed the light into the darkness beyond the staircase. It washed along the house's foundation wall, glinting as it passed over a half-window, too coated with spiderwebs and grime to let light in from the outdoors.

The beam reflected off something white, as tall and wide as two high school lockers hitched together. I fanned the light over it again. An old metal cabinet, 1960s. Kala would have loved it. My brain engaged. It was white. Not dirty. Someone had cleaned it off or used it a lot, and recently.

Yes! I bit my tongue to keep from shouting out loud.

I hurried toward it as fast as I dared, sweeping the floor with my light.

I yanked on the cabinet's latch. Locked tight.

Excitement pushed into my blood. Locked was good. Locked meant something special was inside. This was it. But how to get it open?

My brain flashed back. The wardrobe in the attic. Kala had picked the lock, but doing it had proved to be unnecessary.

I went up on my tiptoes, feeling along the top edge of the cabinet. My fingers found something. Bingo. The keys!

Barely daring to breathe, I pulled them down. They were on a chainsaw-shaped fob, like Claude's key ring. But this ring only held a single small key. Old. Steel.

I slid the key into the cabinet's lock. A perfect fit.

I turned the key. A click rang out and the lock released. I yanked the door open.

The Art of the Decoy

Empty preserve jars lined the top shelves. Shoe boxes filled with gladiola bulbs sat on a lower one, no doubt saved from last year. Balls of twine. Scissors. Garden stakes.

No decoys. Not even anything that hinted at them.

Damn it. I slammed the cupboard door. The clang reverberated through the darkness, ricocheted off the foundation walls.

What was I thinking? The decoys weren't down here. I was fooling myself and wasting time.

I turned to leave. This was useless. I had to get out of here. *Now*, before someone came home—

The blinding brightness of a flashlight hit my eyes.

Chapter Thirty

The interrogation room was stark white. Concrete block walls. The stench of stale sweat and disinfectant hung in the air. I'd sat in a similar room the day I was arrested for selling stolen property. It was one place I'd sworn never to end up in again. But here I was, and this time I was going to jail for sure. Unlawful trespass. A charge I couldn't deny.

A sick feeling tumbled in my stomach. That wasn't the worst of it. This wasn't just about me being found in someone else's cellar. There was the missing Bouchard collection. There were the other robberies. The murder. And I still didn't know if there was manufactured evidence out there on the internet, waiting to be discovered. I certainly didn't know how long— months, years—it might take the FBI and their cyber team to untangle everything to their satisfaction, or if they'd ever reach that point.

I bent forward, elbows on the table, head in my hands. Tears stung my eyes as the events of the last few hours replayed in my mind, cliché as scenes from a B movie. The blaze of the sheriff's flashlight. His voice echoing across the cellar.

"Franklin County sheriff! Put your hands up!"

I'd frozen, unable to move. Then a million excuses for being in the cellar had spilled from my mouth, "I wasn't doing anything wrong. I didn't break in. I was looking for Claude . . ."

The sheriff had clamped handcuffs on my wrists and marched me to the cruiser, immune to my pleading. "Watch your head," he'd said, shoving me inside.

I'd messed up everything. Everyone in the antiques and art world would assume I was a criminal, even if I got out from under this. Everyone in town would, too. We wouldn't be able to buy or sell anything. We'd lose the business my grandparents had worked so hard to build. Kala would lose her job. We'd lose our home.

The real thieves would laugh at my stupidity. They'd literally get away with millions. I could end up in a cell next to Mom. Matching mother and daughter prison jumpsuits, not at all the life I'd envisioned and one that would make Nina gloat for sure.

I tightened my hands into fists. *No, damn it!* I couldn't—I wouldn't give up this easy. My grandparents would've told me when things looked the bleakest, it was time to knuckle down and work harder. Tuck would've said the same thing.

Unlocking my feet from around the legs of the chair, I planted them on the floor in front of me. I had to keep fighting. No mother-daughter jumpsuits in my future.

I drummed on the edge of the table, thinking. How was I going to wiggle out of this? There had to be a way. For one thing, how had the sheriff known I was at the farm, let alone in the cellar? I'd made sure no one had followed me.

The electronic buzz of a lock opening vibrated from the interrogation room door. The sheriff paraded in with a balding blond man in a navy blue suit and tie. Behind them was Shane. His face wore a cool professional expression, somberness unnervingly devoid of any bite of anger or chill of contempt. His eyes held no hint of the kindness they'd radiated that first day in his probation office. No hint of familiarity. No glimmer of understanding.

Cold sweat iced my back. I glanced at his forearms, hoping to buoy myself with the furtive pleasure that they'd never failed to give me.

His shirt sleeves were rolled down, buttoned around his wrists. Only the edge of his vintage Omega wristwatch was visible.

I shivered as the fight went out of my spine. He wasn't here to support me. He was on their side. Any evidence I'd given him could be used against me.

The guy in the suit sat down in the chair at one end of the table. He set a folder in front of him. "I'm Senior Special Agent Latimore with the FBI. I believe you are familiar with Detective Payton and Sheriff Gage."

Shane took the chair at the other end of the table, while the sheriff went to stand at attention near the door, chest out, lips pressed into a smug smile. I shuddered. The sheriff reminded me uncomfortably of Graham, standing all puffed out at the back of an auction, certain he'd spotted a valuable piece all the other dealers had overlooked, certain he'd own it before the end of the day.

I looked at Latimore, lowered my eyes submissively, and nodded. *Yes,* I knew both Shane and the sheriff. It seemed wiser to nod than to say anything aloud. I needed to stay silent. Well, actually I needed to request a lawyer and then stay silent. I needed to call Tuck too.

"Would you like something to drink? Water? Coffee?" Latimore asked.

"Water would be great, thank you," I said stupidly. That's all it took for the same verbal diarrhea that I'd given the sheriff to start spewing out again. "I wasn't doing anything wrong. I went there to see Jean-Claude—"

Agent Latimore cut me off. "I'm not sure you realize how much trouble you're in, Ms. Brown."

"I—do. It's just—" I glanced at Shane. His face went taut, a welcome hint of recognition that I took as a warning to shut my mouth. Except I currently wasn't sure how I felt toward Shane, or if I trusted his opinion, for that matter.

Latimore opened the file. "Did you have permission to be in Jean-Claude Bouchard's home?"

"Ah—" I looked at Shane, then back at Latimore. I knew not to answer that question. Still, they were the experts and I had information that might help them—and me. "I know I have a right to stay silent. But I want to cooperate. I want to tell you what I know."

"We appreciate that," Latimore said.

I gulped a breath. "Detective Payton told you about the missing decoys, that there might be manufactured evidence, and that I didn't take them, right?" No one answered, so I continued, talking faster. "I went to the farm to see Claude, honest." I swiveled, glancing toward the sheriff. "How did you know I was there?"

Latimore rested a hand on his file. "Sheriff Gage was watching the farm for suspicious activity as part of several ongoing investigations."

I felt myself pale. I must have driven right past his cruiser, hidden somewhere near the farm. Shane had warned me to stay clear of the Bouchards'. He'd tried to protect me. My voice faltered. "I didn't break in. The bulkhead door wasn't locked."

"What did you hope to gain by going into the basement?" Latimore pressed.

"Um—" I stalled. I didn't want to lie, but I didn't want to incriminate myself any more than I already had.

His voice deepened. "Are the missing decoys in the basement? Did you go back to collect them?"

Heat blazed across my cheeks. "No. I told you, I went there to talk to Claude. No one was home, but I thought there might be something important in the cellar." I looked at Shane. "Police go with their gut feelings sometimes, don't they?"

"Did you find the decoys?" Latimer said, drawing my attention back to him.

"No, but—" I swallowed dryly. Hadn't they offered to get me some water? "I did an appraisal of the collection. I have a copy. I documented everything. I know what pieces the Bouchards originally had and what's missing. I even took photos of wide tire tracks at their farm that might belong to the thief's vehicle. I got photos of spare tires in Frank Bouchard's garage. They're off his restored Corvette. At one point, I thought they'd match the tracks at the farm." I took a breath, then continued. "Earlier today, someone taped a doll's head in a plastic bag onto my van window. I have photos of it too." I met Latimore's eyes. "I'm sorry. I know this sounds confusing. Please, just give me back my phone and I'll show you the photos. They'll make it easier to explain."

Latimore glanced at the sheriff. Without a word, the sheriff left the room, I assumed to get the phone he'd taken from me at the farm. It felt like a remote possibility, but maybe if I was helpful enough, then Latimore would let me go.

I opened my mouth again, speaking louder and faster, if that was possible. "At first, I thought Nina took the decoys as part of an insurance fraud scheme. Then I started thinking Frank stole them. He's slippery and out for what he can get."

I pressed my lips together. At this point, I wasn't about to mention Mom's relationship with Frank and Nina's possible revenge motive if I could avoid it. Sure, I'd told Shane in the Wise Dollar parking lot, but maybe he hadn't spilled everything to the FBI. It only made my family look more complicit in the thefts.

Latimore folded his hands on the table. "Go on, please."

"Supposedly, Claude overdosed the afternoon before the robbery. He claims someone poisoned him. Nina claimed she spent that night at the hospital, but she was actually with Felix Graham, at least early on. She had a fight with him, about him hiding the fact he was friends with Frank, her estranged husband. One of Graham's employees witnessed the whole thing. Don't you think it's suspicious that the night Claude got sick and went to the hospital, his farm-house was robbed?"

I raised a hand, to let them know I wasn't done. "That wasn't the only odd thing that happened. Pinkney Woods had the plates stolen off her car. They reappeared a few hours later. Scandal Mountain police know all about that. Pinky also told me Frank Bouchard's Corvette spent that whole night in the Jumping Café's parking lot—that's what makes me now think the wide tire tracks at the farm came from a different vehicle, despite the looks of the Corvette's spares."

Latimore sat back and stretched his legs out, eyeing me. Without flinching he asked, "When was the last time you were at the Canadian Museum of History?"

I stiffened. It was impossible to tell for sure if Latimore was accusing me of being involved in that robbery or not. My throat tightened. "About four years ago, as a tourist. I'm not a thief—or a murderer. I'm trying to help you."

Latimore sat up, gaze hard on mine. Voice forceful. "Then you should tell us everything you know about this as of yet unreported Bouchard robbery. From the beginning." His tone moderated. "First, let's go over again what we're going to see on your phone."

"Sure," I said. It didn't seem like he could possibly believe that a thief would photograph evidence of their own crime. Except the photos weren't the only thing on my phone. If the police or the FBI's nerds got hold of it, they'd find personal texts and emails connecting me and Shane. Maybe it was a bad idea to let Latimore look at the phone. If I refused, would they need a search warrant? Then again, I'd sent photos of the terrifying doll's head to Shane's personal account. He might have immediately shown those to Latimore, and perhaps divulged our relationship already. "Ah—" I stalled for a second. "Like I said, it's probably better if I explain while I show them to you."

Shane leaned forward, his voice hushed as he changed the subject. "Can you tell us anything about the car you saw pull into Frank Bourchard's chalet last Saturday. Who was driving it? Did you notice anything different when you went into the house after they'd been there?"

I nodded, only after realizing with that simple bob that I'd confessed to illegally entering Frank's house as well—not once but twice. Still, it was probably wiser to follow Shane's prompts. I couldn't believe he didn't care about me at all, and it wasn't like anyone else could possibly be on my side.

"If I were you, I'd answer the detective's questions," Latimore said.

"The first time the door was open. We went inside because we wanted to make sure Frank was okay. The place was super clean, but that might not mean anything. The door was still open the second time," I said. "I didn't look around closely. There was nothing new or missing that I noticed. None of us got a good look at the people in the car. It was a gray SUV, or silvery gray, but you know that already. There was a bicycle rack on the back. I'm certain of that."

I stopped talking as the pieces of information I'd just given dovetailed with other details I knew.

"What is it?" Shane asked.

More pieces joined with the others, and I could only gape for a moment. Then all my thoughts came out in a rush. "I saw the same car yesterday in Burlington at Felix Graham's store, I'm almost a hundred percent sure. It was a silvery gray Ford Explorer. Massachusetts plates. It belongs to a couple. A man and a woman from Boston. Book dealers. They had a meeting with Graham. They were at our store yesterday and might be there right now to pick up a cabinet. They could've been the ones who taped the doll's head to the van. I saw the same woman at Fisher's auction—"

Latimore raised a hand. "Slow down. Did you notice anything else?"

I thought again. There had to be something solid that could connect Frank and Graham, and the couple in the Ford

Explorer, to the robbery at the farm—and perhaps to the other thefts as well.

"Oh, my God!" I said as the memory of the bicyclists I'd followed around Dead Man's Curve brought something else to mind. Not just what I'd seen and heard, but details from my research. I'd even wondered at the time how the seemingly incongruous works of art had tied in with the other stolen items. "At the Canadian Museum of History the robbers took a rug by Ozama Martin. *Le Velo Jaune—The Yellow Bicycle.* In Boston, someone stole an Ozama Martin piece entitled *The Great Race.* That's of bicycles too, isn't it?"

Latimore's eyes brightened and he leaned forward. "Go on."

"The Explorer from Massachusetts had a bike rack with two identical bikes on it. Do thieves sometimes keep souvenirs of their crimes—things they personally collect? There weren't any bicycle things taken at the Bouchards' that I know of. Still, that might not mean it wasn't the same people, right?"

As I looked from Shane to Latimore and back, the last of the somberness on Shane's face fell away. He nodded, acknowledging the bicycles were something vital, perhaps something the police and FBI hadn't realized, or a detail they hadn't released to the public.

Latimore cleared his throat. "Thank you, Ms. Brown. That'll be enough for now."

He looked away from me, as if my comment had made him uneasy. Had I come too close to the truth? Or perhaps I was close, but not perfectly on target?

I sat up even straighter as a strong possibility came into focus. "The actual thieves aren't bicycle fanatics, are they? The robberies—in Canada and Boston, even the Bouchard collection—were committed by people hired to get specific items. The people pulling the strings are the bicyclists. The masterminds are the couple from Boston with the Explorer, the people who were at Frank Bouchard's house, and Graham's and our stores, not to mention Fisher's auction. They're the ones affiliated with organized crime and black-market antiques and art."

I squeezed my eyes shut, letting my mind flip through details as I searched for a stronger link between the couple and the crimes, not flipping fast like the nightmare I'd had about the Canadian museum robbery, but slowly like the grainy, washed-out video of the Stanstead murder, panning inch by inch across a blur of what I'd seen: The SUV leaving Frank's house. The woman in the bathroom at Fisher's. Their car in Graham's parking lot. Two bicycles. His and hers, most likely. Them in Graham's office. My thoughts zeroed in on her. Tall, fit, bicycle shorts. A vibrant and cylindrical-shaped crossbody bag decorated with geometric stripes in pink and yellow set off by a black background. Its strap was flat and sturdy—and turquoise.

A sick feeling surged up from my stomach as another strap pushed into my mind. I pressed a hand against my stomach, almost unable to keep from vomiting. The robber's head was covered with a plastic bag. A yellow nylon cord wrapped his neck. But his wrists—

My eyes flashed open. I locked my gaze on Latimore's face.

"What color strap was around the wrists of the dead man in Stanstead? The video was washed out. It looked light blue, but it was really vibrant turquoise, wasn't it?"

He went still, as if afraid the slightest movement might confirm my thought.

I looked at Shane. His gaze was down, hidden from my probing eyes and question.

I wet my lips. "Both times I saw the woman, she was carrying a cylindrical crossbody bag with a turquoise strap. My friend Jimmy is an avid bicyclist. He has a similar bag. It's a handlebar bag for bikes, I'm sure of that now."

Latimore raised an eyebrow. "But you first saw the woman with her bag at Fisher's Auction House after the body was found in Stanstead, right?"

I nodded, then backtracked. "When I saw the Ford Explorer at Graham's store there were *two* identical bikes in the rack. The strap could have come off a second handlebar bag—*his* bag. He didn't have one with him at Graham's antique shop. I'm certain of that." I tasted bile at the back of my throat. "My friend Jimmy's handlebar bag has a nylon safety cord as well as the detachable strap, a cord like the one around the man's neck."

The door to the interrogation room opened and the sheriff returned with my phone in hand. Good timing for Latimore and Shane, who seemed eager to not address my suppositions about the cord and strap, and the possibility of the Boston couple being criminal masterminds behind a large string of theft-for-hire robberies.

More than anything, I was certain now the Bouchard collection theft was connected to the Massachusetts couple and the other robberies. Why else would the FBI have had the county sheriff's department stake out the Bouchard property? Why else would the FBI be questioning me?

The sheriff walked across the room to Latimore, gave him my phone, and whispered something in his ear. I only heard a quick mumble, but Shane's attention winged toward them as if he'd caught the gist. Then, for the briefest second, Shane glanced my way and smiled.

My pulse picked up. It looked like something good had happened. Something in my favor.

Latimore slid the phone across the table toward me. "You can forward those photos you mentioned to Detective Payton. I believe you have his email. If you did that right now, it would be helpful."

Latimore's movements were less starched, and his tone hinted at finality. Together they gave me the distinct impression he didn't expect me to give the phone back to him, and that would only happen if they were going to let me go. I also hadn't failed to notice he'd said it would be helpful if I forwarded the photos, rather than demanding I do it, a slick, subtle difference. Still, I didn't want to get my hopes up or rock the boat by asking what was happening. Instead, I did as he asked without another word. No reason not to. I wanted them to have the evidence. The more helpful I was, the better it would look if there was manufactured evidence out there somewhere.

Once that was done, I looked at Latimore. "Am I free to go?"

He got to his feet. "For now. We expect you to stay in the area. No leaving the state or country."

"Of course, I understand." I smiled at him. Then I thought of something I hadn't considered. "What about my van? Where is it?"

The sheriff spoke up. "Here in the impoundment lot. There's paperwork we need to go over in the front office. After that, we'll bring it around to the visitor parking area for you." He paused. "There's a gentleman waiting for you in the lobby."

"Angus Tuckerman?" I asked. Who else could it be?

"I believe that's his name," the sheriff said.

Every muscle in my body urged me to rocket for the door, but I pushed myself out of the chair slowly, so politely even Grandma would have been impressed. I also kept my rising tide of questions to myself. How had Tuck known I was here? Why were they letting me go?

The door buzzed as Latimore opened it. "Thank you for your cooperation, Ms. Brown. We truly appreciate it." He handed me one of his business cards. "If you think of anything else or have questions, feel free to call me anytime."

"Thanks," I said.

Latimore stayed behind in the room, while Shane and the sheriff walked out with me.

The sheriff moved ahead, striding down the concrete-walled hallway toward the front office.

Shane rested his hand on my shoulder and hushed his voice. "You have Claude to thank for this. He returned the sheriff's phone call and said you had permission to be on his property and in his home. You got lucky this time, Edie. No unlawful trespass charge—or anything else."

I had no doubt Shane's walking me out was preplanned, just as I believed Latimore had a reason to include him in the interrogation. But I also suspected Shane's giving me this information was his own doing, and I was very grateful to have the questions answered.

"Thanks for telling me," I said with a smile. "I am sorry. I should have listened to you about staying away from the Bouchards'."

"Let us do our job from here on out and everything will be fine."

I nodded, *yes*. I couldn't bring myself to lie to him out loud. The FBI and police were the experts, but I'd uncovered things they hadn't. I couldn't back off now. This wasn't just about saving my butt, the business, or our home. There were ruthless criminal masterminds getting away with murder and with hiring thieves to steal art, beautiful pieces like the Bouchard decoys, pieces that deserved to be cherished and treated with respect. They were reflections of history, of artists' souls and culture, worth more than being hidden away in top-secret storage vaults until things cooled down, worth more than being relegated to a black-market currency. Traded by organized crime for drugs, or for ego, or worse.

We went a few more steps in silence. Finally, Shane let out a heavy sigh. "You're not going to back off, are you?"

"Do you really want me to answer?"

He shook his head. Then, as we reached the front office, he swiveled and walked back the way we'd come.

Chapter
Thirty-One

Once I'd collected my bag in the front office and finished up with the sheriff, I found Tuck waiting in the lobby. Well, not exactly waiting in the traditional sense. More like he was giving a horticulture lecture.

He stood by a window with his back to the room, instructing a gray-haired woman who hung on his every word. Judging by the cleaning supplies nearby, I assumed she was a custodian. Another younger woman listened closely from a chair on the other side of the room.

"If you keep the other plants out of the hot sun and feed them regularly, they'll come back." Tuck plucked a bedraggled African violet from the windowsill. "This one? Honestly, I'd toss it. I'll drop off one of my latest hybrids for you later this week. A deep purple bloom with pink speckles. It's superb."

As I walked toward them, he turned to me and smiled. "There you are."

"Ready to go?" I asked.

"I bet not as much as you are."

"You can say that again." I hoisted the strap of my bag higher on my shoulder. A lot more time had passed since I'd been caught in the basement than I'd have preferred. It was late afternoon, almost suppertime already. Plus, a new host of questions had taken root in my head since I'd found out Tuck was here. Where was Kala? Alone at the house? Had the couple been there already? I was pretty sure I wasn't going to like the answers.

As I waited for Tuck to say goodbye to his new friends, a cramp pinched my neck. I massaged it to ease the ache. I swear Tuck drew postmenopausal women like auction signs drew dealers.

Finally, we were out the door.

The fresh air cooled my lungs, adding to my surging sense of determination and glorious freedom. Tuck draped an arm around my shoulder and snuggled me close. I leaned against him. Maybe this wasn't over, but at least I wasn't trapped in the interrogation room anymore.

"Where are you supposed to pick up your van?" he asked.

I gestured to a closed gate in the chain-link fence that surrounded the impoundment lot, just beyond where his Suburban waited in the visitor parking area. "Someone's supposed to bring it out to me."

Tuck chuckled. "Maybe it'll be freshly washed and waxed."

"That would be nice," I said. I was grateful that he was attempting to lighten the mood instead of jumping down my throat about trespassing. Going into the cellar had been a stupid move, but I didn't totally regret it. At least I'd learned one thing: the decoys weren't there.

We crossed the short distance to the gate, then I turned to him. "How did you know I was here, anyway? I never got around to asking for a phone call."

"That guy of yours is a good one," he said.

"Shane? He called you?" I let the whole "your guy" thing go over my head.

"He phoned the house. Kala talked to him."

"Where is Kala?" I asked, concerned. "You didn't leave her at home alone, did you?"

He laughed. "Hold your horses. Don't worry." He glanced toward the Suburban.

As I followed his gaze, the car's door opened, and Kala hopped out.

"Hey, jailbird," she called to me as she jogged over.

"I was worried about you. Did the couple show up? What happened?" I asked.

She snorted and waved the question off. "You were right. They were after your grandfather's books. Tuck told them they were already sold, the whole enchilada."

Tuck interrupted. "They scared the bejesus out of me. Too nice, like *extremely* so. After they left, Kala and I tossed around theories about them being with Graham and the doll's head. We came up with some pretty unsettling ideas."

"Well, whatever you came up with, I can guarantee you it's worse . . ."

As we walked toward the impoundment lot gate, I told them what I'd come up with in the interrogation room. About the couple from Boston being the masterminds behind all the robberies and affiliated with organized crime. "It's like a pyramid scheme," I clarified, "with crime bosses and the couple at the top, then Graham, then the actual thieves who don't know who's really pulling the strings. I'm betting the couple and Graham made sure there aren't any links or evidence that leads back to them, at least nothing that will hold up in court. The local thieves or someone they've framed will take the fall for the robberies, like us."

"Framed—or murdered," Kala said.

I nodded, then told them about the woman's handlebar bag, how the strap and cord matched the ones in the video of the assassinated thief. "They couldn't have come off her bag," I clarified. "But there were two identical bikes on the SUV. His and hers. It's quite possible he has a bag too."

"Whoa." Kala shuddered. "That's seriously incriminating."

"Especially if the FBI locates his bag and its cord and strap are missing," I said.

Tuck took me by the arm, pulling me close against his side as we walked. "I wish I could ask you to let this drop. But I know you, Edie. You'd just do it anyway." His voice quieted, barely above a whisper. "And—for your information—I'm not planning on letting you out of my sight from here on out."

I rested my head against this shoulder. "Actually, that's a huge relief. You're right, I don't want to back off, but that doesn't mean I'm not terrified."

Kala spoke up. "I have some good . . . Well, more like strange news. The imposter account's gone, totally scrubbed. And there's no other evidence against any of us online, and I looked deep."

"Are you sure?" I asked. "I thought the internet was forever."

"Usually. Depends on, you know, *skills*. It also makes perfect sense in light of what you just said about people making sure there aren't links or evidence leading back to them."

"You mean Graham and/or the Boston couple created the imposter?"

"Could be, or they hired someone. Maybe from another country," she said.

Tuck let me go. "There's one thing I don't understand. Are you thinking, with this being a pyramid-type scheme, that Frank was only dealing with Graham and didn't know the couple since they're high up in the organization? They were at his chalet."

"That doesn't mean anything," Kala said. "The couple could've been at his place searching for the decoys. Maybe Frank didn't hand over the collection to Graham or leave it off where or when he was supposed to."

I shrugged. "All I know is that couple from Boston are ruthless. Who knows what they would have done if Frank had been home and withholding the collection?"

Tuck stopped walking as we reached the impoundment lot gate. "So you don't think Graham has the collection?"

"No, I don't. There's a reason the couple hasn't left town yet, and yesterday Graham and the pair looked cozy as anything. There's no bad blood between them. My bet? The two of them and Graham are doing the same thing we should be doing right now. They're trying to figure out where Frank and the collection are." I frowned at the gate. "Which would be a lot easier if they'd hurry up and bring the van out."

I was about to mention that the other dangling thread was Claude's poisoning, when I noticed the outline of a low, red car in the shadows on the far side of the lot. I couldn't see it clearly from where I stood.

"Is that Frank's Corvette?" I asked, as much to myself as to Tuck and Kala.

Walking faster, I covered the short distance to the fence. I bent close, squinting through the chain-link and into the shadows. It was a red Corvette all right. Older model. Meticulously restored. Vermont license plate. It was a mirror image of the one Frank had been driving the night he came to the house.

"If they have Frank's car, do you think they're holding him here?" Kala asked.

"The FBI agent who questioned me was the man in charge. Why would he spend time on me if they had Frank?"

Tuck scratched at his cheek, considering the question. "Maybe Frank wasn't willing to talk . . ."

As I stared at the Corvette, Tuck's voice faded into the background. We'd gone through Frank's chalet top to bottom, but the Corvette hadn't been there. We hadn't searched it.

Sweat rolled down my spine and the certainty that we'd found the decoys sent the neurons in the back of my head snapping and prickling. I looked back at Tuck and Kala. "What if Frank stole the decoys using a different vehicle, then transferred them into his Corvette and never took them out?"

Tuck stared incredulously. "You could be right."

"You think the FBI have the decoys in their possession?" Kala asked

The drone of a familiar engine sounded, and my van pulled into sight, approaching and then waiting as the gate automatically inched open.

I folded my arms across my chest and tapped my foot. It seemed like Shane would have mentioned if the FBI or police had found the collection. He knew that would end my search. He'd phoned the house and told Kala I was here. He'd warned me against going near the Bouchards'.

I eyed the open gate, the van now pulling through. There was plenty of room for me to sneak past and get inside. If I ran, I could get to the Corvette in less than a second. Logic said, if the decoys had been in the car, the FBI might have already removed them. Still, I couldn't shake the feeling they were there.

I glanced at Tuck. "I've got to know for sure."

He grabbed my shoulder. "No, you don't. What we're going to do is get your van. Then, if you want, we can go back inside the building and ask to speak with Shane."

"Listen to him, Edie," Kala said.

"All right," I grumbled. But I quivered with the need to run and look.

A young officer climbed out of the van. He nodded. "You're all set."

I pointed at the Corvette. "Is that Frank Bouchard's car?"

The officer glanced to see what I meant, then back at me. "I'm not at liberty to share that information."

"Edie," Tuck said warningly.

I looked directly at the officer. "Did you find anything inside it?"

His stance widened. He gestured at the van. "The keys are in the ignition. You're free to leave *now*."

"Can I just look inside the Corvette. It'll only take a second. It's important. I need to—"

The officer turned away, striding back through the open gate.

Tuck had me by the arm, gripping hard. "No."

I gritted my teeth and squeezed my eyes shut, trying to move past my belief that the collection was in the car. But images flashed in my mind: The decoys lined up across the table under the attic window: a drake mallard, a goldeneye hen, a pair of teal, the lone black duck, and shorebirds, including Gracie's ballerina bird and the plover from the appraisal event. Plus, the other pieces we'd found in the boxes and trunk. Beautiful folk art. Pieces of history. I couldn't let this go. I had to know if they were safe.

I opened my eyes, yanked out my phone, and called Shane.

"Hello? Edie?" he said apprehensively.

"Frank's Corvette. Why didn't you tell me it was here?" I asked.

"It wasn't something you needed to know. It's police business."

"Have you searched it? Do you have Frank in custody?"

"Go home, Edie. Please."

I lifted my chin, jaw fixed.

Behind me, Tuck groaned. "We're in for it now."

"I'm not leaving," I said to Shane. "I don't care if I have to stand here all night by this gate. The decoys are in that car. I know it."

"Trust me. If we'd found them, I'd have told you," he said.

I shifted the phone to my other ear. "The decoys *are* there." I hardened my tone. "Drug dealers—people in organized crime—build secret compartments into cars, right? Maybe Frank did the same thing. Maybe you did look, but it's not like sniffer dogs can detect wooden birds."

His voice edged toward anger. "Seriously, I need you to back off."

"No. Come out here and let me look in the Corvette—or I'm not leaving."

He huffed out a long breath. Then there was silence. I could picture him, pressing a hand against his forehead. "All right. Promise, after that, you'll go home."

"Deal," I said. It was only a half lie. I still had to talk to Claude, thank him and warn him about Nina, Frank, and the couple. I also wanted to find out if he had any idea who'd poisoned him. Then I'd go home. Maybe.

For what felt like forever, I paced between Tuck and Kala and the impoundment lot fence. Finally, Shane appeared on the other side of the gate with the officer who had brought out the van.

The stern look in Shane's eyes made me want to lower my gaze, but I kept my head held high. I couldn't explain how I knew the decoys were in the car if the FBI had missed them. Maybe there was a simple answer, like a wrecker service had just delivered the car and it hadn't been searched yet.

"Remember, you look and then you leave," Shane said. His voice held no room for compromise.

"You won't regret this," I said.

He shook his head. "I'm glad you're sure about that."

Shane motioned for us to follow, then led the way into the impoundment lot. Tuck, Kala, and I followed a step behind. The officer trailed by a few more yards, as if he would've preferred not to be involved.

As we walked, Tuck moved in close to me and whispered, "Claude was right about you, *petit carcajou*."

I smiled at him. "Tell me you'd have it any other way."

He rested a hand on the small of my back. "I wouldn't change a thing."

When we reached the Corvette, Shane took out a key and unlocked the car. He opened the passenger side door. "Go ahead and look. See for yourself. But don't touch anything."

I turned to Shane. On the phone, he hadn't answered my question about whether Frank was in custody or not. If he wasn't, then that raised another question. "Why is the Corvette here?"

"It was found abandoned near the Canadian border," he said, ice cold.

"Oh." I felt myself pale, taken aback by his tone—and I wasn't the only one, Tuck and Kala retreated a step, and the young officer flinched uncomfortably.

"Any more questions?" Shane asked. He jutted his chin at the car. "Are you going to look or not?"

I stepped forward, leaning partway into the Corvette.

My breath tangled in my throat, but my eyes saw nothing other than pristine black leather, black dashboard, black floormats. Every inch of the interior was dark, newly restored and as spotless as the counters in Frank's kitchen, cleaner than his carpet, less the trails of footprints where we'd walked. Was it possible I was mistaken? Maybe the decoys were here at one point, but now were gone?

I swiveled back to Shane. "How long has the car been here? When was it abandoned? Yesterday? Last Thursday?"

Shane rested back on his heels. "We have no idea when it was deserted. It was found a couple of hours ago." His voice lowered. "Are you done?"

"No," I rasped. My mind flailed, searching for answers. "I need to look in the trunk. This is an older model. It has a trunk, right?"

"I believe so." He glanced at the young officer.

"The CSI team already searched it," the officer snapped. "There isn't anything. No fingerprints. No stray hairs. Certainly not a carved duck."

Shane's attention came back to me. "Okay, we'll look in there. Then we're done."

I shadowed him to the rear of the car, my pulse pounding with hope. Sure, I had total faith that the CSI team had done a faultless job. Still, I was on fire with belief.

Shane opened the trunk, then stepped aside. "Go on, look."

Heart in my throat, I moved closer. Like the rest of the Corvette, the interior of the trunk was redone in black. It was also totally empty and spotless. In fact, the trunk looked like no one had ever used it, at least since the car had been restored.

"Satisfied?" Shane asked.

I shoved my hands in my pockets to keep from touching anything, then stepped even closer, studying the interior. I wasn't done yet, and I hadn't been kidding when I'd brought up drug smugglers retrofitting vehicles. That wasn't a TV show myth. It happened in real life—and this was about folk art that was worth as much as a multimillion-dollar haul of cocaine or heroin.

I felt a touch on my shoulder. Tuck. "I don't see anything," he said. He bent closer and whispered, "Trust your gut."

But it wasn't a hunch I needed right now. Unsubstantiated feelings weren't proof in the eyes of the law. I needed real evidence. I needed a decoy.

Behind me, the late afternoon sunshine fanned low across the impoundment lot, slicing past where Kala stood, and brightening the interior of the trunk with a flush of light.

I tilted my head, studying the space from a different angle, like it was a fine piece of porcelain and I was searching for imperfections without the benefit of touch or a blacklight.

Against the backdrop of solid black, I spotted something: a chip of wood the size of my baby fingernail, lying where the side panel met the floor, brightened by a streak of light.

My breath stalled. It was tiny, but I knew what it was in an instant.

I pointed at the chip and glanced over my shoulder at Shane. "You saw my appraisal on TV, right? Do you remember what I said about the plover's tail?"

He frowned, as if thinking back. He'd watched the show at least once, he'd told me that. He had to remember. He loved decoys.

Shane leaned forward, one hand resting on the edge of the trunk. When his gaze went to where I was pointing, his mouth went slack and words came out, almost mechanical, "You said there was a chip in the tail that had been broken out, then glued back in."

"That's the chip," I said. "It's exactly the right size and shape."

I felt the young officer come up behind me, bending forward to take a look. "I can't believe the team missed anything."

Tuck cleared his throat. "Opening and closing the trunk lid could have knocked it free from somewhere."

"It's awful tiny," Kala said. "I might have missed it."

I didn't care where the chip had been hiding or that it had been missed before. I needed to find a whole decoy, and nothing in the world could've convinced me that there wasn't one to be found. The prickles at the base of my skull said there was more here.

In a heartbeat, I saw the Corvette's trunk differently. Its shape was off. The interior was a touch too narrow for the width of the car. Also, a seam in the side panel closest to me was slightly wide and uneven. In fact, the more I looked at the side panel, the stranger the whole thing appeared—crude for a meticulously restored Corvette.

I scrunched forward and reached into the trunk. There had to be a way to remove the panel. If I wedged my fingernails into the seam, maybe I could yank it off.

No! I backed away from the car as if it were burning hot. As much as I longed to see what was behind the panel, Shane had said not to touch anything. I'd come too far to mess up now.

I met Shane's gaze. "The trunk's side panels are fake. I'm sure of it."

A gleam of eagerness sparked in his eyes. He nodded, then turned to the officer. "See who's still here from the CSI team. Tell them to bring their equipment. I'll call Latimore."

As FBI agents and police officers poured into the impoundment lot, Tuck, Kala, and I retreated to watch from a distance. The team set up video equipment and lighting. They put on hooded jumpsuits and gloves. They measured everything with painstaking precision, recording each step in detail.

As late afternoon slipped closer to sunset, I began to think they'd never get around to prying open the panel. Finally, an officer took out a screwdriver and wedged it into the seam.

Unable to hold back any longer, I rushed forward. My body tingled with anticipation as he wriggled the screwdriver and pushed down on it.

Pop! The panel came free, revealing a large, darkened compartment.

My legs trembled. I moved in even closer and bent forward, certain I was right but afraid of what would happen if I was wrong.

"We need more light," someone shouted behind me.

In response a spotlight flashed on, brightening the compartment and reflecting off what appeared to be a dozen bubble-wrapped parcels, each the size of a breadbox.

I blinked to adjust my eyes to the brilliant light. Within one parcel, I could make out the familiar outline of the plover. Another held the drake merganser. Other bundles and decoys were partially visible.

"Thank God," I murmured. The collection was safe.

I stepped back, giving the agents and officers room to work and rejoining Tuck and Kala as I watched the plover being removed from the compartment. This was good. *No*, it was fantastic and amazing—

My excitement wavered.

It was fantastic, but it didn't mean the danger was over for us.

I lifted my chin and set my jaw. We wouldn't be safe and in the clear until everyone involved in the theft was caught, especially the couple from Boston.

Chapter
Thirty-Two

A few minutes later, the three of us decided it was time to head home. As tempting as it was to stay and gloat while the CSI team ripped the rest of the Corvette apart, I suspected the FBI and police had seen more than enough of me for one day, especially Shane.

As we reached the van, the *brrring* of my phone filled the air.

I checked the caller ID, then answered in a flash.

"Hey, Pinky," I said, motioning for Tuck and Kala to listen in.

"After your generous donation to the needy children," Pinky said cheerfully, "I thought you'd like to know that those people you were asking about are here now. In the pub. Together."

"You mean Graham and Nina?" I asked.

"Yup."

"Hmm . . . Thanks." I was grateful she was keeping an eye out, but unsure what to do with the information. Nina and Graham's relationship wasn't a mystery anymore, and confronting Graham about his connection to the robberies at the café wouldn't get us anywhere. Finding evidence against Graham would take finesse and time, if it was even possible. Besides, Nina wasn't a threat anymore, now that the stolen decoys had been found in Frank's car. Still, the information did raise one important question. "Is Nina's daughter with them?"

"Nah, Gracie's grandfather showed up. Last I heard, he was watching her until after the fireworks—and putting down more than a few beers, from what I understand."

"Thanks a lot," I said.

"No problem. Just don't forget about Board Game Night. It's Thursday."

I hung up, then glanced at Tuck and Kala. "We've got two vehicles here. If either of you want to go home, I totally understand. I'm going to the festival. I have to catch up with Claude and thank him for keeping me out of jail. I need to tell him what we've found out about Nina and Frank, and that the decoys are safe. He deserves to know. I'd also like to ask who he thinks poisoned him."

Tuck scowled. "You remember what I said about not letting you out of my sight? I meant it."

"You're not getting rid of me, either." Kala grinned.

* * *

It was twilight by the time we reached the Jumping Café. The shadowy front parking lot was jammed with cars, and the darkening field behind the restaurant was rapidly filling. Tuck scored a parking spot for the Suburban on the edge of the road. I wedged the van into a nearby space. Kala had ridden with me. I'd spent most of the trip telling her about Pinky and warning her that the Board Game Night invite had to do with Pinky's personal interest in her. Kala shrugged it off, and I was left uncertain how she really felt about the whole thing.

Together, we rushed toward the festival, skirting groups of people and dodging traffic. The flea market tents now glittered with strings of colored lights. Smoke and the aroma of roasting chicken rose from the barbecue pits. Music from a country band blared from hundreds of speakers. People shouted. People danced. Everywhere shadows, lights, movement, and noise.

As busy as it was, the inward flow of traffic had begun to thin out, now trickling slowly toward the back fields. Horns tooted every now and again. Headlights gleamed.

"Let's hope Nina stays in the pub with Graham for a while," Tuck said. "It's not like we can talk openly to Claude with her around."

Kala hushed her voice. "You don't still think there's a chance Nina poisoned him?"

I shook my head. "Tuck and I saw her when the ambulance arrived. She was truly shaken."

"Maybe Claude got into some amped-up weed by mistake," Kala suggested.

"It wasn't an accident," Tuck said. "My bet's on Mudder. We've been ruling him out completely, but Claude himself said there was bad blood between him and Mudder's side of the family."

I lengthened my stride. "Either way, we need to hurry. Once the parade award ceremony and fireworks are over, there'll be a stampede to the parking lots. It'll be impossible to spot Claude then."

"We could cover more territory faster if we divide up," Kala suggested.

I shook my head. "We need to stick together this time. Watch each other's backs. Don't forget, the couple from Boston is still on the loose. They know we were looking for the collection, but they don't know we found it. They could come after any one of us thinking we have information they need."

Kala giggled, then inched up the hem of her hoodie to reveal something holstered at her beltline. "That's why I brought my friend."

I stared. "Is that a gun? You had that at the police station?"

"Meet Taz—the Taser."

Tuck chuckled. "You know, Kala, I'm liking you better all the time."

"My mama didn't raise no fool." She grinned, a wide, proud smile.

As we started through an opening in the security fence, my phone rang.

It was Pinky again.

"Everything alright?" I asked.

Tuck and Kala moved in to listen. "I don't know where you are or what you've got in mind, but the wicked witch has left the castle."

I swallowed hard. "What are you talking about?"

"Nina's left the pub. Graham's still here. He asked for dinner plates, so I'm guessing she's getting them some chick—"

Tuck elbowed me. "Ah—Edie, you might want to hang up."

Five yards ahead of us, Nina stood. In her hands were two boxes from the barbecue. Her pale face was mottled bright red. Her eyes were as dark as black amethyst. She swayed as if drunk.

"Never mind," I said to Pinky. "I know. She's getting chicken."

As I stashed my phone, Nina pursed her lips. "Two losers and their helper. I have half a mind to call the police right now."

Kala stalked forward. "Go ahead. It's not like you're lily white."

Nina laughed. "Lily white. That's quite the way for *you* to put it."

I considered rushing forward and putting a hand on Kala to stop her from reacting to what clearly was a slur, but before I could she moved even closer to Nina and snarled, "So why did you bring the decoy to the appraisal event?"

Nina's glare went past Kala, pinpointing me. "You think you're so smart, don't you? I'd already been told the collection was somewhat valuable." Her upper lip lifted in a nasty smile. "I'd planned on hiring your mother. Having her accused of . . . let's just say I counted on the outcome being emotionally and financially pleasant. But then—" Her glare darkened. "I had a good idea I'd been double-crossed when the collection went missing, but I wasn't foolish enough to rule you out."

"You really thought it might have been me?" That explained why her reaction in the attic seemed genuine.

"I wasn't certain. But at the time, I figured you were clever enough to make sure I got the collection back, one way or the other. There also was the bonus of knowing your mother was watching as you dug yourself deeper into a hole." Her voice lowered to a hushed growl. "Frank, that sneaky little skunk, he'll get what's coming to him too. Him and his cohort Mudder."

Kala stepped more squarely between Nina and me and looked her in the face. "How about your buddy Graham? He really didn't know what he was getting into when he hooked up with you, did he?"

She looked down her nose at Kala. "Shut up. No one cares what you think."

"At least this black girl's daddy didn't have to pay bribes to get her into college."

The red drained from Nina's face, leaving only stark white. "What are you talking about?"

Behind me Tuck murmured, "Ah—maybe we should go?"

"I'm not done," Kala said. She lifted her chin, glowering at Nina. "You know exactly what I'm talking about."

Nina hissed. "That was my brother. Not me."

Kala scoffed. "Yeah, right. I forgot, you're the juvie hall princess. I bet your daddy is proud of you. Shoplifting, more shoplifting . . . Assaulting an officer."

"Who told you that?" she shrieked.

Kala's hand went to her beltline, to Taz.

This time I snagged Kala by the shoulder, pulling her back. "Enough."

Nina pushed forward, inching past us and through the security fence opening. "You're going to regret this. All of you."

"Doubt that," I said. I had no idea what Kala had been talking about, but Nina didn't know that any more than she knew the decoys had been found. I called after her, "Enjoy your dinner. Your little revenge plans are over now. The FBI has Claude's decoys."

Nina spun back and gawked at me. "Who told you that? Frank took them, didn't he?"

She turned again and flew off toward the café door, boxes of chicken clenched tight.

"Well, now," Tuck said. "What do you suppose Graham's going to think of that news?"

"I have no idea." I glanced at Kala. "What was that all about? Bribing her way into college? Juvie princess?"

"I was going to tell you in the car, then we got talking about Pinky." She shrugged. "After I got bored trying to find any trace of the imposter, I called in a favor for shits and giggles. Turns out you're not the only one who had a brush with the law."

"Nina?" I said, shocked.

"She might've wondered if you took the decoys at first. What she knew was that one look at her so-called sealed juvie record would make her a suspect too. Between all the bribes and bail, it's a miracle Nina's daddy didn't go broke."

Tuck interrupted. "I hate to break up the party. If you two still want to find Claude, we better get to it before Nina finishes giving Graham an earful and decides it's time to collect Gracie and leave."

"You're right," I said. "Let's go."

We rushed away from the security fence, toward the barbecue area.

Kala went up on her tiptoes. "I don't see Gracie or Claude anywhere. Do either of you?"

"Not me," Tuck said.

I scanned again. There weren't any kids and parents by the pits grabbing up their free after-parade dinners, no one at the picnic tables either—or beyond them by the flea market tents. In fact, those areas were emptying out as the bulk of the crowd flooded toward the carnival games and the field where the award ceremony and fireworks were staged.

A *bang* resounded overhead, announcing the start of the show. Lights flashed, sizzling across the sky. White. Yellow. Blue. Red.

A group *ahhhhhhh!* echoed from behind the carnival games as another whirl of light exploded. Smoke fogged the air, turning twilight into darkness. The sulfur smell from the fireworks tickled the inside of my nose.

Tuck turned back toward us. "The award ceremony must be over already. We need to hurry."

As we headed into the game area, I motioned for them to follow me. I scooted between two tents, leading them down the narrow alley, but not toward the bandstand and where the thickest throng of people would be on their blankets staring up at the fireworks.

More lights exploded. The haze of smoke turned everything into shadows. The band picked up its beat, matching the blasts of light. *Bang. Crackle. Hiss.*

Kala poked my shoulder. "Shouldn't we be heading toward the crowd?"

"I want to try somewhere else first." I walked fast, moving quickly toward the darkest corner of the festival grounds. "When Nina told me about Claude's suicide, she mentioned he thought he had cancer because he needed to pee all the time. We know he's been drinking tonight. That's bound to make him have to go even worse."

Tuck laughed. "I believe up in Stowe, I mentioned a similar thing about my old man bladder."

"So where are we going?" Kala asked.

307

I glanced at her. "The portable toilets. If Claude's in line there, he'll be easy to spot. If he's not, then we'll check the crowd."

The outline of the porta-potties came into view, two dozen of them sitting just inside the security fence, by the exit to the back field and parking area. A guy dressed as a clown stumbled out of a porta-potty and slouched into a plastic chair by the exit. The stomach-churning sound of someone vomiting emanated from behind a dumpster.

Kala hooked her arm with mine. "This was a good idea, but that's kind of ruining the whole festival experience for me."

"Just be glad we can't smell it."

Bang, bang, bang, fireworks resounded overhead. A gold spray fizzed across the sky, sputtering and exploding again. *Bang.* It erupted into blue pinwheels. More gold whirls filled the sky.

"I'll kill you!" a woman shouted. Not far from us.

"Did you hear that?" Tuck asked.

"I think so." I held perfectly still, listening for the voice to come again.

Bang! Crack. Sizzle. Pop. Pop. Pop. A fresh volley brightened the sky, illuminating the porta-potties.

Crack! The sound of wood hitting metal came from the darkness nearby—just outside the safety fence, from somewhere in the parking area.

I wheeled toward the sound, listening even harder.

Thump. A fist hit flesh.

"Where are they!" a man demanded.

"I told ya, I don't have them," a familiar voice screeched.

"Mudder," I gasped. I started toward the voices. Where the hell was he?

Tuck and Kala were close behind as I pushed my legs to a sprint, running half blind through the exit and into the dark parking area.

Bang, bang, bang, more rapid fireworks detonated. Lights strobed, illuminating us and the chaotic mass of parked cars. Just ahead, the man from Boston had Mudder in a headlock. Rivulets of blood flowed down Mudder's face.

The outline of a woman appeared, holding something. A bat.

She swung. *Crack!* It caught Mudder in the knees.

"*Maudit*, bitch. I don't know where the stupid decoys are," he groaned.

She pulled the bat back, readying to swing again. "Damn Canuck."

"Stop!" I screamed, rocketing forward.

Kala was beside me, Taser out.

"Call 911," I shouted to Tuck.

I pushed myself as hard as I could, no fear, no thought other than saving Mudder. *Flashes of light. Heat. Cracks. Bangs . . .* The day my grandparents died, I'd run as hard as I could across the landing strip, across the field and into the light of the fire. The memory of the single-engine plane exploding boomed in my head as I raced toward Mudder and the couple.

The man spotted me and released Mudder from the headlock.

Mudder slumped to the ground, his bulky shape vanishing into the darkness next to a car. The woman turned, sprinting away. The man was close behind her. A car door opened, light fanning out. More explosions overhead, spotlighting them and their Ford Explorer.

Kala dropped down next to Mudder. She pulled off her hoodie, pressing it against the gash in his head. Blood seeped between her fingers.

Tuck was on the phone. "We need an ambulance. Police. State police. FBI . . ."

The Explorer roared to life, headlights flaring white across the parking area.

I couldn't do anything the night my grandparents died, other than run and then freeze in terror. But I wasn't about to let that happen this time. Never again.

I turned on my heels, flying through the gap in the security fence, darting past clusters of people. Racing between vendor tents. The Explorer wouldn't get out of the rear parking area fast. It was a field, rutted, unlit, packed with cars. I had a minute. Maybe two. I could do it.

Keys in my hand, I raced by the picnic area to the barbecue pits, trying to remember exactly where I'd left the van. I pressed the panic button on the van key. A screech rang out.

I followed it to the van, only a few yards away. As I leaped into the driver's seat, I heard a squeal of tires and saw the Explorer careen onto the main road. In a flash of light, I caught a glimpse of the bike rack on the back. No question it was them. And their going after Mudder confirmed my theories. Mudder and Frank had taken the decoys at Graham's behest, but the couple were the ones at the top of the scheme. The masterminds. The organized crime connection.

I shoved my phone in its cradle and slammed the van into gear. The police were on their way, but this was Vermont. Endless back roads. Endless escape routes. I had to keep the couple in my sight.

In a heartbeat, I was behind the Explorer, flying down the road. I pressed the phone button on the hands-free control and commanded, "911."

A voice filled the van. "911. What is your emergency?"

"I'm following a gray Ford Explorer. Massachusetts plates. We're on Wild River Road. Six miles north of Scandal Mountain village."

The Explorer hit the gas, shooting away, vanishing into the darkness.

I stomped on the accelerator. Their taillights once again came into view. The glare of an oncoming car's high beams blinded me for a second. I blinked, regaining my vision.

Time seemed to slow. The world became a deadly blur of taillights and speed. Fields and farms flashed by. Headlights streamed past. Darkness returned.

"Are you in danger, ma'am?" the operator asked.

Ahead of me, the Explorer's taillights faded. I punched the gas, going 65. 70. Their car was powerful. But I knew the road, every inch of it. Every turn off they could take. Every frost heave and pothole. Or I used to, at least.

"We just passed Cliff Road. Almost to Dead Man's Curve. Call Detective Payton with the state police. Tell him it's Edie."

The operator said something about not pursuing. I blocked out her voice as we neared the deadly bend. Thank God there were no bicycles at night.

I tapped the brakes, slowing slightly. Still way faster than normal. I couldn't give them room. I couldn't let them escape.

I soared past the speed limit sign: 25 miles per hour. I was going 50. People had died here. Teenagers on prom night. A bride on her wedding day. Mom almost killed us here. The black ice. The car spinning and spinning. But Mom was a terrible driver, always had been.

The Explorer's taillights vanished as it squealed around the curve, sliding sideways. Dear Lord, let them lose control. Let them roll the car. Let them go into a ditch. Over the bank . . . Let them be pinned inside.

I couldn't breathe. Those were horrible things to wish on anyone. It was all I wanted.

The van's tires gripped the pavement, holding tight as it skidded around the curve. My headlights fanned the road ahead, illuminating the pavement, the edges of the road. No broken guardrails. No spray of smoke from a crash. No SUV lying bottom side up. Only the Explorer's taillights, growing brighter now as I gained on them.

I punched the accelerator to the floor, not far behind. Just beyond the Explorer, the glow of Townline gas station's floodlights brightened the road. Behind me, the distant sound of police sirens began to wail.

I wiped one hand down my pants leg, drying off sweat. This was almost over. The police would catch them. Mudder and Nina would spill what they knew. The truth would come out.

I refocused on the Explorer, a hundred yards ahead, nearing the gas station. As it reached the station's floodlit entrance, it swung off the road and winged past the gas pumps, barreling toward the station's other exit. What the hell?

Too late, I realized what they intended. I jammed on the brakes as the Explorer shot back out onto the road, slid into a ninety-degree turn, and then drove straight at me, headlights on high beam.

I hit the gas and swerved into the other lane. Chicken was not my game.

They veered, matching my move, still coming straight at me.

I jumped on the brakes and aimed for the side of the road. I'd take my chances with the field. I knew this road. There weren't any ledges or trees here. Just bushes. Just swamp and pasture. It was up to the police to catch the couple now—

Except, what if they escaped?

They hired thieves to steal art. They relegated antiques to nothing more than black-market currency. They killed people. Traded for drugs. Traded for ego, and worse.

I couldn't stand by and do nothing. Not now. Not ever again.

"Screw it!" I cranked the steering wheel, fishtailing back toward the center of the road. The Explorer loomed in front of me. I stepped on the gas. If I didn't slow, they'd give in and take the ditch.

They veered toward their side of the road—

And back!

The scream of metal against metal rang out as we sideswiped each other. The steering wheel ripped from my hands. The van spun sideways, hurtling across the road, over a bank. One side hit the ground. For a long, terrifying second, I felt myself and the van rise into the air. Weightless. Then I slammed forward. The seatbelt pinned me. The airbag slammed me back against the seat.

Darkness. No headlights. No dash lights. Only black inside the van. No sound, other than the hiss of escaping steam and the distant wail of sirens.

Pain radiated from my ribs and forehead. I clenched my teeth against the discomfort and moved my trembling fingers along the seatbelt. I found the release and pressed it. The belt unfastened. I fumbled for the door latch. Nothing. Only crumpled metal. What if the couple came after me? Trapped in here, I'd be at their mercy. I couldn't stay in the car.

Adrenaline roared into my veins. I launched myself sideways, slamming the door with my shoulder. The door creaked open. Only a foot.

I shoved again, pushing and wedging my way out. My knees buckled and I sank to the ground. Soggy. Wet. Darkness all around me. Pain knifed across my ribs. Something warm trickled down my face: blood. Still, my legs and arms weren't broken.

The flash of blue lights appeared on the horizon. Sirens, moving fast.

I could see the bank the van had gone over now, rising in front of me, brightened by the strobing lights. Above that, the road stretched.

My muscles resisted, but I got to my feet and struggled up the bank. Ahead, cruisers appeared. Fire trucks. Beyond them, past a line of guard rails and the road, a flare of white headlights pointed skyward. The Explorer. It had crashed.

Had the police captured the couple?

Had they escaped?

Or had I killed them?

Chapter Thirty-Three

I was sitting on the ambulance's tailgate when Shane arrived. There was no missing him as he sprinted through the flash of red and blue lights, across the road and over to me.

"What did you think you were doing?" His voice hovered somewhere between anger and relief. "You're lucky to be alive."

"They drove straight at me, then I—" My voice died in my throat. My mouth tasted bloody. My ribs ached every time I took a breath. I suspected black and blue was spreading across where the seatbelt had pinned me in place. But that didn't matter. What mattered was what had happened to the couple—and no one would tell me, not the officers from Scandal Mountain, not the ambulance attendants, not the state police.

"They're in rough shape, but alive and under arrest," Shane said. "They're being transported to the hospital."

My throat clenched and I rasped, "Thank goodness."

His lips pressed together as he hesitated, then he said, "The handlebar bag you mentioned was in their car."

"Really? His bag. Were the strap and cord missing?"

"Unfortunately, it wasn't that one. We believe it's the bag the woman was carrying. But it's going to help with the

315

investigation nonetheless." He looked down at the water bottle in my hands and shook his head. "That was a very dangerous thing you did, chasing after them."

I ignored that, and I ignored my uncertainty as to how finding her bag could help the investigation. I trusted that Shane knew what he was talking about. Instead, I asked something more vital. "How about Mudder? Is he okay?"

"Latimore's with him at the hospital. Mudder started talking as soon as the first officer arrived on the scene. They couldn't keep him quiet, even in the ambulance."

"I don't think he knew the couple was behind the robbery," I said. "Or anything about the Canadian heist."

"That's what he's claiming too." Shane glanced over his shoulder, as if to make sure no one was within earshot. His gaze came back. "There's no question the couple are high up in a syndicate. Mudder was a disposable flunky. They purposely kept him out of the loop."

"He and Frank did steal the collection then?" I asked. I was ninety-nine percent sure, but I had to know for certain.

Shane nodded. "Mudder admitted to borrowing the truck they used that night. They switched license plates to make it harder to trace."

"So the tracks at the farm were from that truck?"

Shane rested a reassuring hand on my knee. "The photos you took will help verify if Mudder's story is true or not. He says they transferred the decoys to the Corvette at the café. After that, Frank was supposed to meet up with a buyer. Mudder has no idea the decoys weren't sold. He's convinced Frank made the deal, then took off with all the money."

"Is the FBI thinking Frank's dead? Assassinated, like that guy in Stanstead?"

"Actually, no."

"Why not? It makes sense. Frank might have found a better buyer and changed his mind about selling the decoys to the couple. They wouldn't have tolerated that kind of betrayal."

Shane smiled as if amused by my guesses. "That would tie everything up in a neat little package."

"You have a better idea?" I asked, slightly peeved.

"I shouldn't be telling you any of this. Most of it is currently only speculation." He fell silent and folded his arms across his chest.

I jumped to my feet, planning on giving him a playful punch to get him to spill the rest, but a wave of dizziness drove me back down onto the ambulance's tailgate. I closed my eyes, waiting for the vertigo to pass.

After a second I said, "Tell me what happened to Frank. Please."

"If I do, will that satisfy enough of your curiosity that you'll let the FBI and the police take it from here?"

I opened my eyes. "Sure. Cross my heart."

He squinted as if he didn't believe me, then relented. "The decoys weren't the only thing in the Corvette—and, by the way, the whole collection wasn't there."

"It wasn't?" I frowned at him. "How can you be sure? I know how many decoys were taken because of the appraisal. The FBI hasn't seen that—unless they got hold of Nina's copy."

"We know because Mudder said he kept the geese the night of the robbery. He claims he snuck them across the border into

317

Quebec and gave them to his grandmother, Maria Bouchard Joyce."

I shook my head in disbelief. "I'd say that sounds sweet, but Mudder stole them from her brother—and poisoned him." I looked at Shane. "Mudder confessed to drugging Claude, right? I can't think who else could've done it."

"He said something about giving Claude macaroni and cheese." He raised an eyebrow. "Don't you want to know what else we found hidden in the car?"

I nodded. I couldn't begin to imagine what it was, but Shane was beaming like it was the best discovery of all.

"We found evidence that Frank has an offshore bank account in the Bahamas. At this point, Latimore suspects he funneled Nina's trust fund money into it for years. We believe Frank panicked after the robbery, abandoned the Corvette, and took off to Canada. He's probably in the Bahamas on a beach by now."

My head whirred as I tried to rethink everything I'd learned and assumed. I pressed a hand against my upper chest, tender from the bruises. "I never stopped to consider that Frank might have simply run away."

Shane grimaced apologetically. "Actually, your theory about Frank having found a better offer could be true. If that buyer didn't appear for a meetup, or if Frank found them dead, that could explain him abandoning the decoys and running. A lot of seemingly irrational behavior is rooted in fear-induced panic." His voice quieted. "The FBI's patient. They'll catch up with Frank, sooner or later."

I met his eyes. I really was starting to feel drained. "Would you mind giving me a lift home? The paramedics checked me out. Looks like my ribs are probably just bruised. I passed their concussion evaluation. They said I'm fine to go home, but I have no idea where my phone is. I'm not even sure where Tuck and Kala are."

"Last I knew, they were at the café being questioned. I told them I'd stay with you."

Shane slipped an arm around my waist, supporting me as I got down from the ambulance's tailgate, then making sure I was steady on my feet before helping me across the road. I tucked in close against him, a sense of well-being radiating through me as I relaxed into his protective strength. When we reached his Land Rover, he opened the passenger door and gave me a hand up.

"Thanks," I said, settling into the seat. I caught his gaze. It was probably my exhaustion, but talking about everything that had happened was starting to feel surreal, like we were discussing characters from a crime novel instead of real life. That was, except for one player too connected to my real life for comfort—and who I suspected had intentionally reeled me into this whole mess by sending Nina to my table at the appraisal event. A suspicion recently reinforced when Nina confessed that she'd known the decoys had value that day.

Shane tapped a finger against his temple. "You want to tell me what's going on in there?"

"I was just wondering about Felix Graham. Is he going to get off scot-free?"

He shrugged. "That's a hard call."

I shifted in the seat, facing him fully. "Seriously, what's your best guess? I've got a good idea. I just hope I'm wrong."

"Honestly? People like Graham aren't your garden-variety criminals. They cover their tracks and have money for the best lawyers. If I were to bet, I'd say we won't find solid enough evidence to make it worth going after him. His past record is squeaky clean."

"You mean, Graham won't even get a slap on the wrist?"

Shane's gaze lingered on mine, making my pulse beat harder, a quick, jumpy rhythm. "Don't worry," he said. "The FBI won't forget about Graham—and neither will I."

And I won't either, I thought.

I reached toward Shane, brushing his jawline with my fingertips when he moved closer. "I really am sorry for all the trouble I caused you."

"I owe you an apology too," he said. "Not just for following you the other day. That was part of my job. Everything was, but I should have told you anyway."

The tension in the air eased a little. I wanted to keep the mood going, so I smiled coyly and then teased, "Speaking of the FBI. What's the chance of me getting that two hundred and fifty thousand dollar reward? You know, for information leading to the arrest of people involved with the museum robbery?"

He laughed. "I'd let that one go, if I were you. There are a number of things you could still be charged with. Grossly negligent operation of a motor vehicle, interfering in a criminal investigation . . . Do you want me to go on?"

I flipped my palms up in mock surrender. "All right, then. How about no charges instead of the reward?"

He eyed me suspiciously. "I could talk to Latimore, see what he can do. Are you willing to stay away from the Bouchards and out of this from now on?"

"I promise, no more trouble," I said. Well-chosen words aren't exactly the same as a lie, right? I still had business with Claude.

Chapter Thirty-Four

I woke up the next morning to a vase of lilacs and a huge basket of African violets on my bedside stand. As the paramedics had predicted, I ached all over and dark bruises spanned both sides of my upper chest. Still, I made my way downstairs to the living room without much trouble.

Kala was ensconced on the sofa with her laptop, listing fresh merchandise on eBay.

"You don't need to do that," I said. "Yesterday wasn't a picnic for you, either."

"Messing around on eBay is therapy, like shopping, only I'm making money instead of spending it. By the way, we currently have a fun bidding war going on for a penknife I listed a few days ago. Victorian. Fourteen karats. The price is already up to twice what I expected it to go for."

"That's fabulous." I hobbled to the window and gazed out. The driveway looked empty without the van sitting there. Unlike me, with its bent frame and smashed front end, the van wasn't going to recover.

"Edie?" Tuck walked into the room with a phone in his hand. He held it out to me. "There's someone who'd like to talk to you."

I reached for it, only realizing my mistake at the last second. Tuck hadn't said who was on the other end. That could only mean one thing. Mom.

I raised a hand to ward off the phone.

"Edie," he said firmly. "She's worried. She knows you were in an accident."

My jaw tensed, but I surrendered. I hated arguing with Tuck.

I put the phone to my ear and turned back to the window, looking out. "Hi, Mom. Are you doing okay?"

"Edie, sweetheart. I was so worried when Tuck told me you'd been hurt. I'm still shaking all over."

"I'm fine. It was nothing, really."

"You need to be more careful. He said the accident was near Dead Man's Curve. That's a horrible spot. I went off the road there once myself. There was black ice. You were with me. Do you remember?"

The fact that Mom hadn't mentioned I went off the road after sideswiping a couple of criminal masterminds led me to believe Tuck hadn't told her about the robberies. Well, that or anything else, including the involvement of her boyfriend, Frank.

"Mom," I said. "The accident was only near the curve."

"Well, you need to slow down. You always had a lead foot . . ." She went on about how she hadn't been able to sleep since she'd gone to prison. Her bed was too narrow. The cell block was noisy. She wanted to teach an art class and they wouldn't let her. She shouldn't be there. She wasn't guilty.

I massaged my chest, easing a twinge of pain. I didn't say anything in response to her last comment. I wasn't sold on her being completely innocent of forgery, any more than I had been totally innocent when I got caught for selling stolen property. But after the last few days, the possibility of Mom being set up had taken root in my mind. There were any number of people who'd undoubtedly celebrated her imprisonment—like Rosetta Ramone, Martina Fortuni, and Rene St. Marie, not to mention Graham—and who'd love nothing better than to see us bankrupt and forced to sell our business.

As Mom paused for a breath, I momentarily considered asking her about Frank, then I remembered the prison phone line wasn't private. Besides, Frank was out of the picture, at least as far as romance with her was concerned. He'd latch onto another woman down in the Bahamas, probably in less than a week. Still—and despite his being a womanizer and having played my mom—I wondered if on some level Frank had cared about her. Maybe it was just wishful thinking, but had he come to the house that night in an honest attempt to warn me off? To keep me from getting framed for the robbery he'd already decided to commit? Had he been trying to protect me for my mom's sake?

My gaze went from the empty space the van had occupied to the carport. Tuck's Suburban was parked under it. Next to that was another car, covered with a tarp.

"Hey, Mom?" I interrupted her monologue.

"Yes? What is it, darling?"

"Since you're not home and my van is . . . Well, it's dead."

"Dear, you don't need to ask. Of course, you can borrow Grandpa's Volvo. Just promise me no wild rides."

"Don't worry, I'll be careful."

I took a deep breath, building up my nerve. Now that I'd reached this point, I realized it had been inevitable. "Mom, there's something else."

"Does it have to do with that man—Shane? Tuck told me about him."

My face heated. "No. Shane's just a close friend."

"Well then," Mom said. "What is it?"

I glanced toward Tuck, and said to her, "I've decided to stay home until you get back. Run the business for you."

Tuck smiled like he'd sold a whole truckload of African violets to the FBI Art Crime Team. Kala looked up from the laptop and gave me a thumbs up.

"That's nice, dear. I'm sure Tuck will appreciate the help," Mom said.

For a moment, my breath bottled up in my chest. Finally, I pushed past it. "Mom, I love you."

* * *

For the next couple of days, I felt too stiff and sore to do much of anything. Eventually I pulled myself together and used the excuse of wanting to take the Volvo to the car wash to escape from the house. It was true to a degree. The Volvo was a sweet car that deserved special care in every sense of the word. What I neglected to mention was that I planned on going to the Bouchards' first.

I still hadn't thanked Claude for telling the sheriff I had permission to be in the cellar. On top of that, our bills wouldn't pay themselves and he owed us for the appraisal. I'd even called Pinky to make sure Nina and Gracie would be at dance class instead of home. Nina might not have stolen the collection, but she was unquestionably a nasty piece of work and wouldn't be happy to see me at the farm.

The Volvo glided up the driveway and over Claude's rickety bridge. I blew out a relieved breath as the house came into view. His truck with its wooden tailgate was parked under the maples and there weren't any other vehicles around. Claude himself sat on the front porch, wearing his old barn coat, sipping on a beer.

When he spotted the unfamiliar car, he tipsily lurched to his feet and folded his arms. They unfolded as I climbed out.

"Wasn't sure I'd see you again, *mon petit carcajou*." He tottered out to meet me.

"I wanted to apologize for trespassing and thank you for what you said to the police."

He harrumphed. "I didn't say that just for you. You were searching for my decoys, and the *maudit* thief. One hand washes the other, eh?"

I nodded, then put on a more businesslike tone. "There still is the matter of the appraisal. You owe me a check or a trade—or we could talk about auctioning the collection." I figured with Claude, getting right to the point was best.

He squinted. "I'd be open to discussing an auction, if I had my birds back."

"The FBI haven't returned them?" I didn't know how the timing worked in situations like this, but it seemed crazy for them to hold on to his property.

"I call one person and they tell me to call someone else. Those brain-dead FBI people don't know their butts from a hole in the wall—"

I cut him off. "Say I could get through to the right person and get the decoys back for you, do you promise we could talk after that?" A horrifying possibility leaped into my head. What if Nina and/or Frank as co-trustees still had legal rights to the collection? What if one or both of them stepped in and hired

Graham as the intermediary agent for an auction? We'd be cut out of the deal and there wouldn't be anything I could do about it. I looked at Claude steadily. "What about Nina and Frank's involvement?"

A twinkle of sly confidence glinted in his rheumy eyes. "We don't need to worry about them. I had my lawyer dissolve the trust a few days ago, only took my signature and ten minutes in his office. From now on, everything will be between you and me. All I want is to make sure Gracie's future is secure."

"Your lawyer isn't worried about Nina or Frank putting up a fight?"

He glanced at the house. "Nina wants to make this place all fancy. She wants to show it off to her family. I don't trust the woman, especially now. But I can put up with her and her foolishness, if it means I get to have my Gracie around." He wiped his hands together as if washing them clean. "No one's got to worry about Frank anymore."

I nodded. "The FBI thinks he left the country."

"They told Nina the same thing." He swiveled back to me, his voice lowering. "I always trusted Mudder until he fed me that mac and cheese. I got sick five minutes later."

When he fell quiet, I said, "I never believed you tried to kill yourself."

"Mudder swore my sister Maria made it, but it didn't taste like her cooking. Tasted better, like the casseroles Frank used to make when he lived here—good cheese with crumbled Ritz crackers and Canadian bacon on top."

Ritz crackers? Canadian bacon? My mind reeled back, flipping through the contents of Frank's kitchen. There had been Canadian bacon in the fridge and Ritz crackers in the cupboard, and prescription medicine in the bathroom. Everything he'd have needed to create poisonous mac and cheese.

My thoughts went deeper, to the desiccated pieces of tire track in Frank's garage, wide enough to possibly belong to a Corvette—or to a pickup.

I glanced over my shoulder at Claude's truck with its wooden tailgate and wide tires. He'd been on his way to the garage to retrieve it when he left the hospital in a hurry. By then, he would have suspected Frank was the one who'd poisoned him.

"Frank always was a swine—" He stopped abruptly, then said, "Did you notice something's missing?"

I jolted from my crazy speculation and glanced around. "No. What?"

Claude wet his lips. Then he looked directly in my eyes as if watching for my reaction. "I got rid of the pig."

I felt myself pale. Hadn't he just called Frank a swine?

I shook myself back to reality. "You mean, you had that enormous hog butchered? Made into bacon and ham. Wrapped and put in your freezer." When I got home, I needed to remind Tuck and Kala that there be no more horror movies or jokes about razorbacks or serial killers feeding their victims to pigs. All the teasing was starting to get to me.

"*Maudit* animal. Always getting into the garden, eating anything it could get its jowls around." He motioned for me to follow. "If we're going to be partners, I should show you this."

Totally confused, I followed as he teetered past the dumpster and kept going. He stopped just short of the cellar bulkhead, in front of the rusty chest freezer. He took a key ring from a pocket in his barn coat, unlocked the freezer, and opened the lid. "Take a look."

I hesitated. What did looking at a butchered pig have to do with partnerships and auctioning decoys? I liked Claude, but maybe I'd been wrong about him. Maybe he wasn't another Bucky Sanders with a crude exterior and above average smarts. Maybe Claude was just nuts.

I stepped closer to the freezer, looked inside.

At the bottom, on a mat of old cushions, partially covered in bubble wrap, was a long-legged, long-necked bird. A life-size blue heron with pristine paint, superbly carved crest and wings and tons of personality. Breathtaking. Essentially priceless. It was the most beautiful decoy I'd ever seen.

"Whoa," I said, stepping back, unable to breathe. "That's not bacon and ham."

Claude snickered and pushed the freezer lid closed. "That's for sure. The pig was nasty. I didn't butcher it for food. I killed it and got rid of the body." He was silent for a moment. "I don't want anyone to know about the heron. What's in this freezer belongs to Gracie and no one else. For later, when I'm gone."

In the world of art and antiques, it's all about the story.
Stories add value.
The wilder the story, the higher the value goes.
It's just, sometimes—like in the case of the blue heron in the freezer—those stories have to wait to fully come to light.

—Edie Brown